A BRIDE AND GROOM FOR SALE

For all her beauty, education and fabulous wealth, Geraldine lacked an aristocratic name. The scion of America's leading family, Steve Courtlandt lacked money. So Geraldine's father forced Steve to make her his bride.

Obediently, she agreed to stay with the marriage. But could a real man love a woman he had not taken by choice? Furthermore, should he want to live on her money?

When an old flame returned to claim Steve's heart, chance took the trio to a ranch in the West. Suddenly, the Courtlandts were plunged into danger and a deadly plot that tested their strength and power to love.

ACROSS THE YEARS
BEHIND THE CLOUD
A CANDLE IN HER HEART
A CERTAIN CROSSROAD
FAIR TOMORROW
GIVE ME ONE SUMMER
HERE COMES THE SUN
HILLTOPS CLEAR
HOW CAN THE HEART FORGET
IT'S A GREAT WORLD!
A KEY TO MANY DOORS
LIGHTED WINDOWS
LOOK TO THE STARS
MY DEAREST LOVE
RAINBOW AT DUSK
THE TRAIL OF CONFLICT
WHEN HEARTS ARE LIGHT AGAIN
WHERE BEAUTY DWELLS
WITH BANNERS

EMILIE LORING
THE TRAIL OF CONFLICT

*This low-priced Bantam Book
has been completely reset in a type face
designed for easy reading, and was printed
from new plates. It contains the complete
text of the original hard-cover edition.*
NOT ONE WORD HAS BEEN OMITTED.

THE TRAIL OF CONFLICT

*A Bantam Book / published by arrangement with
Little, Brown and Company*

PRINTING HISTORY

William Penn edition published 1922

Grosset & Dunlap edition published 1951

Bantam edition / February 1969

2nd printing .... April 1969	4th printing .. December 1969
3rd printing ...... October 1969	5th printing .. September 1970

New Bantam edition / March 1971

2nd printing .... May 1971	5th printing .. December 1972
3rd printing .. November 1971	6th printing .... July 1973
4th printing .... May 1972	7th printing ...... October 1974
8th printing .... May 1981	

ISBN 0-553-14521-5

Published simultaneously in the United States and Canada

PRINTED IN THE UNITED STATES OF AMERICA

17 16 15 14 13 12 11 10 9 8

THE TRAIL OF CONFLICT

I

"THAT is your ultimatum, Glamorgan? My boy for your girl or you scoop up my possessions and transfuse them into yours?"

Peter Courtlandt tapped the arm of his chair nervously as he regarded the man who sat opposite in front of the fire. The two men were in striking contrast. Courtlandt seemed a component part of the room in which they sat, a room which with its dull, velvety mahogany, its costly Eastern rugs, its rare old portraits and book-lined walls, proclaimed generations of ancestors who had been born to purple and fine linen. He was spare and tall. His features might have served as the model for the portrait of Nelson in the Metropolitan Museum. His eyes were darkly luminous, the eyes of a dreamer; his white hair curled in soft rings over his head; his hands were long and patrician. Glamorgan was built on the Colossus plan, large head, heavy features into which the elements had ground a dull color, a huge body without the least trace of fat. Only his eyes were small. They looked as though they had been forgotten until the last moment, as though the designer had then hastily poked holes beneath the Websterian brows to insert two brilliant green beads. He was a handsome man in a clean-souled, massive way; moreover he looked to be a person who would crash through obstacles and win out by sheer persistence.

He flung the remains of his cigar into the fire as he answered Courtlandt. With the cushion-tipped fingers of his large hands spread upon his knees he bent forward and fixed his interrogator with his emerald gaze.

"That statement sounds raw but it's true. I've been playing my cards for what you call a scoop for some time. Fifty years ago my mother brought her family from Wales to this country. We had come from the coal

1

region. Coal was all the older children knew, so we drifted to Pennsylvania. Until I was seventeen I picked coal. Occasionally I saw the stockholders who came to inspect the mines. One day your father brought you. You passed me as though I were a post, but right then and there I learned the difference between mere money and money with family behind it. That day I laid my plans for life. I'd make money, Lord, how I'd pile it up; I'd cut out the dissipations of my kind, I'd marry the most refined girl who'd have me, and I'd have one of my children, at least, marry into a family like yours. My grandchildren should have ancestors who counted. Well, I got the girl. She had good Virginia stock behind her. Geraldine was born and after five years Margaret, and then my wife died. I began to pile. I denied myself everything but books, that my girls could be fitted to fill the position I was determined they should have. I——"

Peter Courtlandt's clear, high-bred voice interrupted. There was a trace of amusement in his tone:

"Did you never think that your daughters might develop plans of their own? That they might refuse to be disposed of so high-handedly?"

"Margaret may, but Jerry won't. Since she was a little thing she's been brought up with the idea of marrying for social position; she knows that my heart is set on it. Why, I used to visit her at school dressed in my roughest clothes, that the difference between me and the other fathers would soak in thoroughly. Oh well, smile. I acknowledge that the idea is an obsession with me; every man has some weak joint; that's mine. I'll say for Jerry that she never once flinched from owning up to me as hers. I've seen the color steal to her eyes when I appeared in my rough clothes, but she'd slip her hand into mine, for all the world as though she were protecting me, cling tight to it, and introduce me to her friends. The girls and teachers loved her, or she couldn't have got away with it. Her friends were among the best at college. Oh, she'll marry to please me. Even if she didn't want to, she'd do it to give Peg a chance; she's crazy about her, but I know her, she won't go back on her old Dad. Besides, Courtlandt, I have a firm conviction that a person can put through any worthy thing on which he is determined. How else do you account for the seeming miracles men got away with in the World War? The test is, how much do you want it? I've gone on that principle all my life, and it's worked, I tell you, it's worked!"

He waved away the box of cigars Courtlandt offered and pulled a vicious-looking specimen of the weed from his pocket. He stuck it between his teeth before he resumed:

"After I left the coal-mines I beat it to Texas, got an option on land there and began to make my pile in the oil-fields. I worked like a slave days and studied nights. I didn't mean to give Jerry cause to be ashamed of her Dad when she did land. Then I set my lawyer to looking up the affairs of the Courtlandt family. I found that you had a boy, handsome, upstanding and decent. I had him well watched, I assure you. I wasn't throwing Jerry away on a regular guy even if I was stuck on your family. I found also that your money was getting scarcer than hen's teeth. I took the mortgage on this house, on every piece of property in your estate. I knew when the boy chucked his law course and went into the army. I had him watched while he was overseas and I know that he came through that seething furnace of temptation straight. On the day your boy marries my girl and brings her to this house to live I'll turn your property over to you free and clear. It is in fine condition and will give you a handsome income. It won't be sufficient for you and the young people to live as I want to see them, but I'll take care of that. You've known me now for three months. You know that I'm absolutely on the level in my business dealings. What say?"

Courtlandt rose impetuously and stood with his back to the fire, one arm resting on the carved mantel.

"Good Lord, man, I'm not the one to say. It isn't my life that's being tied up. This property can go to the ——" he stopped, and looked about the beautiful room. He stared for a moment at the portrait of a seventeenth century Courtlandt which hung opposite, then up at the beautiful face of the woman in the painting set like a jewel in the dark paneling above the mantel. Her eyes looked back at him, gravely, searchingly. His voice was husky as he added quickly, "I'll talk with Steve to-night and if he——"

Glamorgan nodded approvingly.

"I'm glad you named him Stephen. It was Stephanus Courtlandt whose estate was erected into the lordship and manor of Courtlandt by William the third, wasn't it? You see I know your family history backward. I never buy a pig in a poke," with rough frankness. He rose and stretched to his great height. The man watching him thought of the Russian bear which had roused and shaken himself with such tragic results. "Why don't you and Steve run in town to-night and have supper with Jerry and me after the theatre?"

"Thank you; if Steve has no engagement we will."

Glamorgan thrust his hands deep into his pockets and glowered at the man by the mantel.

"I'll leave you now to deal with him. You might mention to Steve the fact that if he refuses my offer I foreclose within forty-eight hours."

The blood rushed to Courtlandt's face as though it would burst through the thin, ivory skin. He touched a bell, his voice was cold with repression as he answered the threat:

"I'll talk with Stephen this evening. Judson, Mr. Glamorgan's coat," to the smooth-haired, smooth-faced, smooth-footed butler who answered the ring.

The big man paused a moment, his little green eyes flames of suspicion.

"You'll let me hear from you to-morrow? No shilly-shallying, mind. A straight 'Yes' or 'No.' "

"A straight 'Yes' or 'No' to-morrow it is, Glamorgan. Good-night! Judson, when Mr. Stephen comes in ask him to come to me here."

After his guest had departed Courtlandt snapped off the lights and plunged the room in darkness save for

the soft glow from the blazing logs. He sank into a
wing-chair before the fire and rested his head on his
thin hand. What a mess he had made of things. He had
lost his inheritance, not through extravagance, but because he had not been enough of a business man to
steer his financial ship clear of reefs during the last
years of swiftly shifting values. To have the Courtlandt
property swept away! It was impossible. He didn't care
for himself but for Steve and Steve's children. He was a
liar! He did care for himself. It would break his heart
to have this old home, which had been the manor, fall
into the hands of an erstwhile coal-picker. The town
house was different. The location of that had followed
the trail of fashion, it had no traditions, but this——
He rose and paced the floor then returned to his old
place before the mantel and listened. There was the
sound of whistling in the hall, virile, tuneful, the sort
that brings a smile to the lips of the most sophisticated.
"The Whistling Lieut.!" Courtlandt remembered Steve
had been called in the army. He dropped his head to his
extended arm and stared unseeingly down at the flames.
What would he say——?

"Holloa, Sir Peter! Fire-worshiping?" a clear voice
called buoyantly. "You're as dark in here as though you
expected an air-raid. Let's light up and be cheerio, what
say?" The speaker pressed a button and flooded the
room with soft light. "Judson said you wanted me. Shall
I stay now or come back when I've changed?"

Courtlandt senior straightened and looked at his son
with the appraising eyes of a stranger. He admitted to
himself regretfully that the boy looked older than his
twenty-seven years. He was tall and lean and lithe, not
an ounce of superfluous flesh on him. He stood with his
feet slightly apart, a golf-bag dragging from one arm,
his other hand in his coat pocket. His black hair had a
rebellious kink, his eyes were dark blue, his nose clean-
cut, his lips and chin hinted at a somewhat formidable
strength of purpose. Courtlandt's courage oozed as he
regarded those last features.

"I—I merely wanted to ask you to give me this

evening, Steve. I—I—well, there's business to be talked over."

The son looked back at his father. A slight frown wrinkled his broad forehead. He started to speak, then lifted the golf-bag and went toward the door.

"The evening is yours, Sir Peter."

His father listened till his whistle trailed off into silence in the upper regions. His dark eyes clouded with regret. Steve had adapted his selection to dirge tempo.

As father and son smoked and drank their coffee in front of the library fire after dinner, Peter Courtlandt found it even more difficult to approach the distasteful subject. He talked nervously of politics, labor conditions and the latest play. His son watched him keenly through narrowed lids. He emptied and filled his pipe thoughtfully as he waited for a break in his father's flood of words. When it came he dashed in.

"What's the business you wanted to talk with me about, Sir Peter? Fire away and let's get it over. Anything wrong?"

The elder man bent forward to knock the ashes from his cigar. The gravity of Steve's "Sir Peter" had moved him curiously. It was the name his wife had called him, which the boy had adopted when he was too grown-up to say "Daddy." Silent seconds lengthened into minutes as he sat there. The quiet of the room was subtly portentous. There was a hint of unsteadiness in his voice when he finally spoke.

"It's all wrong, Steve. Everything we have is mortgaged to the gunwales."

"But I thought——" The end of the sentence was submerged in stunned amazement.

"That we couldn't go broke? Well, we have. We lose everything we have to-morrow unless——" He dropped his head on his hand.

"Unless what?" prompted Steve.

Courtlandt leaned his white head against the back of his chair and looked at his son with haggard eyes. His voice was strained, humiliated.

"Unless—unless you marry Glamorgan's daughter."

"What!"

The exclamation brought Steve Courtlandt to his feet. The color surged to his dark hair then ebbed slowly back again. His lips whitened.

"Look here, Sir Peter, you don't know what you're saying! You've forgotten that we are living in the twentieth century. Marry Glamorgan's daughter! I've never seen her. I didn't know the old piker had a daughter. What does he know about me? I've never spoken to him more than twice and then when I couldn't help it. I don't like him, he's——"

"Sit down, Steve. Stop raging up and down the room. I want to tell you all about it."

The younger man flung the cigarette he had just lighted into the red coals and dropped into a chair. He kept his eyes on the fading, flaring lights of the fire as his father told of his interview with Glamorgan. The muscles of his jaw tightened, his blue eyes smoldered as he listened.

"What sort of a girl would let herself be traded like that?" he demanded when his father paused.

"That is for you to find out, Steve. I started to have Judson turn the Welshman out of the house after he made his astounding proposition, to tell him to go to the devil—then I thought of you. That I had no right to fling away your inheritance without giving you a voice in the matter. The Courtlandts have held some of the property since the first of the family came from Holland in the seven——"

"Oh, I know all about those old boys; it is what their descendant is up against that's worrying me. Have you tried Uncle Nick?"

The slow color tinged Peter Courtlandt's face.

"Yes. I've appealed to Nicholas Fairfax twice. But you know as well as I that he has never forgiven your mother and me for not letting him have you six months out of every year. He contended that as you, the only son of his sister, were to be his heir, he should have an equal share in bringing you up. Your mother and I couldn't see it that way and so——"

"But I spent every summer there until I went overseas—and, oh boy, how I worked. While my pals were vacationing I was ranching, and ranching under Old Nick is no vacation. I'm as capable of running the Double O now as Ranlett is. Lord, the nights I've come in so stiff that I'd fall on the bed with my boots on. I'd got to shoot and rope, ride and round-up, drive a tractor, know the difference in the quality of the wheat-seed and the grades of cattle. Nick wasn't contented with my doing things as well as his outfit, I'd got to go them one better. But I loved the life and I'll confess that I love Old Nick in spite of his fool ideas."

"I'll try him once more, Steve—but——"

"I'll be darned if you will. Isn't there some other way we can raise money until I——"

"My boy, what can you do? What can you earn at present? You finished your law course after you came out of the army, but it will be several years, as times are now, before you can more than support yourself."

"You don't think I'd touch a penny of the old coal-picker's money even if I married the daughter, do you?" interrupted Steve furiously. "I'd break stones in the road first. Look here, be honest now, what would you do if we lost this place?"

"Blow my brains out," with passionate impulsiveness; then as he saw his son's face whiten and his jaw set, he realized the effect of his words. "No, no, Steve, of course I didn't mean that. The Courtlandts have never been quitters. I swear I wouldn't break the record. Forget that sob stuff. You and I would go somewhere together and I—perhaps I'll keep younger if I have less leisure."

"When are you to give Glamorgan his answer?" Steve seemed the elder of the two now, seemed to have taken the reins into his hands.

"To-morrow."

"To-morrow! Before the girl sees me? Before she has been given a chance to decide whether the encumbrance which goes with the name and social position is worth her thirty pieces of silver?"

"Try not to be bitter, Steve. Remember that when a big man has an obsession it's in proportion to his bigness, and you'll have to admit that Glamorgan's a giant in his world. You have a chance to see the girl before to-morrow. Her father suggested that we run in for supper with them tonight after the theatre. I have a feeling that the daughter is willing to sacrifice herself to make the great dream of her father's life come true, just as you are willing to sacrifice yourself for me—no, don't deny it,"—as his son impetuously opened his lips. "I haven't lived with you for twenty-seven years without knowing some of your mental processes, my boy. If it were only myself I'd tell Glamorgan to go to the devil, but the property will be yours after me and your children——"

Steve interrupted with a short laugh.

"My children! It's going some to make a mess of my life for prospective children. Take it from me, they'll keep on playing with the angels for some time yet."

"Then don't make a mess of your life. Is—is there any other girl? Are you in love, Steve?"

His son thrust his hands hard into the pockets of his dinner coat.

"I've never been swept off my feet at the sight of a girl's face, if you mean that according-to-fiction stuff. Before I went across I thought Felice Peyton——"

"Felice! But she married Phil Denbigh while you were away and now——" He stopped in perturbed realization of what had happened.

"And now they've separated and Felice is cynical and hard. I know that. I never really approved of her in my heart, her ideas, her ideals—oh well, she hasn't any; she wouldn't recognize an ideal if it tapped her on the shoulder. Her plan of life wasn't mine, but somehow I was eternally tagging after her. Moth and candle stuff, I suppose."

Courtlandt stared into the fire for a moment before he raised his head and looked at his son.

"We won't go on with this, Steve. It's taking too

many chances. I'll tell Glamorgan in the morning that he can foreclose and be———"

"No you won't, at least not until we have met the daughter. Have you ever seen her?" then as his father shook his head, "I'll give you a close-up of the lady. Amazon variety—look at the size of Glamorgan—little eyes, prominent teeth, a laugh that would raise the dead and, oh boy,—I'll bet she's kittenish." He glanced at the tall clock in the corner. "I'll tell Judson to have the sedan brought round. We'll have just time to array ourselves for the sacrifice, and motor to town before the theatres are out."

As the older man's eyes, turbulent with affection and anxiety met his, he exclaimed with a sporting attempt at a laugh:

"I'll bet a hat, sir, that when the lady sees you nothing short of being the Mrs. Courtlandt will satisfy her soaring ambition. She won't stand for being merely Mrs. Stephen. By the way, what's the prospect's name?"

"Geraldine. Her father calls her Jerry." Courtlandt senior laughed for the first time that evening. "That's a great idea of yours, Steve. I hadn't thought of offering myself. Perhaps as she only wants the name and position she'd take me and let you off. Your mother would understand," with a tender smile at the woman over the mantel. Her lovely eyes seemed to answer his. For an instant a look of unutterable yearning saddened the man's eyes—then he straightened and looked at his son.

"But no, Glamorgan expressly stipulated that he'd have you for a son-in-law or———"

The light died out of Stephen Courtlandt's face as he muttered furiously under his breath:

"Glamorgan be hanged!"

II

THE telephone in the luxurious living-room of their suite rang sharply as Daniel Glamorgan and his daughter entered. The girl looked at the instrument as though she suspected a concealed bomb in its mysterious depths, then appealingly at her father. He took down the receiver.

"Yes. All right. Send them up." He replaced it with a click. His grim mouth softened into a self-congratulatory smile. "Courtlandt and his son are down-stairs," he announced. "Did you order supper, Jerry?"

"Yes, Dad. The table is laid in the breakfast-room. Leon will serve it when you ring. I'll—I'll go to my room and leave my wrap."

His green eyes dilated with pride as he regarded her.

"You look like a princess to-night, my girl."

"I feel like a princess. They're usually disposed of to a title or some little thing like that, aren't they?" she asked with a laugh which held a sob of terror.

"Look here, Jerry. You're not losing your nerve? You're not going back on me, are you?"

She met his eyes squarely.

"I am not, Dad. The fewer ancestors one has behind one the better ancestor one must make of oneself. When I make a promise I make it to keep. I promised you that if Stephen Courtlandt asked me to marry him I'd say 'Yes.'"

Glamorgan's eyes glistened with satisfaction.

"You have the right idea, Jerry. Here they are now," as the bell rang.

"You meet them. I'll take off my wrap—I'll——"
In sudden panic the girl entered her room and closed the door behind her. She leaned against it. Her heart beat like mad. In the process of making the dream of her father's life come true was she wrecking her own

life? But he had been such a wonderful father—and— to be honest with herself, the romance and tradition and social standing of the Courtlandt name made an alluring appeal to her. She had envied friends at school and college for their careless references to their grandfathers; her earliest recollection was of a room full of hot, grimy miners in a little home near the coal-fields. To marry into the Courtlandt family in America would be commensurate with marrying into a dukedom in England. She breathed a fervent prayer of thanksgiving that her father's ambition hadn't urged him in that direction, also that character had counted with him before social position when he selected his prospective son-in-law.

Her shimmering wrap dropped to the floor as she crossed to her dressing-table and gravely appraised her reflection in the mirror. Was the girl staring so intently back at her fitted to preside over the Courtlandt Manor? She tested every detail of her appearance. Her orchid evening gown set off her arms and the curves of her white shoulders to perfection. Her hair was of glistening brown, brown shot through with red and gold where its soft waves caught the light. Her eyes were brown, large and dark and velvety, like deep pools reflecting a myriad of tiny gold stars now when she was deeply moved and excited. Her mouth seemed fashioned for laughter. The lips were vivid and exquisitely curved, and when they smiled a deep dimple dented one cheek. Her ringless hands were slender and beautifully formed.

"Dad says that you have Mother to thank for your hands," she told the looking-glass girl. She lingered before the mirror, aimlessly moving the gold and enameled appointments on the dressing-table. She dreaded to enter the next room. Her life might be changed for all time, doubtless would be, for she would marry Stephen Courtlandt if he wanted to save his estate enough to take her on her own conditions. She flushed then whitened. Perhaps he wouldn't want her after all. Well, that would soon be settled. Better to have the awkward meeting over as soon as possible. She picked up a large feather fan that was a shade deeper than her gown. As she touched it she felt armed for any contingency, and not without reason, for a fan in the hands of a beautiful woman is as effective as a machine-gun directed by an expert rifleman. Jerry swept her vis-à-vis a profound courtesy.

"I'll say you'll do, Mrs. Stephen Courtlandt," she encouraged with gay inelegance. The laugh still lingered on her lips and lurked in her eyes as she entered the living-room.

The three men who had been looking into the fire turned. The girl's heart went out to the elder Courtlandt in a rush of sympathy. His head was so high, his face so white, his eyes so full of hurt pride. The younger man's face was quite as white, his head quite as high, but there was an aggressive set to lips and jaw, a mixture of amazement and antagonism in his eyes, then something else flamed there which she couldn't diagnose as easily.

"He looks stunned. What did he expect, the pig-faced lady?" the girl thought contemptuously even as she advanced with extended hand and smiled up at the elder Courtlandt.

"Mr. Courtlandt, you seem like an old friend, my father has spoken of you so often," she welcomed in her charming, well-bred voice which had a curiously stimulating lilt in it.

The color rushed back to Peter Courtlandt's face, the expression in his eyes changed to one of relief and honest admiration as he bent over her hand.

"I realize now how much I have lost in not accepting your father's invitation to call before. Will you permit me to present my son, Stephen?"

Jerry crushed down an hysterical desire to laugh. It was so ridiculous, the casual, pleased-to-meet-you attitude of the three persons whom her father was moving at his will about the checker-board of life. She murmured something in which the words "a pleasure" were alone audible. Steve acknowledged them stiffly. Her eyes met his with their faint scornful smile which she felt masked so much. They held hers for a second before she turned to her father.

"Shall we go out to supper?" With engaging camaraderie she slipped her hand under Peter Courtlandt's arm. The expression of his eyes when they had first met hers had won her tender heart. "We'll let the younger set follow us," she laughed. He shook his head.

"I defy Steve to feel as young as I feel now," he asserted with a gallant promptness which delighted her.

At supper she devoted herself to him. He laughed and jested with her and but for his white hair looked almost as young as his son. Steve, angered by her persistent avoidance of himself, broke into their conversation with a banality which caused his father to look at him in amazed incredulity.

"Are you enjoying New York, Miss Glamorgan?"

Jerry regarded him for a moment from under long lashes before, with a smile which she was sure made him want to shake her, she answered:

"Immensely; but this is not my first winter in the city. Dad and I have made our headquarters here since I grew up." She turned to his father, but Steve refused to be ignored.

"Do you like it?"

"Like it? I love it! It's so big, so beautiful and—and —and so faulty," her pose of indifference had fallen from her like a discarded veil; she was all eager enthusiasm. "I—I like to be where there are many people. I would starve for companionship, not food, in the wilderness." Steve raised his brows and smiled unsmilingly.

"Then you believe in love?"

The color burned over her face to her scornful eyes. "He is willing to marry for money yet he dares sneer at me about love," she thought angrily, even as she looked up and deliberately studied him. She laughed a gay little mocking laugh.

"Believe in love? Of course I believe in love; don't you? But what an absurd question to ask. As though you would champion the tender passion." She saw his

eyes darken and his jaw set before she turned to his
father. She was contrite, a little frightened. What had
possessed her to antagonize him like that? A poor way
to begin a partnership which she had hoped would develop into a real friendship.

"Jerry, take Steve into the living-room and give us
some music. Mr. Courtlandt and I will smoke here,"
commanded Glamorgan, as his servant, who fairly ex-
uded efficiency, passed cigars and cigarettes.

"Perhaps—perhaps he would prefer to stay here and
smoke," the girl suggested hurriedly, for the first time
losing her poise. She caught a glint of challenge in
Stephen's eyes and rose. Her color was high, her breath
a bit uneven as she smiled at him with bewildering
charm. "After all, why should I make suggestions? You
are quite old enough to decide what you want to do
yourself, aren't you?"

"Yes. Quite old enough and quite ready to decide
for myself," he answered as he stood aside for her to
precede him into the living-room. "Do you play or
sing?" he asked as he followed her to the piano. The
instrument looked as though it were loved and used. It
was her turn to be a trifle scornful.

"I play and sing. Does it seem incredible that I
should?" She seated herself and dropped her hands in
her lap. "Shall I play for you?"

"Please." He leaned his arms on the piano and
looked down at her, but she realized that his thoughts
were not following his eyes. "I am not in the least musical, but we had a chap in our company overseas who
could make the most shell-shocked instrument give out
what seemed to us in the midst of that thundering in-
ferno, heavenly music. Sometimes now a wave of long-
ing for the sound of a piano sweeps over me, played by
someone who loves music as that boy loved it. Do you
know—Schumann's 'Papillions'? That was one of his
favorites."

For answer she played the first bar of the exquisite
thing. Once she glanced up. The eyes of the man lean-
ing on the piano, not blue now, but dark with mem-

ories, were an ocean removed from her. It was a minute
after the last note was struck before they came back to
her face. He drew a long breath.

"Thank you," he said simply, but his tone was better
than a paean of praise. Then the softness left his eyes.
There was aggressiveness and a hint of irony in his
voice as he said stiffly:

"My—my father has given me to understand that
you will do me the honor to marry me."

A passion of anger shook the girl. She valiantly
forced back the tears which threatened, rose and faced
him defiantly. Her slender fingers smoothed out the long
plumes of her fan. There should be no subterfuge now,
she determined, no cause for recrimination later.

"Your father, doubtless, has told you also that my
father is willing to buy your name and social position
for me with a portion of his fortune. A sort of fifty-
fifty arrangement, isn't it?" she added flippantly, with
the faintest flicker of her bronze-tipped lashes. Courtlandt shrugged.

"If you wish to put it so crudely."

She took a step back and clenched her hands behind
her. Her beautiful eyes were brilliant with scorn, her
heart pounded. It seemed as though it must visibly
shake her slender body as she answered:

"Why not? If we speak the truth now it may save
complications later. You know that my father wants me
to marry you and—and why. I frankly confess that I
sympathize with his ambitions. I want the best of life
in my associations. Your father is in difficulties of one
sort—my father is in difficulties of another sort—if a
lack of family background can be called a difficulty—
and it appears that with our help they can accommo-
date one another. I'd do anything for Dad—he has
done so much for me." She set her teeth sharply in her
under lip to steady it.

"Then—then you are not afraid to marry without
love?" His eyes were inscrutable.

"Without love? For the man I marry? No, not as long
as I have no love for any other. I might love a man

when I married him, and then—love comes unbidden, oftentimes unwanted and pouf!—it goes the way it came, and no one can stop it. You know that yourself."

"Not if it is real love, the love of a man for the one woman," he defended.

"Is there such a thing? I wonder?" skeptically.

If he felt a temptation to retaliate he resisted it.

"Then I may conclude that you accept me?" he prompted with frigid courtesy.

"Yes, that is——" a nervous sob caught at her voice. "If—if you will agree to my conditions. Dad has promised me an income of a hundred thousand a year. I will keep half of it in my possession, the other half you are to have to use as you please."

Courtlandt's eyes were black with anger, his knuckles white. He was rough, direct, relentless as he answered:

"You are indeed determined to make this a business affair. But understand now that I won't touch one cent of your cursed money. Whatever arrangement your father wants to make with you and my father is his affair and yours, but you are to leave me out of it absolutely. That's my condition. Do you get it?"

"Yes, I get it." She colored richly, angrily, then paled. Even her lips went white. "There is one thing more. I—we—this marriage is really a bargain—money for social position. Let it be only that. Need there be anything else? You must understand me—you must," in passionate appeal. She laid her hand on his arm. He looked down at her with disconcerting steadiness. His face was stern.

"Yes, I understand. You mean a marriage stripped to its skeleton of legal terms. No mutual responsibilities, no mutual sacrifices, no—no love. That is for you to decide. The Courtlandt debt is far too great for me not to accept any terms you may dictate. It shall be as you wish, I—promise."

Her brown eyes were brilliant with unshed tears as she held out an impulsive hand.

"Thank you. You make the arrangements seem bleak and sordid, but you have given me back my self-re-

spect. Now I feel that it is an honorable bargain between us two. You are to be perfectly free to come and
go as you like, and I shall be free, too—but there is
one thing I promise you, I—I shall never harm the
name I take."

He looked down at the hand he held for an instant
then released it.

"I knew that when you came into the room to-
night. Will you marry me soon?"

"Whenever you like. Will you—say good-night to
your father for me? I——" With a valiant effort to
steady her lips, she smiled faintly, opened the door of
her room and closed it quickly behind her.

Peter Courtlandt was the first to break the silence
as father and son motored home. He made an effort to
speak lightly.

"Well, my boy, your close-up was wrong. Geraldine
Glamorgan has neither prominent teeth, nor little eyes,
nor a kittenish manner; in fact, I don't know when I
have seen so beautiful a girl so singularly free from the
barnacles of vanity and self-consciousness."

"Kittenish!" his son repeated curtly. "She's far from
kittenish. She's an iceberg, and what's more she has the
business instinct developed to the nth degree. Believe
me, she's a born trader."

III

GERALDINE COURTLANDT slowed down her car to enter the river road. The sun was setting in a blaze of
crimson glory, a few belated birds winged swiftly into
the west. Lights on the opposite shore flickered for a
moment as they flashed into being, then shone with
steady brilliancy. Lights appeared on the few boats
swinging at anchor in the quiet water. Lights in house
windows beaconed a steady welcome to home-comers.
What individuality there was in lights the girl thought.

Those across the river seemed entirely municipal and commerical, those on the boats carried a silent warning, those in the windows seemed warmly human.

The turmoil in Jerry's heart subsided. She had driven miles that afternoon through the cold, exhilarating rush of December air, trying to forget Steve's tone when he had refused her offer to drive him to town that morning. Had she been married only a month? It seemed as though centuries had passed since she and Steve had stood before the altar with their few witnesses and exchanged marriage vows. She shivered. If she had realized how irrevocable they were, their solemn admonition, would she have had the courage to marry to please her father, she wondered.

"And forsaking all others keep thee only unto him as long as ye both shall live?" The question had echoed in every sound at the wedding breakfast in her father's apartment; she had read it deep in Peggy's eyes as they had met hers from across the room; it had kept time to the revolution of the wheels as she and Steve had motored out to the Manor in the late afternoon. Her lips twisted in a bitter little smile as she remembered Sir Peter's tactful suppression of surprise when they had told him that there would be no wedding journey. She and Steve had decided that under the circumstances such a function would be nothing short of farcical, besides he would not ask for leave from the office. Sir Peter had quite suddenly decided to go on a hunting trip.

The girl's brows wrinkled in a troubled frown. She knew now that she had done a grave injustice to Steve, to herself, when she had consented to her father's proposition. Well, the deed was done, her only course was to turn her mistake into a stepping-stone toward ultimate good. That was the one way to treat mistakes remedially, she had learned in her twenty-three years. Repining proved nothing.

"Every engaged couple ought to have the marriage service read aloud to them at least once a week. That would give them pause," she murmured with fervent

conviction. She ground on her brake just in time to
avoid running down a "ROAD CLOSED. DETOUR" sign.
The black letters on the white board danced weirdly
before her eyes for a moment. She must cure herself of
the reprehensible habit of driving with her mind miles
away. She turned into the side road and drove slowly.
Detours were notoriously rough even if they sometimes
offered adventure, she thought whimsically.

The upper windows of the Manor reflected the setting
sun through swaying, bare branches. They shone like
molten mirrors as Jerry turned into the tree-lined avenue which led to the house. At the foot of the garden
slope she caught the shimmer of the river. Already she
loved the place. The great house had "home" writ large
all over it. It bulged, it loomed, it rambled in unexpected places as though it had grown with the family.
And yet, in spite of the additions, it remained a choice
example of early architecture. It was as though a benef-
icent fairy, versed in the arts, had presided over the
alterations.

As the girl entered the great hall, where logs blazed
in the mammoth fireplace, she had the sense of being
enfolded in warm, tender arms. If Steve would not be
so frigidly courteous she could be quite happy, she
thought resentfully. At breakfast each morning during
these interminable weeks he had politely asked her pref-
erence for the evening. Should they motor to town for
the theatre, dance, what should they do? And she,
dreading to bore him more than he was already bored,
and hating to face the curious eyes of his world which
had been set agog at their marriage, had replied to each
suggestion:

"I prefer to remain in this lovely country, but please
go yourself. I really shouldn't be in the least lonely."

He had refused to take advantage of her suggestion.
Every night they dined together with great formality,
she in the loveliest frocks of her hastily assembled
trousseau, he in correct and immaculate dinner clothes.
The only time there seemed the least sympathy between
them was when she was at the piano, in the library, and

Steve smoked in the big chair in front of the fire. He kept so absolutely still, usually with his eyes on his mother's portrait. Was he dreaming dreams, she wondered. Had there been a girl without money whom he loved? Did he know what "the love of a man for the one woman" meant? She should never forget the tone in which he had asked that question. She was standing in the hall, her coat off, when she thought of that. She shook herself mentally and dragged her thoughts back to the present. She spoke to her trim maid who came to take her coat:

"Tell Judson to serve tea in the library, Hilda. I—I'm cold."

She was half-way to the fireplace in the long room before she discovered that the wing-chair in front of it was occupied, occupied by a queer, elfish type of man who regarded her with a poorly suppressed snort of disdain as she paused in surprise. The skin stretched over his high cheek-bones till it shone like mellowing, yellowing ivory. His colorless eyes glittered as with fever, his forehead reared to where his coarse white hair brandished a sort of kewpie-curl. A black cape, of wool so soft that it looked like velvet, lay across his thin, stooped shoulders. From under its folds his hands protruded, clasped on the top of a stout ebony stick. They were gnarled and distorted with rheumatism. His voice, true to type, was high and slightly cracked as he spoke to the girl after an instant of peeved scrutiny.

"So—you're the new Mrs. Courtlandt, the lady of the Manor, are you? You're the girl who has been traded in to save the family fortune?"

The angry color flamed to Jerry's hair but she stood her ground. She even managed to bestow a patronizing frown upon him.

"Now I know who you are. No one but 'Old Nick' would be so rude. You see your reputation has preceded you." She sank into the chair opposite him and with elbow on its arm, chin on her hand, regarded him curiously. She made a brilliant bit of color in the dark-toned room. The light from the fire fell on her rose-

color sports suit, brought out the sheen of the velvet
tam of the same shade, drooped picturesquely over one
ear, flickered fantastically on her white throat, set the
diamonds in the pin which fastened the dainty frills of
her blouse agleam with rainbows and played mad
pranks with the circlet of jewels on the third finger of
her left hand.

How ill and fragile he looked, the girl thought, pathetically fragile. She had a passion of sympathy for the
old. She would ignore his rudeness. She leaned forward and smiled at him with gay friendliness.

"Now that I have guessed who you are it's your
turn. Tell me how you got here. Did a magician wave
his wand, and presto, an enchanted carpet, or did you
arrive via airroute? I am sorry that there was no one
at the Manor to welcome you. I was detained by one of
those silly detours. Sir Peter has been away but returns
to-night, and Steve—did Steve know that you were
coming? Did—did he write you about—about me?" the
last word was added in an undignified whisper.

"Steve! Do they ever let Steve tell me anything?"

"Now I've done it, he's off!" Jerry thought with an
hysterical desire to laugh, he was so like an old war-
horse scenting battle.

"No. The first I knew of you was when Peter Courtlandt wrote that a marriage had been arranged between
the daughter of Glamorgan, the oil-king, and Steve. Arranged! Stuff and nonsense! What poor fool arranged
it, I'd like to know? Hasn't Peter Courtlandt seen
enough of life to know that when a man who has
nothing marries a girl with a large fortune he's ruined?
If he has any strength of character it turns to gall, if
he's a weak party, he gets weaker—it's hell—for a
proud man. Why didn't they give me a chance to save
the family fortune? I'd have done it if Steve had asked
me, but I turned his father down—I wouldn't give a
penny to save him. Why—why that boy ought to have
married someone who'd count, not a once-removed
coal-picker."

Furious as she was at his insult, Jerry kept her temper. It was so pathetically evident that he was old and disappointed and alarmingly ill. However, there was a hint of Glamorgan's determination in her eyes as she answered coolly:

"You may say what you like about me, but I can't let you disparage my father. He is the biggest thing in my life. After all, why should you roar at me? Steve and I are not the first victims sacrificed on the altar of pride of family and possessions, are we? Sentiment is quite out of fashion. What passes for it is but a wan survival of the age of romance and chivalry. Marriage in that strata of society to which I have been lately elevated is like the Paul Jones at a dance, when the whistle blows change partners—in the same set, if one should happen to go out of it, pandemonium, quickly followed by oblivion."

If he was conscious of the sting of sarcasm in her words he ignored it. His voice was barbed with thorns of irritation as he affirmed:

"Then it is as I suspected; you're not in love with Steve. So love is out of fashion, is it? To be scornful of love is the prerogative of youth; when we get old we treasure it. Well, I warn you now, young woman, that my nephew shan't live the loveless life I've lived. I was born rich. Had I been poor and married, had my wife been my working partner dependent upon me for money, helping me climb, I shouldn't be the wreck of a man I am now."

"What a pre-nineteenth amendment sentiment," the girl dared mischievously. He glowered at her from under his bushy brows.

"You can't switch me off my subject with your flippancy. I repeat, Steve shall have love. I'll get it for him—I'll——" He rose and brandished his stick at the girl. He fell back and leaned his head weakly against the chair. Jerry leaned over him and smoothed back his hair tenderly. He looked up at her with fever-bright eyes and gasped breathlessly:

"I haven't gone—yet. I shan't go till—I've thought of some way to—to yank Steve out of this—this dam-

nable Sam Jones ring you talk about. Give me some tea.
Quick! Give it to me—strong. My fool doctor won't let
me have anything else. What's Steve doing? Living on
your income?" he asked as Judson, after fussing among
the tea-things, at low word from the girl, left the room.

Jerry's cheeks flushed, tiny sparks lighted her eyes
as she countered crisply:

"Don't you know your nephew better than to ask
that question? He is in a lawyer's office working for the
munificent sum of fifteen per." Fairfax choked over
his tea.

"D'you mean to tell me that a son-in-law of Glamorgan the oil-king is an office boy? Between you all you've
made a mess of it, haven't you? What does your father
say to that?"

"He's—he's furious," Jerry answered, as she studied
the infinitesimal grounds in her teacup. She gave the
tea-cart a little push which removed it from between
them. She rose, hesitated, then slipped to her knees before the old man. She looked up at him speculatively for
a moment before she commenced to trace an intricate
pattern on his stout stick with a pink-tipped finger. Her
voice was low and a trifle unsteady as she pleaded:

"Uncle Nick, be friends with me, will you?" A non-
committal grunt was her only answer. "Steve won't talk
to me. He won't listen to reason. Having made his big
sacrifice for the family fortunes by marrying me he is
holding his head so high that he'll step into a horrible
shell-hole if he doesn't watch out. Dad is furious that he
won't live and spend money as befits a Courtlandt, that
is, as he thinks a Courtlandt should live and spend, and
with that fine illogic, so characteristic of the male of the
species, takes it out on me. Steve is so—so maddening.
He won't use the automobiles unless he is taking me
somewhere, although they were all, with the exception
of my town car and roadster, in the garage when I
came here. He just commutes and commutes in those
miserable trains. Commuting corrupts good manners;
he's a—a bear. He and I are beginning all wrong, Uncle
Nick." She met the stern old eyes above her before she

dropped her head to the arm of his chair. "Steve hates the sight of me and I———"

Fairfax laid his stick across her shoulders with a suddenness and strength which made her jump.

"What did you expect? Didn't I tell you that when a poor man marries a fortune his pride turns to gall? Can a red-blooded man really love a girl who would marry for position? You're fast getting to hate him, I suppose?" he demanded in a tone which brought her to her feet and iced her voice and eyes.

"You wouldn't expect me to be crazy about him, would you? He is cold and disagreeable and is evidently laboring under the delusion that the world was created to revolve around Stephen Courtlandt." A contemptuous snort fired her with the determination to hurt someone or something. "You may take it from me that if I had the chance to choose again between disappointing Dad or marrying your precious nephew I'd— I'd disappoint Dad." She was breathless but triumphant as she flung the last words at him. He glared at her.

"So-o, you're a quitter, are you?"

Jerry's face was white, her eyes smoldering coals of wrath. Her voice was low with repressed fury as she flung back his taunt.

"I'm not a quitter. But why couldn't Dad have selected some other aristocrat for a son-in-law? From what I have observed there are plenty of them who need money. Believe me, I'm tired of living in this cold storage atmosphere. I was willing to play fair, willing to keep my part of the contract———" Her voice failed her as she met his grilling eyes.

"Are you fulfilling your———"

"What, Uncle Nick, tea-broken?" interrupted a voice from the door. The old man struggled to his feet as his nephew came toward him. A smile of tenderness dimmed the glitter of his eyes. Jerry's heart looped the loop. How long had Steve been at the door? Had he heard that last rebellious declaration of hers? How would he greet his uncle? She hoped that he would be tender, for no matter how disagreeable Nicholas Fairfax was, he was old and evidently dangerously ill. She was quite unconscious of her breath of relief as the younger man laid an affectionate arm about the elder's shoulders.

"This sure is a surprise and then some, Uncle Nick. Why didn't you let us know you were coming?"

"I knew if I wrote, your father'd invent an excuse to put me off, so I roped Doc Rand and came along. I have no time to waste. I wanted to see the kind of girl they'd sold you to——"

"Then you have seen a fine one who did me the honor to marry me, haven't you?" There was a set to young Courtlandt's jaw which boded ill for the person who differed with him. "Why not come up to your room and rest before dinner? Sir Peter returns to-night and you'll want—here he is now," as the hum of voices in the hall drifted to the library.

Jerry sprang forward with a radiant smile of welcome as Peter Courtlandt entered the room. He seized her two hands in his and kissed her tenderly.

"It's a good many years since I had a welcome home like this," he admitted with a break in his voice. "How are you, Steve? Nick, I just ran into Doc Rand in the hall. He told me that you were here." He held out his hand to his brother-in-law who responded grudgingly.

"I suppose he told you a lot of other stuff, too. Well, I'll fool him."

Jerry gave the hand that still held one of hers a surreptitious squeeze.

"It's good to have you back, Sir Peter. The house has seemed terribly big and empty without you."

"Empty!" echoed Fairfax with his sardonic chuckle. "Fancy a bride of a month complaining of emptiness in a house without her father-in-law."

"How does it happen that you have torn yourself away from the ranch, Nick?" interrupted Peter Courtlandt before Steve, who had grown white about the nostrils, could speak. "The last time you came on you said you would never leave it again."

Fairfax swallowed the bait which never failed to lure

him. His western possessions were his pride, and he welcomed an opportunity to talk of them much as a fond parent does of his child.

"Didn't want to leave. Felt it my duty to come and see what you had done to Steve," he growled. "Greyson, of the X Y Z, is looking after things for me."

"Greyson of the X Y Z! Is your ranch near his?" Jerry demanded. A faint color stole to her face, her eyes were alight with interest.

"It is. What do you know about it?" Fairfax's eyes were interrogation points of suspicion.

"Not much. I met Mr. Greyson last winter, and I——"

"Met Greyson, did you? Humph! So that's what's the matter with him. I suppose the daughter of an oil-king looked down upon——"

"Have you had a profitable year?" interrupted Peter Courtlandt, adroitly getting between his son and the old man. "They tell me that this has been a banner season for wheat."

"They told you right. If the cattle winter safe I shall achieve the ambition of my life, to own the biggest and finest herd of Shorthorns in the country. I'll show 'em a thing or two about that breed of cattle. I tell you, Peter——"

"Mrs. Denbigh," announced Judson at the door.

Jerry caught the look of consternation which Peter Courtlandt threw at his son. She saw also the sudden tightening of Steve's lips. What did it mean? She had met Felice Denbigh once and had been repulsed by her super-golden hair and superb-perfect complexion. Was she an old sweetheart of Steve's? She took a step toward the smartly gowned woman who spoke as she crossed the threshold.

"Mrs. Courtlandt, you will forgive me for this intrusion on your honeymoon, won't you? But——but Steve left his gloves in my sedan this morning when we drove to town, and I came to return them."

Jerry's mind took a dizzy turn or two then settled down to clear thinking. She had a curious sense that with the explanation Felice Denbigh had fired the opening gun of a campaign. So there had been a reason why Steve had refused to allow her to drive him to town. She flashed a glance at him even while she murmured welcoming platitudes to her guest. He had his hand on his uncle's arm.

"You remember Felice Peyton, don't you, Uncle Nick?"

"What's that? Felice Peyton, the girl you were forever running after when you were in college? Well, Miss Peyton, you lost him, didn't you?" asked the terrible old man.

"But—but dear Mr. Fairfax, I'm not Miss Peyton now—I married Phil Denbigh when Steve deserted me and went to war. I——"

"Philip Denbigh!" The old man rose, straightened himself like an avenging Nemesis. "Poor devil! So he drew another blank besides that good-for-nothing philandering mother of his. A mother who wept and begged until she kept the boy from enlisting, and by some hokuspokus got him into Class C.—No, I won't stop," as Courtlandt senior laid a peremptory hand on his arm. "There are a lot of men who are cringing through life to-day because their women did not love them enough to cheer them on to fight in the Great Fight."

Felice Denbigh was white with anger, her eyes tiny green flames. Jerry flung herself into the breach:

"Won't you stay and dine with us informally, Mrs. Denbigh? Poor S-Steve must have been bored to death, surfeited with my society this last month."

"Thank you, no." Felice's self-possession was superb. "I shall pay my respects to the new Mrs. Courtlandt later when she is formally at home. Good-night, Mr. Fairfax. What a pleasure it must be for the family to have your genial presence at the Manor. You don't know how happy it makes me to find that someone remembers Steve's devotion to me. He seems to have forgotten it. Good-night, Sir Peter. Stevie, will you come and start that cranky car of mine?" Then, as he reached her side, Jerry heard her ask softly, "Shall we meet at the same place to-morrow morning?"

Nicholas Fairfax must have heard it also, for the girl heard him mutter:

"Snake!"

IV

As she served coffee in the library after dinner Jerry pondered over those low-spoken words. The firelight set the sequins on her pale blue gown glittering like jewels; it accentuated the satiny sheen of her hair, betrayed the troubled expression in her lovely eyes. Nicholas Fairfax was in his room. He had collapsed when he went up to dress for dinner. Doctor Rand, whom he had brought with him, stood back to the fire stirring his coffee. There was a suggestion of fat and wheeze about the little man. His weather-stained face had the wrinkled effect of a quite elderly, quite plump russet apple. His white hair bushed à la Golliwog. His frock coat was of finest, pre-war broadcloth. The flamboyant effect of his black necktie made the girl think of the bow on the neck of a pet kitten. He tested his coffee before he observed dryly:

"If a man with an under-developed heart-beat and an over-developed blood-pressure will go chasing half-way across the continent to see a pretty girl," he bowed with somewhat ponderous gallantry in Jerry's direction, "what can you expect but collapse? He's crazy about you, Steve, and somewhere he got the fool notion that you were unhappy. That's what started him East. I tried to hold him back. I knew the price he'd pay."

Stephen Courtlandt came suddenly from the window where he had been looking out upon the snow-dusted world. He approached the fire. His eyes looked strained.

"Then you think he won't rally from this attack, Doc?" he asked anxiously.

"It's better for you to know the truth, Steve. He knows. He's wired for Greyson of the X Y Z and——"

"Oh-h!"

The startled exclamation had escaped Jerry's lips before she realized that she had made a sound. A delicate pink stole to her hair as she met Steve's steady eyes. Doctor Rand was apparently quite unconscious of the interruption.

"And sent for your family lawyer. Your father is with him now. I'll go and relieve him. Your cookie sure makes good coffee, Mrs. Jerry. Bring her out to the Double O and invite us old bachelors for eats once in a while. You'd be doing a charity bigger than some you spend your time on here, I can tell you."

"Mrs. Courtlandt would starve for people in that wilderness, Doc," announced Stephen with parrot-like glibness.

"Would she now? Sure, she doesn't look like a child who'd be so dependent on chatter. Well, the Double O isn't in the Dude ranch region, neither is it exactly a wilderness. It's a seething cauldron of society in comparison to some of the places. You knew that Old Nick and Greyson had given the Bear Creek ranch to a returned service man, didn't you, Steve?" then as Courtlandt nodded, "He brought a wife out last spring. She doesn't have a woman to speak to but she reminds me of a meadow-lark, little and quiet but with a voice that sings."

"Do she and her husband live there all alone?" Jerry asked in wonder.

"Yes—that is—there's a range-rider but—but that's another story." Had she not thought it quite out of character Jerry would have sworn that Doc Rand was embarrassed. "We—here I am talking when my patient needs me. It's all your fault, Mrs. Jerry. You shouldn't have vamped me so outrageously. Steve, I want a prescription filled."

"I'll send Carter for it, Doc. Give it to me." He left the room with the slip of paper in his hand. Rand looked after him, then thoughtfully at the girl where she sat in the flickering light of the fire. He set his cup on the tray and patted her hand gently.

"Don't mind Old Nick, child. He's sick and jealous and—and mad about Steve—it will all come right. Things have a marvelous unbelievable way of coming right. That's what I kept telling Fairfax but he wouldn't listen."

"Why—why should he hate me so?"

"He doesn't hate you, he's—he's just afraid for Steve, that's all. He adored his sister—he used to say that when he found a woman like her, he'd marry——" he looked up at the portrait over the mantel. Jerry's glance followed his. The eyes, so like Steve's, were thoughtful, there was a suspicion of laughter in the curve of the lips, the flesh tints were marvelously lovely, a string of rare pearls gleamed softly on the creamy neck. The artist had worked lovingly and had produced a portrait that was humanly, warmly alive, a spirit that dominated the quiet room.

"Steve,—Steve and Sir Peter love her like that too, do they not?"

Rand thrust his hands under his coat tails and flapped them in time with his heel and toe teeter.

"Love her! It is more than love. Betty Fairfax, the name clung even after marriage, makes me believe in immortality. The best of her is living in Steve and it will be handed on to his children. Her spirit is just as much alive for her husband and son as it was the day she left them. That's why Steve has kept straight through temptations which would have lured most chaps of his age. No one can ever tell me, and get across with it, that a mother's influence doesn't live forever. That boy is one of a thousand, isn't he, Mrs. Jerry?"

"Oh—perhaps, as thousands go." She looked up from under her long lashes at his discomfited face. Laughter gleamed through the tears which his tribute to the mother had brought. "You shouldn't pry into the secrets of a maiden's heart," she teased with exaggerated demureness. Rand responded to her mood.

"That's better. A child like you should laugh, not be as serious as you've been ever since I've seen you. Don't let Nick's condition depress you. He may live for weeks and when he does go, it will be a release. He wants it—if—if he can go knowing that Steve's happiness is assured."

"Is anyone's happiness assured?" asked the girl gravely.

"No"—he regarded her with his twinkling gray eyes—"but I'll bet my broncho if anyone's is—it's Steve's. Good-night."

He was gone before Jerry could reply. Her heart felt curiously warmed by his words. He—he evidently liked her if Steve didn't. She went to the piano. Her fingers touched the keys experimentally for a moment, then she quite unconsciously struck the opening bar of "Papillions." The music danced and rose with dainty spontaneity. She drifted into Bach's "Praeludium." Separated chords or flowing melody, she played with a sympathy and sureness which showed the touch of an artist. She knew when Steve came into the room and crossed to the window. As the last note died away she turned. He stood with his hands clenched behind his back. What was interesting him outside, she wondered. She wanted to speak to him but she never yet had addressed him by his first name. It seemed absurd, it was absurd, but she had avoided using it to his face. To continue the avoidance presented difficulties now that his back was turned. She usually waited until he looked at her, which she had to acknowledge was seldom. She ran through the opening bars of "Papillions" again but his back remained obdurately turned to the room.

"I—you——" she halted awkwardly, "I would like to talk to you," she admitted hesitatingly. Courtlandt wheeled and approached the piano.

"Good Lord, don't you know my name that you have to juggle 'I—you——' when you want to attract my attention?" he demanded belligerently. There was a defiant gleam in the eyes which met his.

"It does sound silly, doesn't it—Stevie?" with exaggerated demureness and an exact imitation of Felice Denbigh's voice. "But—but I know yours better than you know mine—I think——" then as he opened his lips to speak she hurried on, "I wanted to ask if you were in love with Felice Denbigh? No—no—don't mistake me," as his blue eyes darkened to purple-black, and his lips tightened, "I'm not jealous—really I'm not —I only wanted you to know that if you are, I'm sorry, terribly sorry. It's a tragedy to love one person and have to marry another."

"How do you know? Are you in love with Greyson?" with rough directness.

His sudden turn of the tables took the girl's breath. She colored betrayingly. She knew that she must be the picture of guilt as she stood there, her color coming and going, her heart beating like a silly tom-tom. There was even a slight unsteadiness in her voice as she evaded:

"I haven't seen Bruce Greyson since last winter," then maddened at her own lack of poise she looked up with frank defiance. "It's a pity that he doesn't live here. He could motor me to town."

He flushed darkly.

"My motoring to town with Mrs. Denbigh this morning was purely accidental."

"But—but—you will never go with me."

"Trolley incomes should avoid limousine ladies."

"Limousine ladies!" Jerry gripped her temper and controlled her voice. "Pardon! My mistake," she drawled maddeningly. "Is—is Mrs. Denbigh divorced?"

"Not yet. What Old Nick said about Phil's mother was true. She did ruin his life. It would have been better for him and for her had he been shot to pieces, than to have him as he is now with this gnawing shame at his heart."

"She—she was not much like your mother, was she?"

"Like Mother?" Jerry thought she had never heard anything so beautiful as that word "Mother" as Courtlandt uttered it. He smiled up at the portrait—"Mother was—well——" he cleared the huskiness from his voice and went on, "As I was saying about Denbigh, remorse got too much for him and a year ago he disappeared, dropped completely out of sight."

"Why didn't Felice go with him?"

"Do you know, I fancy that Phil didn't want her."

"Nevertheless she had married him. One doesn't take the vow 'and forsaking all others' to break it, does one?" gravely.

"I deduce from that that you do not believe in divorce?"

"Divorce! While I acknowledged that there may be situations where it is unavoidable, I hate the word. Always to me it takes on the semblance of Medusa's head in my school mythology, its snaky, hissing locks striking, stabbing, stinging, scarring indelibly. I believe in keeping covenants."

"It's hard sometimes."

"It is, but life isn't intended to be all joy-ride. I've found that out."

"You mean——"

"Nothing which need make you glower at me like that," defiantly. "Do you know, I fancy," with an exact imitation of his earlier voice and manner, "that the future first families of America's 'Who's Who' will be those who can count back at least four generations of ancestors who have, in spite of disappointment and disillusion, poverty or riches, sickness or health, kept their marriage covenants. A curious idea, isn't it? It just came to me. 'A little thing but mine own,'" her tone changed from earnestness to flippancy on the last words. She syncopated a few bars of "Papillions" as though to emphasize her indifference.

Courtlandt thrust his hands hard into the pockets of his dinner coat. The atmosphere tingled with electricity. The girl wondered if he were throttling a desire to shake her. She hoped so. He met her eyes steadily for a moment before he turned to leave the room. Jerry took a hasty step after him.

"Wait, please—if—if——" as he kept on she added

desperately, "Steve, please." He stopped and turned. "If—if you should see Dad—do not mention the fact that Bruce—that Mr. Greyson's ranch is near your uncle's."

"Why not?" relentlessly.

"Because in an attack of homesickness last winter I became engaged to him."

V

In the music-room of the Manor the rugs had been rolled back, the voice of the phonograph released from captivity and the Courtlandts' guests were dancing, at least some of them were. Sir Peter had beguiled Glamorgan to the library for a smoke. The oil-king had cast a gloom over the dinner. Was it because he was disturbed about Nicholas Fairfax, Jerry wondered. To the amazement of all, he and the ranchman had become great friends. It would be like her father to be irritable if he were moved. Perhaps it had been the arrival of Greyson which had infuriated him. Last winter he had quickly made her see the folly of her engagement to the owner of the X Y Z, and now she was grateful to him. She had known at the time that she did not love Bruce Greyson, but that she was in love with love. In a way her life had been a lonely one, and when he had pleaded with her to marry him, she had agreed to a tentative engagement. Now she was glad that she had kept him at a distance, even in those two weeks.

She looked up at Greyson as he sat beside her in one of the deep embrasures of a window. A distinguished looking man, he gave the impression of having lived in great spaces, of having achieved worth-while things, of being absolutely poised and self-assured. His dark hair was tending toward neutral at the temples, his keen blue eyes had fine lines radiating from them, which denoted long-distance gazing. The weather-beaten texture of his skin was emphasized by the immaculate white of the shirt and collar of his up-to-the-minute dinner clothes.

Peggy Glamorgan, as she danced with her brother-in-law, was doing direful things to the heart of young Don Curtis, whose family estate adjoined the Manor. She was a charming, younger model of her sister, except that where Jerry's eyes were brown, Peggy's were a somewhat elfish hazel. She was making the most of a week-end freedom from school discipline. Steve Courtlandt's glance wandered to the two in the deep window. Peggy looked up at him with tormenting concern.

"That's the second time you've lost step, Steve. I protest. I hate being trodden on." Her laughing eyes and mischievously curved lips robbed the words of their sting.

"I'm sorry! Give me one more trial, Peg-o'-my-heart, and I'll do better," promised Steve. He had taken an immense liking to the girl, she was so genuine, so unaffected, so brimming over with the zest of living.

"Nothing doing, brother. Go get Jerry. It's a part of her job to put up with your poor dancing, isn't it? A part of the love, honor and obey stuff? Catch me saying 'I will' to that. Jerry's different. She'd walk over the proverbial ploughshares if she thought duty called." She looked across the room to where her sister sat and added softly, "It's a queer trick of fortune that Bruce Greyson should be your uncle's confidential man and should come to this house."

"Why accent this?" demanded Steve Courtlandt bluntly.

Peggy blushed guiltily beneath his stern eyes.

"That's only my exclamatory style. I meant that it was strange that Jerry should meet him here after—after—I—I wonder if that was what made her cry last night?"

"Did Jerry cry last night?"

"She cross-my-throat-and-hope-to-die swore she didn't, this morning, but her lids were suspiciously pink. Didn't you notice it? Thank you, I should love it," she responded to young Curtis who had been impatiently hovering in the offing. "There really isn't much fun dancing with old married men," she confided in a tone intended to reach Steve. She made her impudent little face at her brother-in-law over her partner's shoulder. He smiled and blew her a kiss as she danced away but her words hurt, hurt because he knew that she was right. He felt years older than he had that epoch-making October night when his father had revealed to him the state of the family finances, and had presented the means whereby it could be remedied. Had he chosen wisely, he wondered; wouldn't it have been better to let the property go than to have married a girl who had so quickly acquired an aversion for him?

He looked across at the two engrossed faces in the window. He'd break that up. Jerry should remember where she was and not give occasion for silly gossip. Already Felice Denbigh, who had motored out from town for dinner, had called his attention to Greyson's apparent devotion. With eyes combative, Steve strolled to where Jerry sat.

"Will you dance with me, Mrs. Courtlandt?" he asked with aggressive formality. In the midst of a sentence, she looked up in startled surprise. Greyson rose.

"I have committed the unpardonable blunder of monopolizing my hostess, Steve," he apologized, "but the temptation to live over a perfect friendship was too great to be resisted. I will beg a dance from your sister, Mrs. Courtlandt."

Jerry's eyes followed him as he crossed the room. They made Steve think of deep, troubled pools when she looked up at him. Was it because Peg had put the idea into his head or did they look as though they had known recent tears? Was she finding her marriage a bar to happiness already? His face was a trifle white, a trifle grim as he reminded:

"Do we dance?"

Without answering she rose, and he put his arm about her. Except for taking her hand it was the first time he had touched her. How slender she was, how soft, how graceful. He could feel her heart pound heavily against his breast. One might think that she was frightened, but with him—that was absurd. Her dancing like her walk was perfection of motion. He was careful of his steps as they danced down the long room. Jerry should have no occasion to echo Peg's reprimand. She stopped.

"Tired?" he asked solicitously, his senses still throbbing from the appeal of music and dance. She shook her head.

"Tired! I don't know what it is to be tired. Some of our guests are not dancing. Mrs. Denbigh is quite alone and looking horribly bored. Peg seems to have appropriated more than her share of men; she is surrounded. Don't you think that as host you should dance with Felice?"

"Presently. I have something to say to you first." He changed his position so that he stood between her and the others in the room.

"Why did you cry?"

She crimsoned even under the tiny curls at the nape of her white neck.

"I! Crying! How absurd. You really should go and dance with your guest——"

"Not until you tell me why you cried."

"But I haven't been crying."

"Oh, yes you have. I——"

"Supper is served in the library, Mrs. Courtlandt," interrupted Judson of the velvet tread. As they left the room in the wake of their guests the butler detained Stephen Courtlandt and said something in a low tone.

"Has Mr. Greyson gone up?" he asked hurriedly and when Judson answered in the affirmative he turned to Jerry:

"I must go to Uncle Nick. I may not be down again."

"Is he——" but he was mounting the stairs two steps at a time before Jerry had finished the sentence. With a feeling of foreboding she entered the library. The guests were grouped around the fire with Judson and a maid serving supper. She stopped in the shadow of the doorway. Upstairs the spirit of an old, weary man was passing, here—the room and its furnishings made a rich background for the shimmering satin of dainty gowns; the firelight played mad pranks with jewels at white throats and on pink fingers, with the glittering buckles on silver slippers; bright eyes were laughing into eyes that pleaded or compelled, young voices were teasing, challenging.

Jerry's breath came unevenly. She had cried last night. It was a rare indulgence for her. She could not tell now why. How could Steve have known? She hoped that none of these chattering boys and girls suspected it. She looked about the room. How she loved it! It stood for all the background she had acquired by her marriage. She loved the old seventeenth century Courtlandt, she held long, one-sided conversations with him when she was sure that she was quite alone. He had given her to understand that a *marriage de convenance* quite met with his approval, that in his day girls married to please their parents. She wasn't so sure of the judgment of Steve's mother. Her eyes, so like her son's, looked down with a grave question in their depths when she appealed to her.

The group around the fire made room as they welcomed her with gay reproof for tardiness. Felice Denbigh inquired impatiently for Steve. Jerry made his apologies and explained his absence. The voices of the guests became hushed. One by one they left, almost tiptoeing through the hall. Peggy snuggled up to her sister when the two were alone.

"Has—has Uncle N-Nick—gone?" she whispered. Then as Jerry shook her head, "If—if he does will you come and sleep with me?"

"I will, dear, but there is nothing to frighten you. Why should there be in the passing of an old man's spirit?"

"But—but he was such a cross old man. What has made you so brave, Jerry? Once you would have dreaded it as much as I—being here at a time like this, I mean."

"Perhaps it is the hours I have spent in the hospital with the sick and wounded soldiers. I have seen so much and felt so much, that death has seemed beautiful, not terrible. Go to bed, child. I'll come in later and stay with you."

She went down the hall. "But he was such a cross old man!" Peggy's obituary of Nicholas Fairfax echoed persistently in her mind. What a tragic thing to have said about one. She couldn't blame her sister. Old Nick had been consistently disagreeable to her and Peg was too young to take into consideration his age and illness. She lingered for a moment before the door of the room in which Nicholas Fairfax lay. Could she help? The nurse came out suddenly and almost collided with her.

"Goodness, Mrs. Courtlandt, you gave me a start! I was just coming for you. Mr. Stephen sent me. His uncle wants you."

With her breath coming hurriedly, her heart pounding, Jerry followed the woman. What could Old Nick want? To continue his insults? She passed into the inner room. The window was open to let in the clear winter air. The old man was raised high on his pillows. Steve held one of the gnarled hands. Courtlandt was behind him. Greyson, as rigid and immovable as one of the mountains of his own country, stood at the foot of the bed. Doctor Rand, his face grave and deeply lined, motioned the girl to take her place opposite Steve, then he and the nurse and Greyson moved back to the outer room. As Jerry bent over him, Nicholas Fairfax looked up into her eyes. They met his tenderly. The tenseness of his expression relaxed, he fumbled for something under his pillow. Jerry reached for him and drew out an open prayer-book. His shaking finger pointed to the page; it was the marriage service.

"Read that—read that—aloud," he commanded in a voice which still held a ring of power.

Slipping to her knees beside the bed the girl read. Haltingly, huskily at first, but as she lost thought of self in the beauty and meaning of the words her voice cleared.

" 'Wilt thou have this man to be thy wedded husband, to live together after God's ordinance in the holy estate of matrimony and forsaking all others keep thee only to him as long as ye both shall live?' "

The gnarled, claw-like hand fell on the book. The old man leaned forward. His voice, weaker now, interrupted:

" 'And forsaking all others keep thee only to him as long as ye both—shall live,' did you mean it, girl, when you made that vow?"

Jerry's face was colorless. There was a broken exclamation from Steve. She laid her hand gently over the icy hand on the book. Her young ardent eyes met his dim ones steadily.

"I did, Uncle Nick."

He dropped back with a faint sigh.

"Then it will be all right—Steve. I was afraid—that I might have—but I meant it for the best—it will come right Doc Rand says—things will come right—marvelously—unbelievably—ri-ght!"

His voice trailed off into silence. The lines of pain and weakness in his face disappeared as though a soothing hand had been laid upon them. The curtains at the open window stirred for a moment and then were still.

VI

CALEB LAWSON paused in the reading of the will of Nicholas Fairfax to peer over his half-moon spectacles. His pursed lips made a red, bulbous blot on his pale face as he regarded the three persons in the library at the Manor. Outside an ice-tipped vine struck with a ghostly tap! tap! tap! against the diamond-paned window. Geraldine sat beside Peter Courtlandt. Stephen stood with his back to the fireplace. The sunlight which streamed in at the window touched the girl's hair and transformed it into a crown of bronze with curious red and gold lights. The lawyer's gaze lingered on her for a moment before he cleared his throat with a force which sent a premonitory thrill down the spines of his hearers and resumed the reading of the bulky document he held.

" 'Lastly, all the rest, residue and remainder of the property both real and personal of which I may be possessed or to which I may be entitled at my decease, I give and devise to my nephew Stephen Courtlandt, to him and his heirs forever, on condition, however, that he take possession and management of my ranch in the State of Wyoming not later than three months after my decease and live there one year with his wife Geraldine Glamorgan Courtlandt. And on the further condition that his said wife, during said year, shall refuse to receive income from the fund her father has provided for her, and shall dispose of all securities and money she may have. If my nephew Stephen Courtlandt or his wife, Geraldine Glamorgan Courtlandt, fail to fulfil any one of these conditions said property shall be divided as follows:' "

The lawyer laid down his papers and looked over the edge of his spectacles at Stephen Courtlandt.

"There is no need of my reading that long list of beneficiaries until I know your decision, Stephen. If your father will take me to his study we'll leave you and Mrs. Courtlandt to talk it over."

"You may proceed with the reading. I refuse to accede to the conditions," Steve announced with grim lips.

"Steve," his father protested, "think it over before you say that." He looked imploringly at the girl beside him but her eyes were fixed on the interlacing fingers which lay passively on the lap of her black gown. "Talk with him, Jerry. Don't let him fling this away recklessly," he pleaded. "Come, Lawson, we'll leave the young people to thrash this thing out."

He followed the lawyer from the room and closed the door. Stephen poked viciously at the coals in the fireplace till a fountain of sparks sputtered up the chimney. Then he backed up against the mantel and with a face from which every drop of color had drained, looked down at the bent head of the girl he had married. He laughed shortly.

"Old Nick had a genius for messing things up, hadn't he? When I heard the first clause of that will, which related to me, even when the condition followed that I was to live on the ranch for a year—nothing but a mad sense of freedom thrilled me. I would be my own man once more, rich enough to pay back to your father every cursed cent he had loaned on the Courtlandt property and then have a living income. I could——"

His eyes burned, the veins stood out on his forehead. Jerry realized for the first time the sacrifice of pride and happiness he had made for his family name. She finished the sentence for him:

"You could have your marriage annulled."

He looked at her steadily.

"That did not enter into my plan. Why, oh why, did Uncle Nick have to wreck the whole thing by involving you? I wouldn't take you if you would go. You married me for what I could give you socially. A lot I could give you out there in the wilderness."

"Nevertheless, I shall go with you."

"What! Why, by your own confession you would starve for people in a wilderness."

"Do you want this fortune?"

"More than I ever wanted anything—except one—in my life."

Jerry whitened at his amendment.

"I suppose that one thing was Felice. In spite of that I shall go with you. I shall fulfil my part of the conditions and after you have fulfilled yours then—then we'll consider."

He strode over to her, seized her hands and pulled her to her feet beside him. His face was white, his eyes searching.

"Peg said that you would walk over burning plough-

shares if you thought duty called; she's right. But—but
I shan't let you make the sacrifice."

"You can't help yourself if I am determined to go.
You don't want to start a scandal in high society, do
you, by refusing to take me? I don't care to go any
more than you care to have me," bitterly, "but—but I
promised. Uncle Nick knew what he was doing when
he made me read that marriage service, 'and forsaking
all others'—I shall be doing that all right. But it was
not a fair-weather vow. If your interests take you to
the ranch I shall go with you."

"What will your father say?"

She shrank away from him but he still had her hands
in his and drew her back. Her lips curved in a disdainful smile.

"I think—I think we shall have what the miners
used to call a 'helofarow.' "

"He will never consent to your going."

"What difference will that make? How can he prevent
it? He cannot take back what he has given your father.
That is all that need concern you," with exasperated
frankness. He flushed darkly at her tone, dropped her
hands, and touched a bell. When the butler opened the
door he commanded curtly, "Judson, ask Mr. Lawson
and my father to come here."

When the two men appeared in answer to the summons Glamorgan was with them. His face was deeply
flushed, his little green eyes snapped with anger.

"Look here, Jerry, what's this I hear about your
going off on a ranch? It can't be done, I tell you.
Steve doesn't need that—that old mischief-maker's
money," his voice broke queerly, but he steadied it and
went on, "Why doesn't he stay here and spend mine?"

"You are quite right, Mr. Glamorgan. I have been
trying to impress your daughter with the fact that she
need not take her marriage vows literally. I am content
to eat the crumbs which fall from my rich father-in-
law's table."

"Steve!" Peter Courtlandt protested brokenly.

Jerry faced her father. Her black gown brought out

the pallor of her face and throat. The only color about her was the vivid curves of her lips; even her usually brown eyes were black.

"I'm sorry if it hurts you, Dad, but I shall go with Steve. He is entitled to his uncle's fortune. What is a year out of our lives? Nothing. I—married to please you. Now I shall interpret my marriage vows to please myself." She was most lovely as she defied him. His green eyes contracted to emerald sparks. The veins stood out on his forehead like cords. Jerry remembered that it was the first time one of his children had gone contrary to his command.

"What will you do for money? That infernal will strips you of everything. Ask Steve for it? I can see you. Come, Jerry, give this thing up. Settle down here at the Manor and be happy."

For the first time since she had come into the lives of the Courtlandts Jerry looked like her father. There was the same determination about her eyes, about her lips.

"Be happy! Does smooth going necessarily mean happiness? Does jogging along on the path beaten by our social set mean happiness? Do you know how I feel, Dad? It is as though Steve and I had come up against an enormous sign-post bearing the startling information, ROAD CLOSED: DETOUR. The detour may be hard going, detours usually are, but they also offer more thrills and adventures than the broad highway. I'm willing to take a sporting chance if—if Steve wants me——"

Young Courtlandt laid his hands lightly on her shoulders and looked down at her with inscrutable eyes.

"I do want you, but remember, if I win out, half of what I have will be settled unreservedly on you. You will have earned it." She looked up at him for a moment.

"Then when you have rewarded me for being a good girl and have paid back Father, you will consider yourself in a position to snap your fingers at the Glamorgans?" He looked down at her with disconcerting steadiness as he answered cryptically:

"I shall consider myself in a position to dictate terms to one member of the family. Mr. Lawson, I accept the conditions of my uncle's will."

VII

WITH each stop of the cross-continent train rain-coated men, with occasionally a woman, entered the car and passed down the corridor to disappear into the compartments. Porters wearing that air of authority and responsibility for which one might justly look in a premier or secretary of state, came and went; conductors punched tickets and answered questions more or less amiably; the wheels rattled and roared and ground ceaselessly; outside the rain descended with a persistence worthy a better cause.

From the window of her compartment Geraldine Courtlandt looked out upon a drenched world. There was nothing to see save a dense white sheet ten feet beyond the window. In an hour she and Steve would reach their destination, the first stop on the detour, she thought with a sudden mist before her eyes. She hoped that the storm was not an omen of what lay before them. She shook herself mentally: "Don't be silly and superstitious," she admonished that Jerry Courtlandt who persisted in having a queer lumpy feeling in the region of her throat whenever she thought of the curious twist the apparently broad, straight road of her marriage had taken.

Her father had maintained his attitude of angry aloofness. He had not come to the station to see her off, she had waited on the platform until the train started, hoping that he would relent at the last moment. He had sent a curt typewritten note to the effect that if she and Steve regained their common sense and returned to the

Manor before the end of the year he would double the income he had allowed them. There were a dozen glorious American beauties in her compartment when she entered it. The roses had set the atmosphere tingling with life and color and love. Jerry laughed happily and kissed each one of them. How like her father it was to write the note with one hand and send flowers with the other.

What difference would it make if her income were doubled if she were disloyal to the promise she made when she married Steve, the girl thought, as chin on her hand she gazed unseeingly out at the rain. "An easy conscience is more to be desired than great riches," she paraphrased to herself as she thought of the weeks when she had been engaged to Greyson. Her heart still smarted with contrition as she remembered how ashamed she had been that she could make so little response to the love he lavished upon her. "Never again!" she said aloud. "I've made two mistakes. Bruce and Steve. From now on I'll do what I know to be right even if I hurt someone else and—and hate doing it. But—but just what shall I do for money?" she questioned with puckered brows.

She opened her beaded bag and poured the contents into her lap. "How are the mighty fallen!" she quoted with a laugh as she looked down upon the collection displayed. A handkerchief, one gold pencil, the key to her safe-deposit box, the membership card of her club, a book of postage stamps. Nothing else. She had carried out the terms of the will in letter and spirit. After her bills had been paid she had transferred her bank balance to her father and had dropped her remaining cash into the box of a Salvation Army lassie as she entered the station to take the west-bound train. The woman in the red-banded pokebonnet, standing on a board to keep her stout boots from the dampness, had looked at the bills crushed into her box, then after the donor incredulously. Such lavish generosity was rare in her experience.

Jerry frowningly regarded the objects in her lap. Not

one cent of money. "Being marooned on a desert island has nothing on being marooned on a ranch without a penny," she mused under her breath. She hastily
stuffed her belongings back into her bag as she heard
an approaching whistle. It was Steve. The queer merry-
go-round of fortune had accomplished one thing, it
had restored Steve's spirits. Since leaving New York he
had been a different person from the morose, touchy
individual she had known since her engagement to
him. He had been companionable, sympathetic in a
fraternal sort of way which had made her wish fervently
that Fate had given her a brother instead of a husband.

"Won't you come in?" she asked as Courtlandt
stopped at the open door, then as he entered, "Is it
time to get on my coat?"

"Not for half an hour." He seated himself opposite
her. There was a new expression in his eyes which set
the girl's heart to beating uncomfortably. She couldn't
define it, she couldn't meet it long enough to define it.

"Jerry," there was an " 'tention company" note in
his voice which brought her chin up defiantly, "I suppose—if you complied with the terms of Uncle Nick's
will you must be rather down and out financially—
yes?" She succumbed to the lure of his smile and the
laughter in his eyes.

"Thought telepathy," she responded gayly. "I was
taking account of stock when you appeared. I have in
this bag, one pencil, one handkerchief, one perfectly
good club-membership card—good, that is, until Jan-
uary first—and a book of two-cent stamps. Those
stamps won't imperil our hopes of the inheritance, will
they?" she asked with exaggerated anxiety. "Caleb
Lawson held me up before I boarded the train. I had to
sign a paper and show him my empty purse to prove
that I was really the Beggar-maid, bare-pursed instead
of barefooted, following my King Cophetua out into
the cold, cold world."

"Your simile is faulty. As I remember it the Beggar-
maid loved the King."

"Also the King loved the Beggar-maid. You're right, the similarity ceases with my lack of funds."

"I shall open an account for you in the bank at Slippy Bend. Until then——" his hand went to his pocket. The girl's face whitened.

"Don't offer me money, Steve," she commanded tensely.

"I'm not offering money. I am giving you what belongs to you. Aren't you earning what Uncle Nick left as well as I?"

"Weren't you earning your share of Father's money when you married me?"

"That's different."

"Why? You refused to take my money. I refuse to take yours."

"You will take it."

Jerry leaned forward, her face as colorless as his.

"Take that 'Hands up!' expression out of your eyes, Steve. I shall not take a cent of your money. You will find that a Glamorgan has as much pride as a Courtlandt if she hasn't several generations of aristocrats behind her." Her angry eyes blazed as he retorted laughingly:

"You forget. You're not a Glamorgan now."

She shrugged lightly.

"More's the pity."

"Do you mean that?" Consternation banished the smile from his lips. He caught her hands in his. "The day Uncle Nick arrived I heard you say——"

"Nex' stop Slippy Bend, Miss. Porter for your bags," interrupted a Jamaican voice with a Chicago accent. Jerry's face flushed with relief as the black head with its gleaming eyes and teeth bobbed in at the door. She pointed to the bags. As the man went out with them she turned to Courtlandt with an embarrassed laugh.

"You've won this time. I had forgotten the porter. You'll have to tip him and the maid for me. However, as this is really a deferred wedding-trip the expenses naturally fall to the groom, don't they?" with reckless daring.

He looked at her until her laughing eyes fell before the glow of his.

"You've said it—if this can be called a wedding-trip—but take it from me, sometime, Mrs. Courtlandt, I'll show you what a real honeymoon can be. Porter, here's another bag."

He followed the black man into the corridor. Jerry settled her smart toque and pinned on her veil before the mirror, but she couldn't see her own face, only Steve's with that curious I'm-biding-my-time look in his eyes. What had he meant about a honeymoon? Did he mean that he and Felice—no, *no,* Steve was not that kind. She looked about the compartment to make sure that she had left nothing. Three roses still glowing with beauty remained of the dozen. She pinned them to the front of her coat. She would take so much of her father into her new life with her.

The wooden shanty which served as a shelter for telegraph, freight and passengers at Slippy Bend was as depressing as rain, flapping shingles and a skewed roof could make it. The road which struggled up a slope to hide between two shabby buildings was a river of mud. A knock-kneed man with a string of slat-ribbed calico horses and cayuses following him, waded downward through the middle of it. Every few steps he would stop to yank a howling, red-eyed bulldog from a hole which had betrayed him. Jerry valiantly blinked back the tears as she watched him. She had never seen anything quite as sordid and depressing as her surroundings. The only note of civilization in the dreary scene was the large, curtained touring car by the platform. As she looked at it, two legs, which had acquired Queen Anne curves from many hours spent in the saddle, wriggled from under the curtains followed by a large body. A Belgian police dog, tawny, noble, aloof, followed the man. Courtlandt who had been busy with the luggage turned with a boyish laugh and held out his hand.

"It sure is great to be back, Pete. Down, Goober, down, boy!" to the dog who, after an uncertain second, had leaped to lick his face. He kept one hand on the animal's head as he turned to the girl beside him. "Jerry, this is Pete Gerrish, who taught me all I know about ranching. He is Uncle Nick's right-hand man. Pete, this is Mrs. Courtlandt."

"He's got me wrong, ma'am. I *was* the old gentleman's right-hand man, but Ranlett's in the saddle now. I'm sure pleased to meet you an' I hope you'll be downright happy with us."

"Thank you, Mr. Gerrish." Jerry felt the tears absurdly near as she looked up at him. He was regarding her with unqualified approval. His large face was cross-currented with fine lines and smiles; his Stetson came close to ears which looked as though the Almighty had designed them as hat-rests and had made a surprisingly good job of it. He carried the marks of his calling in the devil-may-care poise of his body, in his clothing, in his rollicking Irish eyes.

"I'll give Baldy Jennings a hand with the trunks to get 'em out of the rain till the boys get here for them. They're teamin' in. How the devil did yer expect to get all them things out to the ranch over these spring roads, Steve—I would say Chief? The boys has decided that even if they did teach the new owner most of what he knows about ranchin', it won't do to be familiar-like no more. So we've decided to call him chief, ma'am," Gerrish inserted the bit of information to Jerry in the midst of his dissertation on the condition of the roads. "I went up to the hubs gettin' here with no load. By cripes, I don't know what'll happen goin' back."

Jerry was tempted to echo that "By cripes!" later, when the big car laboring through what seemed rivers of mud, foundered in a hole. She unfastened the curtain and looked out. Goober on the running-board, plastered with mud, looked like nothing so much as a model sketchily done in clay as he peered down inquiringly. Gerrish expressed himself in language which the girl was sure was being painfully expurgated because of her. The wheels groaned and choked as they churned up fountains of mud. As she watched the wheel under her Jerry could think of nothing but a gigantic egg-beater gone mad from the futility of its efforts. The back of Gerrish's neck had taken on a dangerous, apoplectic color generated, doubtless, by restraint from the fullest self-expression.

"Would it help if I got out?" she ventured in the lull while the engine rested.

"Haw! I guess if yer did we'd have to haul you out in a hurry or send a rescue-party through to China," Gerrish discouraged while Courtlandt commanded:

"Stay where you are! I'll take the wheel, Pete. We have nothing to put under the back wheels; it would do no good if we had. The engine will have to do the trick."

He threw on the switch. The engine started. The spinning wheels hitched forward, he reversed, hitched forward, reversed, hitched forward till Jerry experienced all of the discomforts, and none of the stimulation, of being aboard ship on a high and choppy sea. Courtlandt grimly pursued his tactics till with a roar from the motor and a lurch which sent Jerry's teeth into her lower lip, the car, looking like an uncanny prehistoric animal which had been wallowing in a mud bath, dragged itself from its hole, skidded with hair-raising irresponsibility, came back to the road and struggled on. The rain stopped. The sky showed shapeless spots of light where the clouds were thinning. Vapors floated lightly above the fields.

It was twilight, a crimson and gold twilight, when Courtlandt turned into the avenue of cottonwoods which led to the ranch-house of the Double O. The air was fragrant with fresh washed earth and the spicy breath which the storm had beaten from the pines. From somewhere a meadow-lark trilled an ecstatic greeting and as though frightened at its temerity as suddenly subsided. The flaming color in the west might have been the glow from a blazing forest, but it was only the sun flinging its good-night over sky and fields and mountains in the whole-hearted Western way.

Against the red light squatted the shadowy shape of the ranch-house.

When the car stopped Goober sprang to the porch and stood as if awaiting orders. In the background hovered two Chinese servants, a man and a woman. Their slant-eyes in their moon faces were ludicrously alike. The woman in her gay silks and embroideries looked like a painting on rice-paper.

Pete and Hopi Soy carried in the bags. At a nod from Courtlandt the woman followed. Steve held the door wide. With a curious choked feeling Jerry entered the house. Then her emotion found vent in a little cry of delight. After the grayness and mud of the ride out the great living-room glowed like a jewel. The color stole through her senses like an elixir and rested and refreshed her. Her eyes shone, her lips curved in a faint smile as she looked about her. The servants had disappeared. She and Steve were alone.

Logs blazed in the great stone fireplace. Safely out of scorching distance a white cat dozed in front of it, her fluffy coat rosy in the firelight, her wide eyes like blinking topaz as she regarded the newcomers. Gorgeous serapes from old Mexico, Hopi saddle-blankets, heavily beaded garments of the Blackfeet, Apache bows and quivers full of arrows, Navaho blankets, skins of mountain lions and lynx there were, each one placed in artistic relation to its neighbor. A profusion of books and magazines, a baby-grand piano, a phonograph *de luxe,* softly shaded lamps, added their note of civilization to the array of savage trophies and over the mantel——

"Why, Steve! There's Mother!" whispered Jerry softly.

For a silent moment the man and girl standing side by side looked up at the tender, laughing face of the woman in riding costume. She didn't seem like a thing of paint and canvas, she was real, vital, alive and welcoming. Jerry was the first to stir. She colored with confusion.

"Steve, I—I beg your pardon! I—I shouldn't have

called her—mother. But I was so—so surprised. It seemed for a moment as if she held out welcoming arms to me." She turned away. Courtlandt gripped her shoulders with a force which hurt.

"She is your mother—I———" he released her abruptly and threw open a door. "These are your rooms. Mine are opposite. You see we have but one story in the ranch-house. Your bags are in your room. Ming Soy will come to help you when you ring." He put his two hands on her shoulders again. "I'm glad that you wore my roses."

"Your roses! Why I thought—I thought———" Her voice was drenched with disappointment. Steve's face was a mask, only his eyes seemed alive as he removed his hands and asked crisply:

"That they came from Greyson?"

"No, Steve, no! How could you think such a thing? I thought that Dad had relented and—and had sent the roses to———" she winked her lashes furiously but not before Steve had seen the diamond-like drops that beaded them. His voice was tender as he comforted:

"Your father will come round, Jerry. Just believe with old Doc Rand that things have a way of coming marvelously, unbelievably right. You are not sorry that you came, are you?"

"I'll say I'm not!" She had essayed an imitation of his voice and words but the emotion which had threatened her all day surged in her heart and betrayed her. Steve caught her hands in his.

"Don't look like that, little girl. You're going to love the life here and the ranch and—and—and Goober," he added with a short laugh as the dog bounded into the room.

VIII

JERRY COURTLANDT sent her horse up the slope and
came out on a bluff above the Double O. As the girl
sat motionless looking off over the plain, an artist
would have labeled the picture she made, "A Study in
Browns," before he slipped it into his mental port-
folio. Her mount, Patches, was a deep mahogany in
color, her riding boots were but a shade lighter than
his satin skin, her breeches and long coat were of
khaki, her blouse was fawn color, her eyes were deeply,
darkly bronze. Rebellious tendrils of lustrous brown
hair escaped from under the broad brim of the campaign hat she wore, one of Steve's army hats with its
gold and black cord. He had insisted upon her using it.
The hats she had brought to the ranch had been urban
affairs, not designed to shade her eyes from the glare of
white roads. As she had had no money with which to
buy another she had taken it.

Jerry pulled it off as she took a deep breath of the
glorious air asparkle with bubbles of life. She loved the
spot. Every day that she rode she stopped to look
down upon the valley. Far away among the foot-hills
a silver stream cleft rocky bluffs, then coiled and
foamed its way until it broadened and flashed in gleaming waterfalls. In places where it boiled and frothed
rustic bridges had been thrown across. Toward the
east lay the sturdily built stock corrals, storehouses
spick and span with whitewash, towering silos. Toward
the west were fenced-off alfalfa fields and beyond them
a mosaic of varicolored pasture-lands, dotted with grazing herds, stretched out to the foot-hills.

Beyond the foot-hills loomed mountains darkly green
with pine and spruce to the timberline, above which
reared sombre, forbidding rock until against the ragged
edge of gold-lined clouds, white peaks flamed crimson

in the slanting sun. Toward the north she could see the gap in the mountains through which the railroad cut. The gap was known as the Devil's Hold-up because of the natural facilities it had offered—and still offered for that matter,—to the class whose pleasing pastime it had been to maintain their divine right in the other man's property at the point of a gun.

Almost beneath her, approached by a broad, well-graded road, lay the ranch-house. Telephone wires from all directions rounded up the activities of the Double O at the office near by. The house was a rambling structure of rudely squared timbers set in fieldstone and cement. Its one story was built around a court on which many doors opened and which was gayly brocaded with shrubs and plants in blossom this late June day.

Where was Steve, Jerry wondered, as her eyes lingered on the office building. She saw him less and less as the days passed, as more and more he assumed the responsibilities of the Double O. He was off before she was up in the morning riding the range or in the dairies or barns until night. She had hardly believed her eyes when on the evening after her arrival, she had seen Steve and Tommy Benson, his secretary, come into the living-room in dinner coats. Courtlandt had answered her unspoken question with the explanation that it had been Nicholas Fairfax's unvarying rule to shed ranch problems at night, and he had found that getting into the dress of the city helped. A man just naturally would curb an impulse to toddle down to the corral if he were in dinner clothes. The two didn't seem to go together.

Steve had appointed Tommy Benson her squire, he himself had so little time to give her. A laugh curved Jerry's lips as she thought of Tommy. He was a slight youth with a face of one of Raphael's cherubs grown up and a book for his inseparable companion. His almost yellow hair was short and wavy, his eyes were a brilliant blue, his skin was as nearly pink and white as human skin can be after it has been ranch-seasoned, his

lips seemed made for laughter. He and Steve had been
officers in the same company and when they returned
from overseas the two had gone to the ranch to recuperate. Tommy had remained there to please his
mother. He was in the throes of a virulent attack of
stage fever and Mrs. Benson had begged him to wait
a few years before he decided upon acting as his career.
She had assured him that if after reflection he still felt
that it was the profession for him she would attend his
première without a qualm. So he had stayed at the
Double O. There was plenty of money back of him
and he had grown to love the ranch life, apparently.

Tommy was taking the responsibility of training the
lady of the ranch seriously, that is as seriously as a boy
could who was forever expressing his emotions and con-
victions in the words of the immortals, Jerry thought
with a smile. She had ridden since she was a little girl
but Tommy was making her proficient in some hair-
raising stunts. Steve didn't know of those but he had
ordained that she was to learn to saddle Patches, that
she must be able to fasten and unfasten gates securely
while mounted, that she was to rope and shoot from
her horse's back.

Her days were full but filled with her own pleasures.
She did nothing for others, she thought ruefully as she
gazed down upon the smoke rising from the cook-house
chimney. Her only link with the outside world was
Sandy, the carrier, whose appearance sent her imagination winging into the past whenever she saw him. The
queer little postman wore a tall gray hat which, Tommy
Benson insisted, was a left-over from the wardrobe of
Gentleman Rick whose zeal as a promoter of pleasure
in Slippy Bend in the nineties had lured men through
miles of wilderness. Jerry often sat on the wall beside
the mail-box to await his coming. He always had news
and a quaint bit of philosophy if he hadn't letters.
Letters! There weren't many for her. She had had hosts
of friends in school and college but she heard from
them seldom now. Her conscience administered a vicious pinch. Yes, it was quite all her fault, she answered

it. The girls apparently had adored her, but she had been unable to accept their devotion with single-minded pleasure. Always in the back of her mind had skulked the ghost of that first home near the coal-fields. Would they have cared for her could they have seen that? After her marriage events had moved too rapidly for her to pick up the scattered lines of her correspondence. However, she no longer had that excuse, her days now were long and uneventful. She would write to every friend she had. It would be like sending out a fleet of ships. How eagerly she would await the return cargoes.

She broke into her own good resolutions with a laugh. To send out letters one must have stamps. She had used the last one she possessed yesterday and to get more she must have money. "Money!" Jerry laughed again as she repeated the word aloud. Conditions were reversed now as to money, she thought as she stared unseeingly off at the mountain tops which pricked the crimsoning sky. Steve had the income from his uncle's large property as long as he remained on the ranch. It would not be his unreservedly until a year from the day they had arrived at the Double O. She had persistently refused to accept money from him. If she wrote to the girls she would need a regiment of postage stamps. If she could earn——

Her eyes flashed earthward from the mountains as she heard the click of a hoof against rock and the creak of saddle leather. A horse and rider topped the slope. It was Courtlandt on his favorite mount, Blue Devil, a horse all spirit, shining blue-black satin. He was a regal creature from his flowing mane to his silken fetlock. He nosed Patches who showed an undignified haste to snuggle up to him in return.

"Did you think you had lost me, Steve?" Jerry asked gayly as she noted the seriousness of his blue eyes and the crease in his forehead which his broad-brimmed Stetson was not drawn low enough to hide. How unnecessarily good looking he was in his riding clothes, she thought. He wore a black tie with his khaki shirt, his heavy riding breeches were tucked into the tops of high boots which laced up the front and had curious sloping heels. He had removed one of his riding gloves and the dark stone of his ring, which bore the seal of the Courtlandts, made the browned hand seem white in contrast. He gave the impression of being absolute master of his horse and of any situation which might arise. Jerry's heart unaccountably skipped a beat as he answered her question.

"No, I saw you from the road. You looked like one of Dallin's bronzes. Where is Tommy?" with quick displeasure.

"Don't glower. I sent him back. I don't want him always at my heels. I love to come up here alone and, figuratively speaking, look down upon my blessings."

"Was that what you were doing when I came up? Your expression belied you. Instead of looking beatific, you looked worried."

She laughed up at him with warm friendliness as she bent forward and confided in a theatrical whisper:

"You are right. I was figuring finances. I have just ——" The color flew to her face as she thought of what he might infer. She stumbled on quite conscious that she was making matters worse. "I'm about at the end of my stamp book and—and—I've developed a sudden fervor for letter writing and—and——" she broke off her breathless explanation as he laid his finely-shaped hand on her saddle-bow. Even back in the Manor days his hands had fascinated her.

"I'm glad that you've brought up the subject of finances, Jerry. The money question between you and me has got to be cleared up, and cleared up now. You've had your way long enough. Don't be foolish any longer, little girl. I——"

"I shall not take your money, Steve. Would you take mine?" then as his eyes darkened stormily, "Oh, truly, I didn't mean to rouse sleeping dogs—but—but I won't take it. I do nothing for you—if I even had anything to do about the house but Ming and Hopi Soy run the household motor noiselessly, perfectly, with every cylinder hitting. If there was anything I could do——"

"There is something you can do."

Jerry's heart flew to her throat. What did he mean? He looked grim and determined.

"W-what is it?" she asked faintly. She put on her hat, tightened her reins unconsciously.

Courtlandt laughed. The sternness left his face. There was an expression in his eyes which she couldn't translate as he teased:

"Don't run, Jerry. You don't trust me over much, do you? To return to finances, if you want to help you can do so tremendously by taking over the accounts and my correspondence. Tommy's had that job but I need him outside. Ranlett's leaving. You'll soon get the hang of the accounting and it won't take much of your time."

"But if it took all I'd love to do it, Steve. Shall I have a desk in the office?" she asked eagerly.

"If you agree to accept a salary."

"But I don't want to be paid for helping."

He turned his horse's head toward the slope.

"That settles it. I shall send to the agency tomorrow for a private secretary." As she did not answer he looked at her with a smile which lighted eyes and lips. "Now will you be good?"

She regarded him with oblique scrutiny. With an adorable imitation of Pete Gerrish she drawled:

"You're sure puttin' it straight, Chief. You win. Now shall we mosey 'long home?" With a touch of spurs she wheeled Patches and headed him down the slope.

"Why is Ranlett leaving?" she asked as their horses trotted side by side along the hard white ranch road. Courtlandt's face reddened darkly.

"Because I thought it time to determine the status of the alien on Double O ranch. Ranlett had a couple of men in the outfit who have not taken out first naturalization papers, even, who had been pointing out to my boys deficiencies of the government. They're flares set here to ignite any chaff of discontent which may be blowing about."

"But you're not against freedom of speech, Steve?"

"You bet I am against the inflammatory brand on the tongue of an alien. What is he in this country but a guest? If a man came to stay in my home and began a systematic undermining of the ideas and ideals on which that home was built, what do you think I'd do to him?"

"I'll say you'd sure put him out, Chief," with Gerrish's drawl and a little rush of laughter.

"I'll say I would. So quick he'd wonder what struck him. Why should the government put up with their vicious patter? It's bad enough when an honest-to-God citizen breaks loose and turns red, but for a man who is here by courtesy—well, as I remarked before, there is no place for him on the Double O ranch. Aliens will keep their jobs here only so long as they conform to my ideas of fitness."

"You're right, Steve. I have never thought of agitators in that light but they are a sort of human slow-match timed to fire a mine of discontent, aren't they? And half the time the mine doesn't know what it is blowing-up about. How do the men feel about Ranlett's defection?"

"I haven't asked them. What's the infernal row?" he demanded as they drew rein at the gate of the court. Jerry looked at him in surprise. His tone was that of a man whose nerves were taut to snapping point. She slid from her horse and dropped the reins. Patches loped quietly but determinedly in the direction of the corral and supper. Blue Devil, with a reproachful glance at the deserter, followed daintily in the steps of his master as Courtlandt and the girl entered the garden. The court was a riot of plants and shrubs. The air was sweet with the fragrance of roses just coming into bloom and rent by agitated yelps and a hoarse, croaking voice.

When Jerry and Steve reached storm centre they saw a combination of scarlet, blue and green, swaying precariously on the top of a shutter. It was José's parrot, Benito, flinging to the breeze the most vituperative epithets a rich and racy vocabulary could suggest. Below him Goober sat on his haunches. Between barks his tongue dripped, his mouth hung open as though in riotous laughter. His tawny eyes flashed ruby light. Tommy Benson, his finger between the pages of a book, his hair rampant, his blue eyes sparkling with mirth, egged on the two as he quoted from his favorite "Ancient Mariner":

> " 'The wedding guest sat on a stone,
> He could not choose but hear;
> And thus spake on that ancient man,
> The bright-eyed mariner.' "

His eloquence incited the bird to renewed effort to express his sentiments. Jerry clapped her hands over her ears and dashed into the house. Steve whistled. The dog bounded in his direction, his quarry forgotten in the job of seeing his master. Courtlandt seized him by the collar.

"What do you mean, you sinner?" he demanded sternly. Goober looked as though he were about to offer an explanation when the gaudy parrot, who had been rocking back and forth on the shutter, croaked:

"Lick him, Bo! Lick him!"

Tommy dropped to the ground and rolled with laughter. José came hurrying out of the house. He swept off his hat with a wide bow. His face had the look of a much-shriveled mummy, his solitary tooth waggled precariously as he talked.

"*Que hay! Señor!* One teeng I tell you. It ees that wild devil of a dog that makes my leetle Benito to curse. *Madre de Dios,* but he ees one—one———"

"You've said it, José," encouraged Benson as he sat up and wiped his eyes. He took his knees in an affectionate embrace. "He sure is one little curser, that Benito of yours. Want me to help get him down?"

"No—no, Señor Tommee. He come to me." He reached up and after a few protesting squawks the particolored bird settled on the Mexican's shoulder. As José left the court with him, the parrot shivered, flapped his wings, winked at Tommy and croaked hoarsely:

"What's all the shootin'?"

Tommy gave vent to a whoop of appreciation before he turned to Courtlandt, who was regarding the ranch-house door unseeingly. He gave him a resounding whack on the shoulder as he ranted:

> " 'How is't with you
> That you do bend your eye on vacancy?' "

"Quit your histrionics, Tommy. Has Pete Gerrish been here for me?"

"Nope. Nothing doing." Benson stroked Blue Devil's satiny nose and rested his face against it as he asked in a low tone, "Any news of those stray calves?"

Courtlandt's brows met in a quick frown.

"No, but of course we'll find them. It's absurd to think a man can get away with rustling in this enlightened twentieth century, that we've got to revert to shooting and——"

"That's what the majority of the world claimed in 1914," interrupted Benson dryly.

"Don't be a blamed pessimist, Tommy. I'm going to take you off the books and use you outside."

"Oh boy!" he voiced the twentieth century equivalent to the nineteenth century "Great Scott!" in delighted approval. "If you do that and Ranlett has been crooked, he hasn't a prayer. I'm the original Sherlock Holmes. Watch me get him! Pete's boys have all they can do now without turning detectives. You'd think that Gerrish had just been put in charge of a new outfit. He's on location every minute, reëstimating the number of head each pasture should carry, weighing up the stock, sifting out the undesirables. Take it from me, old dear, he knows every calf by name, what it's worth now and what it will bring one year from now. He claims that Ranlett has been underselling. I'll ride the fences to-morrow. If you say the word I'll take Jerry along and we'll have a corking time."

"You and Jerry usually have a corking time together, don't you?" Benson showed his teeth in a flashing smile.

"I'll say we do. I don't like to talk about myself, but——"

Courtlandt laughed.

"You don't care for yourself one little bit, do you, Tommy? By all means take Jerry if she cares to go. Beat it down to the corral with Blue Devil, will you? That is if you dare ride him," Steve amended with a laugh.

Tommy mounted with the agility of a monkey, wheeled his horse and declaimed theatrically:

> "I dare do all that may become a man
> Who dares do more is none!"

IX

"Work is the grandest cure for all the maladies and miseries that ever beset mankind.—CARLYLE."

JERRY nodded approvingly at the quotation above her desk in the office. It had been hung there in Old Nick's day and was quite as pertinent in her case as it might have been in his. To be sure, their maladies differed. His couldn't by the remotest possibility have been lack of money, she thought with a laugh.

Steve had installed her at her desk two weeks ago and had then forgotten her, presumably. Tommy Benson was giving her instructions as to her duties, but even his attentions were episodic. Ranlett had departed swearing vengeance in the good old nineteenth century style and Steve and Gerrish were out from morning till night taking account of stock and checking up. Tommy was riding range and being general utility man. Neither he nor Steve knew how closely she had remained at her desk. She must make good and she must accomplish it without taking too much of Tommy's time. As Steve had insisted upon paying her a month's salary in ad-

vance she had surreptitiously sent for a correspondence
course on bookkeeping. She was making Sandy's life
miserable because the material, which she expected
would make her efficient in twenty-four hours, had
not arrived.

Arms on the back of her swivel-chair, one knee in
the seat she twisted slowly about. The room inspired
the same sense of breathless interest it had the first time
she entered it. Two walls were encased in glass. Behind
the glass hung a collection of riding equipment and
firearms. Some of the pieces dated back to the epoch-
making journey of the pathfinders, Lewis and Clark,
some to the first white settlers in the region west of the
Mississippi. There were saddles rich in silver filigree
which had come from the southwest of the cattle country; there were saddles with short round skirts, open
stirrups, narrow and rimmed with iron; some had bor-
ders and emblems stamped on the leather, some had
dark stains. There were chaps, fringed and unfringed,
in infinite variety. There were coiled ropes of rawhide
and of well worn grass; there were guns and knives and
tomahawks, there was a stained and tattered Stars and
Stripes.

"You fairly ooze atmosphere," Jerry mused aloud,
her dreamy brown eyes on the saddles. "If you could
speak what couldn't you tell of romance and comedy
and tragedy. Herds, bad men, *voyageurs,* rustlers, settlers, prairie-schooners and Indians, you must have seen
them all." Her voice had dropped to a whisper. Its
tenseness roused her from what was fast becoming a
vermilion orgy of imagination. She swung her chair
round and dropped into it with a laugh and the reflection, "Pete Gerrish says that when a person talks to
himself he's sure in for adventure."

She picked up a typewritten letter and regarded it
with vainglorious elation. Not so bad! There was a spiral
effect at the end of one sentence but on the whole it was
a creditable affair for a person who had never used a
typewriter till the week before and who was relying on
the hunt-and-punch method for progress. Her already

flushed cheeks took on a deeper tinge as she looked at
the filing cases. Would she ever acquire a feeling of even
bowing acquaintance with them, she wondered; they
were most awe-inspiring.

The sun lay warmly on the fields outside, a gay
little breeze spiced with pine danced in at the open
window, stirred the curls at the nape of the girl's neck
and whisked out again. Jerry looked out longingly,
shook her head. "Remember, you're a daughter of toil
now," she adjured the vagabond impulse which urged
her to be up and away on her horse. She resolutely
turned her back on the tempting out-of-doors and
picked up her letter.

" 'Gentlemen,' " she read aloud, " 'We are shipping'
—now why should I have typed that slipping—'thirty
head of Guernseys on the——' " A shadow from the
open door fell on her paper. Absorbed in her correc-
tions, she spoke without looking up from her desk:

"You are wanted at the Lower Field, Pete. The Chief
just 'phoned that more calves are missing. That——" as
no colorful ejaculation followed her announcement,
Gerrish swore with fascinating facility when he was
deeply moved, she looked up in surprise. The smile
which the thought of Pete had brought stiffened on her
lips. She sprang to her feet and pushed back her chair.
A man leaned against the door, a giant of a man fully
six feet two. In a flash she sized him up. He was of
different caliber from the "boys" of the outfit. No one of
them would have stood with his hat on in her presence.
The stranger's Mexican sombrero, pushed far back on
his head, revealed rough red hair; his eyes were a hard
blue; his nose suggested the beak of a hawk; his mouth
was his best feature, it looked as though it might have
been tender before the insidious processes of discourage-
ment and recklessness got in their work. One temple
gave the impression of having been knocked in and
from the dent to the corner of his lips ran an angry,
wrinkled scar. It contributed a curiously saturnine expression to what in youth might have been a pleasing
face. From feet to waist his clothing was reminiscent of

the army; from the belt up it might have belonged to a rider, even to the gay purple and crimson bandana at his neck. The stranger smiled boldly as his eyes met the girl's. Jerry's heart did a handspring and righted. A fleeting cloud of apprehension dimmed the brilliance of her eyes.

"If you are looking for a job you'll have to come back after five," she volunteered with her best in-charge-of-the-office manner. "The manager is off on the range." She could have cheerfully bitten out her tongue as she noted the smile with which the man received the information.

"I'm no cow-puncher," he answered disdainfully. "I'm not hunting a job here. I'm looking for the railroad. I took the ranch road by mistake, but, now that I am here——" He straightened his great shoulders, pulled his soft hat jauntily over one ear with his big hairy hand, and took a step into the room. "Well, you're too pretty a girl to be left alone, *sabe?* I always had a taste for stenogs."

Jerry's heart did another turn. She hated the man's eyes. Hers flashed to the desk. There was no use trying to telephone, he might stop her; besides, the ranch was an affair of magnificent distances; it would take time for anyone she called to reach the office. Ming and Hopi would be of as much assistance as two Chinese dolls. She must depend upon herself to get rid of the creature. She swiftly computed the relative splashing values of the ink-well and the pot of paste. The ink had it. Her hand crept along the desk.

"Don't come any nearer. If you're wise you'll go at once."

"I get you. Here's-your-hat-what's-your-hurry stuff, yes? But I think I'll stay. I've just come up from the border. You're the handsomest white girl I've seen in months. Come on, be friends. I like that gilt-edged effect in your hair and eyes. Take it from me——"

Jerry was white to the lips. She lifted the ink-well.

"You'd better go or I——"

"What's your business here?" a crisp voice interrupted from the door.

"Steve!"

With the startled whisper the stiffening departed from Jerry's knees. She sank back in her chair. The stranger wheeled with military precision then, in a startled voice laden with pride and affection, cried:

"Comment ça va, mon Lieutenant!"

"Carl! Oh boy, Carl, where did you come from?"

The undertone in Courtlandt's voice brought the tears stinging to Jerry's eyes. Steve gripped the stranger's hand as though he would never let it go. The two patted one another's shoulders with their free hands and beamed with suspiciously bright eyes.

"What good wind blew you here, Beechy?" Steve demanded. "Jerry, this is Carl Beechy, who was my top sergeant in France. That scar he wears was intended for me, and—and—he took it. Carl, this is my—this is Mrs. Courtlandt."

"Mrs. Courtlandt! Your wife, Lieutenant? *C'est drôle, ça!* I—I—thought——" The girl had never seen such contrition as clouded Beechy's eyes as they met hers. There was not a trace of recklessness in them now; they were frankly pleading. She hesitated for a moment, then smiled.

"I'm glad that you came to the Double O, Sergeant Beechy. It was fortunate that you arrived when you did, Steve. Mr. Beechy was just going. You—you might not have recognized him had you met him on the road." Her lips twitched traitorously as her glance flashed to the inkwell on the desk.

Beechy's eyes sent her a wireless of passionate gratitude and admiration. Then he turned to Courtlandt.

"You are the last person I expected to see here, Lieutenant."

"Weren't you looking for me, Carl? I told you——"

"I know, you told me to look you up, but—two years is a long time and I've found men forget. I went to Mexico after I left hospital. I've been drifting till now——" He broke off the sentence sharply. His face had the curious look which tanned skin has when the blood has been drawn away from it. Jerry could have sworn that there was fright in his eyes. Did Steve see what she saw? Evidently not, for he exclaimed:

"When you didn't turn up I thought you'd re-enlisted."

"Me! Nothing doing, Lieutenant. The next time my country calls it'll have to call so loud that I'll hear it at the other end of the world. No, me and the U. S. A. is through."

"That's fool talk, Beechy. I've heard it before. If you were needed you and every man who talks like you would be the first to answer the call to the colors. I know you. You jumped in at the first sign of trouble. You'd do it again. Well, there's a job for you right here."

The man's lips stiffened. A look of dog-like devotion flooded his eyes.

"That's just like you, but—but I can't take it, Lieutenant. I've signed up for—for something else, and you know—there's—there's honor among thieves," with a strained attempt at levity which was belied by his eyes. He looked at Jerry. "I never knew what a man could be till I met the Lieutenant, Mrs. Courtlandt. I'd always thought that a rich guy was bound to be soft, but he's tested steel. I've got to beat it this minute. I—I was telling your wife when I came in, Lieutenant, that I was looking for the railroad and took the ranch road by mistake."

"But you can't go, Beechy. Good Lord, man, you've got to eat somewhere, at least stop for chow. Come along to the bunk-house. I want the boys to know you." He turned to Jerry. "Did you get hold of Pete?"

"No, I couldn't reach him. I—I thought that it was he when Mr. Beechy appeared."

"Let it go then." He looked at her keenly. "Have you been out of the office this week? I thought not," as she colored faintly. "Don't do any more work to-day— please. Let's go, Carl."

Beechy turned to Jerry. He twisted his hat awkwardly in his big hands.

"Good-bye, Mrs. Courtlandt. I hope that you'll—you'll——"

Jerry held out her hand with a smile.

"I shall always remember what you did for your lieutenant, Sergeant Beechy. Good luck; if you don't like the railroad come back to us." He gripped the hand she extended. Jerry gave his a warning pressure as she looked up and saw Steve regarding them intently. With a squeeze which made her see fifty-seven varieties of stars and their collateral branches, Beechy released her hand.

"Let's go, Lieutenant."

Jerry looked after the two as they strode away broad shoulder almost touching broad shoulder. Had they been girls they would have their arms around each other's waists, she was sure. What strange friendships the war had welded. Braggadocio had slipped from Beechy like a garment the instant he recognized Court-landt's voice. He had assumed an entirely different personality. Dr. Jekyll and Mr. Hyde. The soldier was a much safer citizen than the man of peace, she told herself with a reminiscent shiver.

She picked up the papers on her desk, then dropped them. Steve had been emphatic about her going out. Suddenly she felt that she couldn't endure four walls a moment longer. She must be in the open. She pulled down the top of her desk and dashed through the flowering court to the house. She called Ming Soy to bring lunch to her room. She telephoned the corral to send up Patches.

In her cool, silvery gray linen riding clothes Jerry drew an ecstatic breath as she gave Patches his head. He pirouetted for a moment then settled to a steady canter. On all sides spread fields and pastures in luxuriant greenness. Beyond them mountains swept to hazy, purple heights. In one of the fields a rider turned and looked at her as she passed. She leaned forward in her saddle, opened a gate and closed it; she hoped the man had noticed with what ease it had been accomplished. Great blooded Shorthorns turned ruminative eyes upon her; she had seen women with that same expression when at a society function another entered as to whose social status they were in doubt. Off in a pen a perfect specimen of pure-blooded Ayreshire bull pawed the ground and sent showers of earth spraying on his satiny back. Where the trail left the flower-dotted meadow a spring bubbled from under a mushroom-shaped rock. Jerry dismounted and knelt for a drink, more for the feel of the sparkling water against her lips than because of thirst.

Where should she go, she wondered as she mounted Patches. She had an inspiration. She would make a neighborly call on the wife of the ex-service man at Bear Creek ranch. Jerry had never seen her, but Sandy the Carrier, who was the artery for news in the county, had told her that she was lonely.

The water was high in the stream. The banks were pink with wild roses and among their denseness the meadowlarks kept up an invisible chorus. Jerry forced Patches to a coquettish prance across the rustic bridge. It was there that the apex of the B C triangle of land forced its way between the Double O and the X Y Z. She knew the place; Tommy had shown her the dividing fences. From where the rushing water narrowed and whitened over a rocky bed an aged pack-trail staggered into a cuplike ravine. Rejuvenated by the sunshine in the hollow it straightened and sprinted straight as an arrow for the foot-hills. The sun shone warmly on lustrous fields. The air was spicy with the breath of pines. A rabbit hopped from cover and scurried back again.

As Patches, with ears pricked, silky neck preened, stepped daintily along the trail the girl sang happily:

> " 'My road calls me, lures me
> West, east, south and north;

> " 'Most roads lead me homeward,
> But my road leads men forth—
> To add more miles to the tal——' "

The last word was broken in the middle as they rounded a clump of cottonwoods and came suddenly upon a horseman with a small bunch of sheep. He jerked his hat low over his eyes as the girl hailed him.

"Good-afternoon! I am looking for Bear Creek ranch. Will you direct me?"

Without answering in words the man pointed toward a clutter of buildings in a slight depression. Back of them a scantily timbered hill, in places rich with grass dotted with grazing sheep, gave the impression of an animated Corot. Before Jerry could speak the stranger had galloped off.

"A responsive party," she soliloquized. "Was he afraid of me, I wonder? He registered guilt, all right. If he is the owner of B C ranch Uncle Nick and Bruce Greyson were buncoed. That man is hiding something."

A woman flung open the cabin door as Jerry rode up. She was young and pretty. Her clear, full eyes reminded the girl of Ox-eyed Juno. She was dressed in a bungalow apron of hectic design but scrupulous neatness. A wistful smile trembled on her lips as she asked:

"Have—have you lost your way?"

Jerry Courtlandt shook her head and slipped from the saddle. The gold in her brown eyes predominated as she fastened Patches to a post and approached the door.

"Lost? No, I came to call. I am Geraldine Courtlandt, your neighbor at the Double O."

The woman's face colored a delicate shell pink. Her expression was radiance tempered by incredulity.

"How—how nice of you, Mrs. Courtlandt, how human. I—I am Mrs. Jim Carey. Nell Carey. Won't you come in?"

Jerry liked her dignity. She showed no consciousness of the difference between her three-room shack and the luxurious ranch-house from which the visitor had come. "Thoroughbred," thought the girl as she preceded her hostess into a small but immaculately clean room. With a happy laugh tinged with excitement, Nell Carey waved her to a seat.

"Do make yourself comfortable. If you'll excuse me for a moment I'll bring some tea. The kettle has just boiled. You won't vanish while I'm gone, will you? Promise. I have a horrible fear that your being here may be nothing but an iridescent dream."

Jerry's heart smarted with self-reproach. What heathens people can be and yet be neighbors, she thought. Here was this girl, and she was a girl in spite of that betraying heap of white sewing on the machine in the corner, craving companionship, and she spent hours and hours riding about the country with never a thought of being neighborly. She looked about the room. What part of it wasn't taken up by a roll-top desk was filled by a table fairly groaning under its load of magazines. Three chairs and the machine completed the furnishings; that is, unless a worn violin case in a corner came under that head. She hastily cleared an end of the table as Nell Carey entered with a tea-tray.

"Thank you. You are the first woman who has been inside my house since I came here a year ago," she announced breathlessly. Her eyes glowed, her cheeks were flushed. "Of course Jim has flivvered me to town, but—but I haven't met anyone whom I cared to have here. Cream?"

The loneliness of it, Jerry thought, as she watched her hostess pour thick cream into the fragrant tea with hands that trembled. Then she remembered that she had been at the Double O three months, and that except for Ming Soy and Mrs. Simms, the foreman's wife at Upper Farm, she had not seen a woman. Curious that she had not missed them. Doc Rand had been as neighborly as his busy life permitted; Bruce Greyson had been away from the X Y Z since her arrival. With Steve and Tommy she had been absolutely content. Why? Her thoughts bolted on a tour of investigation; she dragged them back to answer a question from her hostess:

"Not another cookie, thank you. I've been a gourmand, but they are delicious."

"Jim likes them."

"I wonder if I saw your husband by the stream?"

"No. Jim left yesterday on a hunt for help. He'll only be away four days but it seems years to look forward to. You must have met our range-rider, Bill Small. He dropped from the sky, figuratively speaking, ten months ago. I call him the Man of Mystery. He never talks about himself, never mentions his people, never has letters, but he's a shark for work and he plays beautifully. That is his." She nodded toward the violin case in the corner. "The boys from the Double O and the X Y Z hit the trail for the Bear Creek every chance they can get to hear him play."

The sun topped the cap of a mountain like a mammoth red button as Jerry leaned from the saddle and held out her hand.

"You will come and see me, won't you?"

Nell Carey's lips quivered betrayingly.

"Of course, if you really want me. But it will be after——" Jerry gave the hand she held an impulsive squeeze.

"I'll come here again before that. Aren't you madly happy? I must hurry or they'll have the entire outfit hunting for me. Good-bye!"

As she reached the pack-trail she turned and waved and the woman standing alone by her door waved back. What an atom she seemed in the wide spaces about her. As she rode Jerry's mind was full of the home she had left behind. What courage Nell Carey had had to follow her man into a wilderness like that. And now a little child was coming. She thought of her father, of his anger because his daughter had insisted upon accompanying the man she had married to the Double O ranch with all its luxury. Men were curious creatures.

The sun had disappeared, fluffy islands of cloud, pink, lemon and violet, floated above the tops of the mountains, the sky was fast purpling, there was a suspicion of razor-edge in the crystal-clear air as Jerry unlatched the gate by the road and closed it after her. She gave Patches his head and raced toward the ranchhouse. In the distance she saw two horsemen galloping toward her. Steve and Pete Gerrish! She glanced guiltily at her wrist watch. She was late. Did Steve care enough to be anxious? The thought gave a tingling sense of excitement. As she came near the two riders she touched Patches with her spurs, then pulled him up suddenly. He stop-slid on his haunches, a bit of circus-variety of horsemanship which Tommy had taught her. She pulled off her broad-brimmed hat with a sweep reminiscent of José at his best and called gayly:

"*Que hay, señors! Buenos dias!* La señora has been on a wild devil of a ride, yes?"

She laughed up into Steve's white face. He moistened his lips as though they were stiff. She had worried him then. Pete Gerrish's eyes regarded her with frank admiration.

"Can she ride, Chief? I want to know! Can she ride! Steve is scared, ma'am. There's a lot of strangers snooping round and he——"

"Where have you been, Jerry?" Courtlandt had recovered his voice.

"Don't beat me, Steve!" Patches was loping along between Blue Devil and Gerrish's big sorrel. Encouraged by the foreman's quickly suppressed "Haw-haw" at her pleasantry, she went on, "I've been to Bear Creek ranch for tea."

"To the B C alone?"

"Do I look as though I carried concealed escorts?" with tormenting charm. "I had an acute attack of conscience. It occurred to me that I had been something of a heathen to ignore little Mrs. Carey, though I didn't know that she was little when I went. I only knew what Sandy had told me, that there was a woman at Bear Creek hungering for someone of her own sex to talk to."

"You are to be commended more for your conscience than your common sense," retorted Courtlandt dryly. "Don't do it again." They reached the ranch-house steps as he spoke. He slipped to the ground and before Jerry could protest had lifted her from the saddle. She felt the muscles of his arms twitch in the second he held her. Before she could speak he had gathered up the bridles of the horses and started for the corral. The brown depths of the girl's eyes were troubled as she looked after him. What menaced the good-comradeship which their arrival at the Double O had established between herself and Steve? Now he reminded her of a wary foe thrusting and retreating on the slightest pretext. What could she have done to change him so? She looked up at Gerrish, a puzzled question in her eyes. He shook his head as his met them.

"We mustn't mind if the Chief does act a little locoed, ma'am. He's walkin' right into trouble. It's Ranlett the Skunk, saving your presence. Somebody's cayuse got rid of some hobbles when the fence was cut where the Double O and the X Y Z join, and a bunch of calves has disappeared. There ain't hide nor hair of 'em to be seen. But, shucks, don't tell the Chief I told you. I'll mosey 'long now."

Jerry looked after him with narrowed eyes. "Where the Double O and the X Y Z join," Pete had said. That was where Bear Creek ranch came in! Like a movie close-up came a vision of the solitary horseman she had hailed, the man who had dropped from the air, who never talked about himself or his people, who never received letters, the Man of Mystery.

X

COURTLANDT backed his horse suddenly into the shadow of the quaking aspens which were fluttering their gold in the sunshine. He adjusted the field-glasses which he carried slung from his saddle-fork and looked intently at the bluff which reared from the western bank of the stream. He was right. There were two men there. The day being Sunday, ordinarily he would have thought nothing of it, but disturbing things were happening every day now and Instinct and Caution were riding close to his saddle-bow. He had the sense of living on the thin crust of a simmering volcano. He couldn't distinguish their faces, but he would be willing to swear that the men belonged to the Double O outfit.

Above the roar of the stream as it made its way through the cañon formed by the bluff he heard another sound. There was no mistaking it. Steve had heard the curious whirr of a plane too often not to recognize it now. It was not uncommon to have one pass over the Double O, but for some unaccountable reason Courtlandt linked this one to those two skulking figures at the foot of the bluff. He heard its approach for some minutes before it came in sight above the hill which he knew was back of the B C ranch.

"That's queer! Looks as though it came out of Buzzard's Hollow," he muttered as he watched the approaching aeroplane. He focussed his glasses on the men again. They were waving something. Something white. As though in answer to the signal the huge mechanical bird went wing-over-wings and slid gracefully into a barrel-roll, then sailed off into the distance. When Courtlandt's eyes returned from their journey with the plane the two men had disappeared.

Motionless, deep in thought, Steve sat his horse. What baneful force was at work on the ranch? Calves had vanished as completely as though conjured into thin air, curiously enough, though they were the least valuable in the herd. The man who had taken them couldn't know much about cattle. Some of the boys appeared surly and disgruntled. The stand he had taken on the alien question couldn't account for it all. The trouble had started a few weeks after his arrival at the ranch. He had expected that Ranlett would resent having a much younger man than himself in possession, but he had looked for no such series of complications as had presented themselves.

The situation had one compensating side. He had been too occupied with Double O affairs to have much time for Jerry. He said something under his breath. Blue Devil nosed round at him inquiringly. Courtlandt looked at the sun and touched the horse lightly with his heels. It was time to meet her now. To-day they were resuming a custom that Nicholas Fairfax had inaugurated, which was to have luncheon beside the stream on Sunday. Old Nick, young Nick he was then, had announced that the ceremony would stand for church, that he would worship God through nature. He and Doc Rand had provided the fish which were cooked on forked sticks over a fire on the bank of the stream. The work-logged physician's weekly holiday came to be respected in Slippy Bend. Men, women and children endured to the limit before they would disturb the doctor's fishing trip.

Opposite the rendezvous Courtlandt drew rein and looked across the stream. Benson, on his knees on the pebbly beach, was struggling with a fire. He was in khaki riding clothes. A small book protruded from his hip pocket. Steve smiled. To think of Tommy without a book would be like thinking of an elephant without his trunk. Beyond the firemaker a spring bubbled out of the bank in a clear, pure stream, above him the land sloped smoothly, greenly up to a clump of cottonwoods. In the middle of the clearing knelt Jerry. A lovely Jerry in riding coat and breeches, hatless, with millions of golden motes glinting in her hair where the sunlight rested. Her cheeks were flushed, her eyes glowed with friendliness as she talked eagerly with the man who knelt on the other side of the cloth spread between them.

Bruce Greyson! Steve's jaws set ominously. The owner of the X Y Z was passing something to the girl and it seemed to the prejudiced eyes of the looker-on that their fingers touched and lingered. The two had evidently been preparing the feast, for with a satisfied nod Jerry sank back on her heels. She made a megaphone of her hands and called:

"Coo-e-e! Coo-e-e-e!"

From around a bend of the river came an answering shout. In spite of the unaccountable fury which the sight of Greyson in just that spot had roused in Courtlandt, he laughed as his eyes rested on the figure which came splashing down the middle of the stream. It was Doc Rand attired in his usual ministerial black frock coat, with the unusual addition of hip boots of rubber. The effect of the combination would have tickled the risibilities of a stoic, if a stoic has the luck to be blessed with risibilities. A fish basket was slung from one shoulder, his white hair bushed beneath the brim of his Stetson; the sun on his glasses added an uncanny touch. His broad black tie, which he usually wore in a Byronic bow, streamed back over his shoulders. He waved and shouted as Courtlandt rode his horse down the bank and forded the stream. When Steve reached the improvised table Greyson and Jerry sat at discreet distances from it.

"When did you get back, Bruce?" he asked as with cordial friendliness the owner of the X Y Z sprang to his feet and gripped his extended hand. In that instant Courtlandt saw that the whiteness of the hair about the older man's temples was more noticeable, that it added to his fine, upright air of distinction.

"Yesterday. Brought my sister Paula, Vance, her husband, and a friend of hers along. I want you all to dine with us to-morrow night. We'll show these blown-in-the-glass New Yorkers that we are not entirely devoid of the social graces even if we are not in the Dude-ranch neighborhood. Got half-way to the Double O before I remembered that it was the old custom to lunch here Sundays. You'll come, won't you?"

"Come!" Jerry's eyes were starry with excitement. "Yes, thank—oh, what beauties!" as Doc Rand puffed up the bank dangling a string of trout for her inspection.

"Take 'em, Steve. You and the Benson boy can cook 'em. Isn't that an equitable division of labor, Mrs. Jerry? I caught them." He dropped to the ground beside her and pulled off his hat. "These—these fishing trips aren't what they were. I miss Nick," he confided as he mopped his hot brow. Jerry's eyes were tender with sympathy. They wandered dreamily to the illimitable spaces above the purple mountains as she asked softly:

"Where is he, Doctor Rand? Death is such a strange thing. I—I try to keep a brave front to Peggy but—— but I don't care to think about it."

"Why should you at your age? All your thought should be on making your life count for something. It is different with me. I find it profoundly interesting to wonder and imagine what follows this world. For instance, look at the question in this way. At this moment I can send my mind to the Manor; in spirit I'm pacing the terrace with Sir Peter. I can see the boats chugging up and down the river, can smell the queer fragrance which the sun is baking out of the box hedge in the garden, can hear the birds twittering among the vines. If I can do all that now, what will it be when the spirit is not hampered by the body? It will be like flying, won't it? That reminds me! Oh, Steve!"

Courtlandt poked his head above the bank beneath which he and Benson were cooking the fish. A tiny spiral of smoke rose and with it the aroma of sizzling bacon and frying trout.

"Did you see the plane that went over?"

"Yes, Doc."

"I wonder where it came from. It wasn't one of the government fliers. I know their marks. Did you see the pilot do those stunts above the bluff? Curious that he should pull off that cut-up stuff there, infernally risky I call it. He couldn't have been doing it for my benefit. What do you make of it, Steve?"

"Probably some crazy, reckless flier getting ready for a contest," Courtlandt observed, and disappeared below the bank.

Doc Rand and Greyson left directly after luncheon. Benson packed the basket which some of the boys would take back to the ranch before he rode off to Upper Farm on an errand for Courtlandt. Steve helped Jerry mount and swung into the saddle. The girl tightened her rein then held up an arresting finger.

"Listen! The Kreutzer Sonata," she whispered.

From somewhere up-stream came the notes of a violin. There was a rare brightness, an aerial quality to the music that most artists take too gravely. The variations of the slow movements gave the sense of a glorified voice. Jerry drew a long, tremulous breath as the last note died away.

"That must have been the Man of Mystery," she confided in a low voice, as though fearful even at that distance of disturbing the musician. "I don't care if he did drop from the sky, if he never receives letters, he plays like—like an angel—if angels can play," with a laugh. Courtlandt looked up-stream as though mystified.

"I knew a man who played that sonata, just like that, but—but it can't possibly be he. Who did you say you thought it was?"

"Bill Small, the range-rider at the B C. Mrs. Carey told me about him when I called there yesterday. She said that the boys of the Double O and X Y Z outfits trailed over there every chance they could get to hear him play. That reminds me," her beautiful face glowed with enthusiasm, "I—I wonder if—if the boys of our outfit would care to have me play and sing for them? I should so love to do it."

"Care! I know they would. Pete says that they line up outside the court wall after dinner on the chance of hearing you sing."

"Really—really, Steve? I'd rather have that tribute than—than my name in electric lights on the Great White Way. Ask them up this afternoon. We'll have an honest-to-goodness musicale with Signora Geraldina Courtlandta as head-liner. Hurry!" She touched her horse with her heels. "It's a pity that Bruce Greyson didn't wait. He——"

"Your proposition was to sing for the Double O outfit. Greyson doesn't come in on that."

"Ogre! I can hear my bones scrunch between those strong white teeth of yours when you look at me like that."

"Then remember that you're married."

"Are you sure that the ceremony wasn't a dream?" with a provocative ripple of laughter. "Do you know, Steve, somehow I never can think of you as Benedick the married man. You—you are such a good-looking boy." She was the incarnation of girlish diablerie indulging an irresistible desire to torment. The color burned to Courtlandt's temples. He caught the bridle and drew Patches close. His eyes compelled Jerry's.

"Do you know what happens to a person who rocks a boat, Mrs. Courtlandt?" he demanded autocratically.

"Do you know what happens when a person gets unbearably dictatorial, Mr. Courtlandt? This!" She slapped her horse smartly on the hip. Patches threw up his head and broke from Steve's hold. The girl looked over her shoulder. Lips and eyes challenged in unison as she sang mischievously:

> " 'My road calls me, lures me
> West, east, south and north;
> Most roads lead me homewards,
> But my road leads——' "

Patches stepped in a gopher hole, which feat brought the song to an abrupt termination.

When she met him in the late afternoon on the terrace which overlooked the court Jerry was as coolly friendly as though the little passage-at-arms, which had left Steve's pulses hammering, had never taken place. The piano had been moved out and the outfit, in its Sunday best, occupied the rustic seats and benches and overflowed to the turf paths. The girl felt choky as the men rose to greet her. They looked so big and fine, so like eager, wistful boys. She smiled at them through a mist.

"I'll sing what I think you'll like, then you must ask for anything you want. Please smoke," she added, as she realized what it was that had made them seem so unfamiliar. They looked from her to Steve. He nodded. With delighted grins they dropped back to their places and proceeded with the business of rolling cigarettes.

Courtlandt and Benson took their places on the edge

of the terrace. Overhead the sky spread like a flawless turquoise; cameoed against the blue were snow-tipped mountains. The court was gay and fragrant with blossoms. In the dark shadow of the open doorway Ming and Hopi Soy made a patch of Oriental brilliance. Jerry in her filmy pink frock looked not unlike a flower herself, against the rosewood background of the raised piano top, Courtlandt thought. He looked from her to the rapt, weather-browned faces of his men. His gaze came back and rested in fascinated interest on her foot in its pink slipper on the pedal of the instrument.

Jerry sang as she had never sung before, ballads, rollicking melodies. The men drew nearer. When she stopped a swarthy Italian stepped as near the piano as the terrace would permit. His black eyes seemed too big for his thin face, his plastered-down hair suggested infinite labor with brush and pomade.

"What is it, Tony?" Jerry asked with a smile.

"Have you the one grand opera song?" he asked shyly. Jerry was nonplussed. She had not thought of opera for these men. As she turned over her music she asked:

"You like opera, Tony?"

"Vera much, Signora. At home we taka the leetle seester to grand opera even if we have not mucha to eat. We feel that eef the leetle seester hear great music, she be fine lady, not common, not bad—never." His earnest voice broke as he realized that he was being stared at in amazement by the outfit. He mumbled an apology and hurried back to his seat. With a smile at Tony, Jerry placed Tales of Hoffmann on the rack. She sang the Barcarole. As the exquisite, langorous notes floated out over the court the shadows lengthened, the sun dropped behind the mountains. There was no applause when she finished, no one was smoking, the men sat motionless. Where were their thoughts, the girl wondered. With a glance at the crimsoning foot-hills she struck a few chords and sang softly:

> " 'Day is dying in the west;
> Heaven is touching earth with rest;

Wait and worship while the night
Sets her evening lamps alight
Thro' all the sky.' "

With the second verse the men took up the song. To
most of them it brought a vivid picture of mother and
home and the village church at sunset. They sang until
with the last line mountains and foot-hills took up the
words and sent them pealing into space.

That closed the musicale. One by one the men came
forward and thanked Jerry as she stood between Courtlandt and Benson. As the last one left the court Tommy
turned to the girl.

"I'll say that was a wonderful thing to do, Mrs.
Steve." With a quick change of tone he spoke to Courtlandt. "Marks and Schoeffleur weren't here; did you
miss them?"

"Would you expect them to be here?"

"I should have expected it until to-day. Ever since
Marks blew in here from nowhere two months ago
I've been wondering where the dickens I'd seen him.
When that airplane passed over to-day memory flipped
into place the missing piece of the puzzle. He was a
mechanician at the hangar where I tried to develop
wings in 1917."

"You are sure of that, Tommy?"

"Sure as shootin'. What's up? Why that 'Fee, fi, fo,
fum, I smell the blood of an Englishman' scowl, old
dear?"

"Nothing, except that your information confirms me
in my suspicion that Marks and Schoeffleur signaled to
that pilot when he went over."

" 'And still they gazed, and still the wonder grew
That one small head could carry all he knew.' "

contributed Benson in mock amazement.

Up from the corral floated a chorus of men's voices
singing:

" 'Wait and worship while the night
Sets her evening lamps alight
Thro' all the sky.' "

XI

COURTLANDT'S fine brow puckered in a thoughtful crease as he waited in the living-room of the Double O for Jerry the next evening. Benson, on the arm of a chair, bent forward to get the light from the lamp on the book he had picked up. Through the open windows came the scent of pine and dewy fields, the murmur of the distant stream as it thundered and rippled its never-ending triumphal march to the sea, the occasional soft lowing of cattle.

Jerry had been tremendously pleased and excited over Greyson's invitation to dine, Steve thought as he lighted a cigarette and blew the smoke toward Goober. The dog was regarding him with an air of watchful waiting. Was he to be invited to jump on the running-board of the automobile which stood in the drive outside the front door? Courtlandt remembered as clearly as though it had been yesterday what she had answered the first night they met when he had asked her if she liked the city. He could see her eyes now with their golden lights, hear her musical voice:

"I love it. It is so big, so beautiful, so faulty. I—I like people; I should starve for companionship, not food, in a wilderness."

And this was the girl who had been on the Double O ranch for over three months and not a person outside it, except Doc Rand and some neighboring ranchmen, had she seen before she made the trip to the B C. He had been too busy to think of it before and—and he had intentionally kept out of her way. He had thought that he had his course set to avoid danger, but he had come mighty near going to pieces on an uncharted rock yesterday. He tossed away his cigarette as Jerry's door opened. He took an involuntary step forward, then thrust his hands into his pockets. Lord, how impellingly beautiful she was! Her gold-color gown, all film where it wasn't glistening paillettes, was as simple as the most expensive modiste in New York could make it. Her lovely arms were bare. The ranch life had deepened the coloring of her face and throat till her shoulders looked startlingly white in contrast. Steve noted, with a surge of primitive triumph, that the only jewels she wore were a string of softly gleaming pearls and her wedding ring. Sir Peter had given her the pearls when she was married. They had been worn by his wife and before that by his mother. Steve heard Tommy give vent to a sound that was a cross between a swallow and a gasp before he struck an attitude and paraphrased theatrically:

"But soft! What light through yonder doorway breaks?
It is the east and Juliet is the sun."

Jerry laughed and blew him a kiss. Her teeth rivaled in beauty the pearls below them. Ming Soy, more rice-papery than ever in the resplendent embroideries she wore in the evening, followed the girl from her room with a shimmering wrap over her arm.

"Were you casting aspersions on the brilliancy of my costume, Mr. Tommy Benson? This is the first invitation I have received to dine since I left the metropolis and I acknowledge I have splurged. Do—do you like me, Steve?" Her attitude was demure but her smile was adorably mischievous. Courtlandt's eyes flamed, then smoldered.

"You'll do," with an edge of sarcasm. He hated himself as he saw her smile fade. Oh, why the dickens couldn't they have met—Tommy swept into the breach:

"Oh boy, hear the lady, Steve. 'Will I do?' just as though she didn't know that

"'Alack there lies more peril in thine eyes
Than twenty of their swords.'"

"Gracias, señor! Alas, if it weren't for you, Tommy, I should go down to my grave unwept, unhonored and unsung. Now that you have fully absorbed the glory of my raiment hold my cloak for me, that's a dear. Now this maline over my hair. I don't wish to appear before the guest from the effete East like a Meg Merriles."

"You couldn't," encouraged Benson fervently. "You'd—"

"Let's go!" cut in Courtlandt sharply, and led the way to the automobile. He sent the leaping, barking dog back with a curt command which caused Goober to regard him in drooping, tawny-eyed reproach. He took the wheel of the roadster. He kept his eyes resolutely on the road as he drove though he felt as though a magnet of the nth power was drawing his eyes to the girl who snuggled down between him and Benson. At the door of the X Y Z ranch-house Greyson met them.

"It's mighty good of you all to come." His voice was nervous, hurried.

"Good of us! Bruce, you're a public benefactor. You're a candidate for a specially designed, specially gilded halo. Do you realize what a risk you have taken introducing me to your city friends? It is so long since I have dined in state that I am quite capable of committing some horrible social blunder."

Steve's anger flared. Why did she have to admit to Greyson that she had been bored? It was still flickering as he entered the big living-room, a room lined with books from floor to ceiling, with color only in the crimson rug and heavy hangings.

"You see I've come to help you bear your exile, Steve!" greeted a laughing voice. Jerry and Tommy, who had preceded Courtlandt, turned involuntarily. He met the girl's startled eyes. He reddened furiously before he turned to answer the golden-haired woman who had stepped from behind a screen.

"Felice! Where did you come from?" His tone was dazed and strugglingly cordial.

"Have you lost both manners and memory, Stevie? You haven't offered to shake hands; you have apparent-

ly forgotten that I wrote you that while he was at the
Manor Mr. Greyson discovered that I had been at
school with his sister. Paula has come out for the summer and brought me with her. I adore the ranch. Steve,
we'll have some rides that will make those we used to
have take on a pale anaemic blue." She linked her arm
within his and smiled up at him beguilingly.

"Hmp, vamp-stuff!" Courtlandt heard Tommy con-
fide to Jerry before he disengaged his arm from Mrs.
Denbigh's clasp and reminded:

"Have you seen Mrs. Courtlandt, Felice? Jerry, you
remember Mrs. Denbigh?"

"Perfectly. She is one of those persons one never forgets. Mrs. Denbigh, may I present Mr. Benson? Mr.
Greyson, back up your statement, show me that Hopi
saddle-blanket which you claimed yesterday had Uncle
Nick's licked to a finish. That phrase is your bit of
choice Americana, not mine, remember."

Steve's eyes followed Jerry as she moved away with
her host. There was a slightly scornful tilt to her lips.
Greyson looked as though he had been caught stealing
sheep, he decided. Was there a sinister undercurrent at
the X Y Z as well as the Double O? If there were he'd
get to the bottom of that, too. Regardless of Benson's
proximity he burst out:

"Why did you intimate that I had been correspond-
ing with you, Felice?"

The woman's super decolléte frock was no greener
than her eyes, her elaborately coiffured yellow hair
glittered; it hadn't the satiny sheen of Jerry's; her hands
were frosty with diamonds. Even her laugh had a me-
tallic ring as she answered:

"What a literal person you are, Stevie. Have you been
bitten with the nothing-but-the-truth mania? Can't I
interest you in a saddle-blanket? It makes an excellent
smoke-screen for a tête-à-tête." Her laugh tinkled mali-
ciously as she nodded toward the corner where her host
stood with Jerry Courtlandt. Steve deliberately turned
his back and inquired irrelevantly:

"How was little ol' New York when you left, Felice?"

It wasn't to be wondered at that Jerry liked people, people so evidently adored her, Courtlandt thought as coffee was being served in the living-room after dinner. Paula Vance, who though no older than Felice Denbigh, already showed symptoms of middle-aged curves, was officiating behind the massive silver tray with its rare, antique appointments. Her husband, with those three unmistakable L's, liquor, lobster and leisure writ large on his portly person from his terraced chin to his shining patent leathers, Greyson and Benson were listening to Jerry as, with eyes like stars, cheeks flushed, she sat at the piano. She played a low, rippling accompaniment as, in answer to a question from her host, she gave an account of her visit to Bear Creek ranch. Felice Denbigh also had her eyes on the group. She divided her attention between it and her coffee. Her light lashes swept her cheeks as she tapped her cigarette against her thumb-nail and drawled:

"Better give young Benson his time, Steve. Isn't that ranch parlance for discharge? He's in love with Mrs. Courtlandt." The man beside her reddened angrily.

"Don't bring your tainted ideas out into this clean, glorious country, Felice. Benson is——" he broke off to watch Greyson's Jap, a little man with a face like the mask of tragedy who was speaking to Jerry.

"Are you sure that he said Mrs. Courtlandt?" Steve heard her ask in surprise. Then as the man reiterated his message she excused herself to the men about her and left the room. Tommy looked after her anxiously before his eyes flashed to Steve. The latter gave an imperceptible nod and with a murmured excuse to Felice followed Jerry. As he stepped to the porch he saw the golden gleam of the girl's gown at the farther end. She was talking earnestly with a man, a man who was holding a saddled horse. The moon shone down upon the animal's wet sides; he had evidently been ridden hard. What did it mean? Had Glamorgan, by any chance, sent for his daughter? As he strode toward them he heard the girl say breathlessly:

"No! No! Don't wait! Ride as fast as you can. I'll get there some way."

"Jerry!" in his anxiety Steve sent his voice ahead of him. At the sound the man leaped to the horse's back and galloped away into the dusk of the road. The girl strained her eyes after him before she turned.

"There is something queer about that man, Steve; he is a man of mystery," she confided as though Courtlandt's materialization out of the dark was quite what she expected.

"What did he want?"

"He wanted me. Don't look so incredulous. I may be an acquired taste like olives but—some people like me." She abandoned her teasing tone and hurried on, "That man is the range-rider at Bear Creek ranch. Mrs. Carey has been taken suddenly ill, there,—there is a baby coming, you know, Steve. He wanted me to go to her. Her husband is away. They haven't had a telephone put in and it may take hours to get the doctor and nurse from town, he may not be able to get them at all and so—and so he asked me to go and stay with her until he could get help."

"But you can't go, girl, at this time of night."

"Oh, yes, I can, Steve. I'm going. Please ask Tommy to drive me. We'll make better time going in the machine even by the roundabout wagon road. If I rode I'd have to go home first and change my clothes. He can come back for you. Hurry!"

"Back for me! Do you think you go off this ranch tonight with anyone but me? It's rank folly for you to go——"

She caught the lapel of his coat and looked up at him with dewy eyes.

"Suppose,—suppose that it were I, Steve——"

Even in the dim light he could see the soft color steal to her hair. He turned away with a sharp:

"Get your wrap while I go for the car, and give Benson his orders. He'll have to keep a date for me."

The star-spangled night was clear and still as Courtlandt slowed down in front of the Bear Creek ranch-house. The girl beside him shivered as she looked at the lighted windows. He laid one hand on hers.

"Steady, little girl, steady. You won't be able to help if you lose your nerve."

"I know, Steve, I'll be all right as soon as I get busy. I have never seen——" She sprang from the car and ran up the path, her golden gown gleaming in the dim light. As she opened the door Courtlandt heard a sound which sent him from the car. He couldn't sit still. Lips set he paced back and forth, back and forth while a voice inside his head, which didn't seem his voice at all, kept repeating, "Suppose—just suppose it were I, Steve?"

Other thoughts crowded in upon him as he paced like a sentinel, a sentinel in dinner clothes, before the little house. The dawn crept slowly up in the east spraying the dark sky overhead with gorgeousness. It transformed the world into the fairyland of the pantomimes of his boyhood, a world full of magic passwords and talismans. He almost expected to see a shimmering, masked Harlequin tap on the cabin door with his supple wand and a dainty Columbine pirouette out in response.

Whatever it might be outside, there was no illusion behind that closed door. It was raw reality. What wonders women were, some of them, Steve amended. He thought of the girls with whom he had dined and danced in the last two years. Many of them sensation-seeking privateers. Was it after-war reaction which made them so recklessly, flagrantly determined in their attempts to lure? They had succeeded only in repelling him but they had plenty of victims. How they crackled the glaze of their reputations. How they married and unmarried, those people whom he knew, and with what tragic consequences to their children. Felice was a product of the atmosphere in which she lived. He realized now that she would have no scruples in coming between him and the girl he had married if she could. A fragment from Kant which had been the text for a college theme teased at the tip of his tongue. He had it! "No one of us can do that, which if done by all, will destroy society." If this divorce business kept up it would destroy society. Did luxurious social life breed inconstancy of purpose, contempt of covenants?

As though in answer to his question came a vision of Jerry as she had knelt beside Old Nick's bed. He could see her face, the hint of tears under the steadiness of her gaze, hear her voice as she repeated reverently the marriage service.

She would keep her marriage vow at any cost to herself, Courtlandt thought, no matter how she might care for someone else. She was the sort of woman who would stand the wear and tear of daily companionship, making allowance for a man's moods but never knuckling to them. She'd bring him up with a round turn, but she'd laugh while she did it. He couldn't imagine her irritable or fretty or snappy. She had the saving grace of humor. If women could only learn the persuasive value of a laugh as against tears or sulks how many marriages would be saved from the scrap-heap. After all, any poor dumb-bell could get married; it was staying married which proved one's metal.

The color overhead spread with increasing beauty. The last friendly star high up above a mountain twinkled out. Somewhere toward the barns a shrill-voiced, enterprising cock "hailed the smiling morn." A curl of smoke rose lazily from the cabin chimney. The sun shot up through a fleece of clouds; it painted the fields and sloping hillside with radiance. A horse whinnied in the corral, a light breeze sprang up and brought with it the odor of barns, the strong scent of wool. From the road came the labored breathing of a flivver.

"Thank God, someone's coming!" Courtlandt thought. He looked toward the cabin, transformed in the morning light into a habitation of gold. As he looked the lights in the windows went out. What was Jerry doing? Could he have helped? A flivver rattled up and stopped. In the exuberance of his relief Steve opened the door of the car before either of the occupants had a chance. "Mother" Egan, a portly woman whose clothing suggested a starch and soap advertisement, it was so immaculate and standoutish, nodded as she stepped heavily out. Her face beamed with kindliness and sympathetic understanding as she lumbered up to the door. Doc Rand regarded Courtlandt with an incredulous grin:

"For the love of Mike, Steve, what you doing here? This isn't your party——" with a hardened chuckle.

"Cut out the comedy, Doc. I brought Mrs. Courtlandt over to stay until you came. For God's sake get in there and stop those sounds. Send Jerry out."

"What you say goes, Steve. Out she comes. Run the flivver round to the barn, will you? I'm likely to stay here most of the day."

Worn black bag in hand he disappeared inside the house. As Steve started the car a horseman galloped into sight on the road. He stopped his horse with a suddenness that threw the animal back on his haunches, then, after an instant's hesitation he went on toward the huddle of buildings. Steve looked after him curiously. Was he Jerry's Man of Mystery? He deliberately followed the horseman. When he dismounted Steve shut off his engine and jumped to the ground. The rider turned. Steve stared.

"Phil Denbigh!" he exclaimed incredulously.

XII

THE two men faced each other silently. The morning light accentuated the lines on Denbigh's thin, ascetic face, revealed the brooding sorrow in his eyes. After his involuntary halt of surprise Courtlandt sprang forward with outstretched hand.

"Phil, old scout, it's good to see you! But—but what the dickens are you doing here? I know Jim Carey but you're—not——"

"The same. I'm Bill Small, range-rider of the Bear Creek outfit, which extensive outfit consists at present

of the owner and yours truly. It has taken some dex-
terity to keep out of your way, Steve. Your Uncle Nick
got me the job. Curious that I should have turned to
him in my despair, but—but he was the first person I
thought of. I had heard Mother rail about his caustic
tongue. I concluded if she thought that, he must have
a keen sense of justice and fair-dealing. Mrs. Carey
thinks that I dropped from the air or any old place.
Jim went away three days ago and left me in charge.
We didn't think that this—this—was coming so soon.
My first thought when Mrs. Carey called me last
evening was to get hold of the nearest woman and—and
Mrs. Courtlandt seemed to be it. I went to your ranch
first and they sent me on to the X Y Z."

"I can't make you seem real yet, Phil. I'm dazed with
the succession of surprises. Saturday, Beechy, my late
sergeant walked in and——"

"Beechy!"

"Say, 'The Devil!' and be done with it, that's what
your tone implied. What do you know about Carl
Beechy?"

"I've run across him in Slippy Bend. A regular fella
with the ladies, isn't he?"

"So that's it! I'll have to admit that Carl is an easy
mark with the fair sex, but he's all there when it comes
to fighting. I wanted to keep him at the Double O, but
he insisted that he must keep his contract with the
railroad."

"Oh, he did. You're fond of Beechy, Steve?"

"He saved my life, Phil. I was as sure of the man's
loyalty as I was that the sun would rise in the morning."

"Have patience, Steve, you'll get him back. Sadder
and wiser, perhaps a bit damaged, but you'll get him
back."

"Damaged! What do you mean?"

"Nothing specific. I'm judging from what I've seen
the railroads do. I hear Ranlett has left you. Take it
from me, you're in luck."

"I'll say you're right. I haven't had a chance to talk
it over with Greyson yet; he came back from the East

only a few days ago. Uncle Nick relied on his judgment. Good Lord!"—as remembrance of the evening before flashed clear in his mind, "do you know who came with him? Your—your wife."

Denbigh leisurely lighted a cigarette and as leisurely drew a long whiff of it.

"My wife! I haven't a wife. Felice will have her divorce in a few months. Desertion. Mamma Peyton's master-mind directed the campaign. Trust an old-timer like her to know the ropes. Felice didn't love me when she married me; she merely contracted a virulent attack of the war-marriage epidemic. I found that out when you came home. I'm through with women, Steve, that is until I've proved myself a man whose sense of right and justice can't be twisted by them. If I hadn't been weak Mother couldn't have—oh, why go into it? It wasn't her fault; life had been too easy for her; she couldn't bear to be hurt. Well, she has lost me as effectually as though I had been shot to pieces in the Argonne where so many of my friends lie. The effects of gas and shot and shell aren't in it with the intolerable sense of shame which a man, who didn't do his best to get into the war, will carry through the years. God knows, I'm paying for my weakness. Don't mind this outburst, Steve. Forget it! You're the first person I've seen from home. It—it just surged out."

He leaned his head upon his horse's neck. The animal which had been pawing impatiently settled into bronze immobility at his touch. Only his sensitive nostrils quivered. Courtlandt laid a sympathetic hand on Denbigh's shoulder. His voice was unsteady as he protested:

"You're torturing yourself unnecessarily, Phil. The world has almost forgotten——"

"I haven't, Steve, but we'll let it go at that. Don't let Felice know that I am here. When she gets her divorce——"

"But, Phil, can't you and she patch things up? Divorce is a hard thing for a woman to live down."

"Not in our set. Good Lord, man, Felice thinks no

more of it than she would of discarding an unbecoming gown. It's in her blood. It's in mine. Her mother had changed husbands once before Felice was born. Mine changed hers when he was young and unsuccessful. She had the money. When the Fates want to hand it to a man good and plenty they marry him to a girl who has slathers more money than he has." Steve's face whitened. "Was that a door closing? Go quick, Steve. If it is Mrs. Courtlandt I don't want her to see me. Don't tell her who I am." He seized his horse by the bridle and vanished into the barn.

Steve met Jerry beside his car. His jaw set in the manner dreaded by his father as he looked at the girl's face. It was white with violet shadows under the wide, strained eyes. Her exquisite frock was torn where she had caught it on a hook. A long angry burn was visible on the wrist which the sleeve of her wrap didn't cover. Her lips quivered traitorously as she saw Steve's eyes on it. She hastily concealed it behind her back with a valiant attempt at a laugh.

"It's nothing. I hoped that it would escape your ruthless managerial eye. I tried to heat water and I'm not used to a kitchen range. In fact, I don't know what I can do that's vitally useful. When—when I go back to civilization I shall take a course in nursing, then I won't be so absolutely useless at a time like this." Her voice was pitched in a key of nervous excitement, and she shivered as she spoke.

"Come here!" Courtlandt's face was as white as the girl's as he picked her up in his arms and put her into the car. He drew her wrap closer about her shoulders and tucked a light robe about her knees. She sat there tense, unresponsive, but as he started the car she suddenly relaxed with a stifled sob and covered her face with her hands. Steve stopped the car. With quiet determination he put his arm about her.

"Cry it out, child," he encouraged tenderly. When the storm broke he wondered if he had been wise in the recommendation. He was frightened at the tempest of sobs which shook the slender body. He tightened his arm. Then after a few moments, "Was it as bad as that, girl?"

She sat up with a start and drew as far away from him as the limited space would permit. He laid his arm across the back of the seat. She pushed the hair from her forehead and looked up at him through drenched eyes.

"Bad!" she controlled a shudder. "Bad only because I was so powerless to help. An angel from heaven wouldn't have looked as good to me as Doc Rand." There was an hysterical note of laughter in her voice as she continued, "He must have thought I had gone suddenly mad for when he opened the door I flew at him and kissed him." She made furtive dabs at her eyes. "Don't think that I'm constitutionally a cry-baby," she laughed up at Courtlandt shamefacedly. He turned away from her quickly, removed his arm from the back of the seat and started the car.

"Now that you've got your grip again we'll go on. I'm famished," he announced prosaically.

"Now that I think of it, so am I," she agreed with gay camaraderie, but her breath came in a little sob as a child's might after crying, "and—and so are they! look, Steve! Over on that hillside—look!"

She gripped his arm with one hand as she pointed with the other. On the top of a low hill, outlined like shadow pictures against the morning sky, so near that their hanging tongues were plainly visible, were three dark, sinister shapes.

"Coyotes?" the girl whispered as though even at that distance they might hear.

"Timber wolves. See those sheep grazing in the coulée below? They are after them."

"Oh, Steve, can't we do something?"

For answer Courtlandt reached into the pocket of the car and drew his automatic. The shots rang through the morning quiet, the echoes ricochetted back from the hills. The sheep kicked up their heels and scampered off. The wolves stood like creatures of stone for an instant, then slowly, quite without panic, turned and disappeared over the brow of the hill. Jerry shivered.

"Wolves! I thought you were rid of them in this country."

"We are almost. Occasionally the boys bring in reports of the trail of a wolf or a mountain lion. We have a pest of coyotes though, this year. If you want to insult a ranchman or cowboy to fighting mad, call him a coyote; it means the most despicable creature in the animal world. They're cowards. If that bunch of sheep turned and faced a coyote they would terrify him."

"Ranch life is just one problem after another, isn't it?"

"No more than any life which is packed with interest."

"My mistake! Didn't the little boy want his little ranch found fault with? Then he shan't be teased."

As he turned and looked at her she caught her breath, colored richly and apologized. "Don't mind me, Steve. The sudden release from responsibility and the elixir of the morning air have gone to my head. I'll be good, really I will. Did you see the Man of Mystery? I—I somehow have a feeling that he may know something of the missing calves."

"You're wrong. He's all right, he's doing a man's job—*he* isn't troubling me but—but I wish I knew what Beechy had up his sleeve. What had he said to you before I came in that day in the office?" with quick suspicion. His tone sent the color flying to the girl's hair.

"Why—why—nothing—but——"

"Don't perjure yourself," dryly. "Much as I think of Carl I'm not blind to his ways with women. He couldn't have been unbearably raw or you wouldn't have shaken hands with him, would you? I—I didn't like his eyes when he said he had work on the railroad."

"Steve, you are developing nerves; your imagination is running wild. One would think that we were back in the days of armed bandits, when masked men held up trains at the point of a gun. That isn't done now, you know," with gay patronage.

"Perhaps—look up on the hill! The boys are bringing down the horses."

The girl's eyes followed his pointing finger. Nose to tail, close herded by riders, the animals trailed toward the corral after their night of feeding in the hillside pastures. They tossed their manes, they made sportive attempts to escape their keepers.

"How well our boys ride." Steve's pulses responded to that possessive "our."

"They ought to. They are as near old-timers as can be found now. The Double O was Uncle Nick's master-passion. He took up the land when it was the ranchman's paradise, in the years before fence-posts and barbed wire, when cowboys packed guns and drank and gambled away their pay. He adapted himself with amazing success to changing conditions though, and hung on to all the real boys whom he could tempt with pay and the pride of raising thoroughbreds."

As Courtlandt stopped the car in front of the ranch-house, the door was flung open and a girl ran down the steps. Jerry stared incredulously. "Peggy! Peggy!" She was out of the car in a flash and had her sister in her arms. Steve heard one more muffled "Peggy!" before the two entered the house. The surprise following so close upon her night's vigil might be too much for Jerry, he feared. When Peg had written him and begged him to keep her coming a surprise he had weakly consented. He had intended to meet her train but had had to delegate Tommy to take his place.

Jerry had quite recovered her poise when she appeared for breakfast in the court. If there was a trace of *vibrato* in her voice only Courtlandt noticed it. She and Peg had stopped talking long enough to get two hours' sleep. Overhead the sky spread like a Della Robbia glaze, the atmosphere was so clear that the snow-tipped mountains seemed reachable. A tractor in a distant field sounded but a few feet away. The air was sweet with the fragrance of roses, the fountain tinkled musically. Benito, yellow eyes blinking, his gay plumage ruffled till he looked like an animated feather-duster, sidled round and round the rim of the basin.

Peggy regarded her sister with elfish, hazel eyes as she took her seat at the table.

"Ye gods, Jerry, but I'm glad to see you clothed and in your right mind. That green skirt and sweater is a little bit of all right and I'm crazy about your frills; they make me think of the soap-suds you see in the demonstration electric washers, they're so—so fleecy. When you drove up in that vampish gold gown this morning I thought it must be the custom of the country to breakfast in evening clothes and I could have wept. I'd been disillusioned enough. I thought that every honest-to-goodness he-man on a ranch wore chaps and tore about with his six-shooter 'spittin' death and damnation,' but the man who brought out my trunks evidently has a passion for overalls, and Mr. Benson met me at the train looking like a model of the Well-Dressed Man."

Her sister laughed.

"You've been reading Zane Gray et als. Please understand that we are ultra civilized on this ranch after six o'clock."

"Then you'll eat up my news. That smitten salesman of yours at Tiffany's told me before I left New York that he was on the trail of the Alexandrite ring you'd been wanting. It belonged to one of the late royalties. He says that it is a wonder, beautifully set and only two thousand dollars! You'd better write him about it. Of course he can't hold it indefinitely."

"Two thousand dollars!" Jerry regretted the shocked exclamation as soon as it left her lips. She glanced furtively at Steve. His eyes, clear and clean and shining from his out-of-door life, disconcertingly direct, met hers. She looked away hastily. "I'm—I'm not buying jewels now, Peg."

"You're not! Growing miserly in your old age, Geraldine?" with patronizing surprise. "You've been talking of that Alexandrite for——"

"Will you ride the range with your ancient brother-in-law this morning, Peg-o'-my-heart?" broke in Courtlandt. "We'll have lunch at Upper Farm."

"I'll say I'd love it. Will you come, Jerry?"

"No, I have work to do. Behold your erstwhile humble sister the private secretary of the owner of Double O ranch," with laughing empressement.

"Don't work. Sleep, or ride with Peg," cut in Steve sharply. "Remember you were out all night."

"O King Live Forever!" mocked Geraldine gayly. "Just as though I hadn't danced all night many a time and ridden in the park all morning. I shall——"

"Pete Glellish tlell you dat Ranlett make bad pidgin in Lower Flield," interrupted Ming Soy's soft voice at Courtlandt's elbow. "He says, 'Hully—hully—hully!' "

Steve sprang from his chair and caromed into Tommy Benson who had just entered the court and stood beaming upon Peggy Glamorgan.

"What, down already, Miss Peg? Methinks.

> " 'This morning, like the spirit of a youth
>   That means to be of note, begins betimes.'

Why the glassy-eye and furrowed-brow effect, Steve? I hope that you've left me a taste of the honey, Miss Glamorgan?" he reproached as he took his place at the table beside the girl.

"As soon as you've had a bite, Tommy, join me at Lower Field. Bring Peg along. Jerry," Steve Courtlandt's voice was peremptory, "remember, no work in the office and if you don't go with Peg and Tommy stay in sight of the ranch-house if you ride. Don't expect me until you see me. I may not be at home to-night."

He didn't wait for her answer. In his own room he picked up a Colt 45, spun the cylinder, slipped a box of cartridges into his pocket and hurried to the side door. Gerrish, mounted on the big sorrel, held Blue Devil by the bridle. Both horses were prancing nervously, for the parrot, who had climbed to the gutter under the roof, was clucking and calling:

"Gid-dap! Go-long!"

"That bird ought to be shot," Steve growled as with some difficulty he mounted. "What's to pay now, Pete, Ranlett?"

"You've got your rope on the right pair of horns this time, Chief. The fences of Lower Field have been cut."

"Toward the railroad?"

"By cripes, no. Toward the mountains. If 't been the railroad side we might have stood a chance of corralling the Shorthorns, but if they once get into the mountains —Lord-ee, I believe yer uncle'll rise out of his grave an' go after 'em. Them critters was the pride of his life. Ranlett was a low-down dawg to turn a trick like this. Say, do you know anything about thet range-rider at Bear Creek?"

"Why—why—I've spoken to him. You don't suspect him of being in this deal, do you?"

"I ain't suspectin' nothin', but after I'd saw him twice talkin' to Ranlett I sort of got his number."

"You've got it wrong, then, Pete. I happen to know that the man is white clear through."

"Well, I ain't shootin' off my mouth careless when I say that the range-rider's got somethin' up his sleeve. It's my best bet there's going to be fifty-seven varieties of hell blowin' up round this ranch before we get through. If you ask me, I'll say that the crime-wave that's been lappin' the coast has swashed out here in a flood."

"But, Pete, it's impossible for rustlers to get away with their old stuff now."

"You're shoutin', Chief, it sure is, but—they'll find some new ways. I got it doped out your way too, but if it ain't rustlin', what fool thing is that coyote Ranlett up to?"

"Giving us a run for our cattle, I guess. Spite. How many boys can we spare to round up the Shorthorns?"

"I've sent fer the bunch. There's somethin' else phoney that I haven't told yer. It's been open and shut in my mind whether I'd better."

"Shoot, old-timer!" commanded Courtlandt curtly.

"Well, since you fed Ranlett his time he's been moseyin' round Slippy Bend. The other day when I rode over there to see Baldy Jennings, 'bout shippin' them steer, I just naturally dropped into the Lazy Wolf. Our late manager was settin' at a table with two girls and a man. It wasn't my butt-in and I wouldn't have specially noticed the stranger if he hadn't been makin' goo-goo eyes at one of the females out of all proportion to her good looks. She had——"

"Let's pass up what she looked like. Who was the man?"

"I didn't know them, but Saturday you brought the ol' son-of-a-gun of a lady-killer to the bunkhouse yourself. Savvy?"

"You don't mean Beechy?"

"Sorry, Chief, but he's the same. An' unless I'm locoed Ranlett's got the feller's hide nailed to his stable door; he's got him an' he's got him tight."

XIII

BUBBLES the roan, own brother to Patches, and Peggy Glamorgan on his back were radiant youth incarnate. The horse arched his graceful head as though proudly conscious of the loveliness of his burden; the corded muscles of shoulder, flank and leg flexed sensitively under his satin skin with every move of his pliant body. The girl's sombrero had the true ranchero tilt. Her khaki riding costume was as perfect a thing as the cinema-fed imagination of a fashionable habit-maker could conceive; it was only by exercising superhuman restraint that he had refrained from adding buckskin fringe and a six-shooter. Tommy Benson regarded her as though hypnotized. He caught a quizzical expression in Jerry's eyes as she stood on the porch, and colored hotly. He swallowed hard and sprang to the saddle. With obvious effort to regain his poise, he touched his horse with his heels and with a theatrical sweep of his right arm declaimed:

"Let's go! 'Once more into the breach, dear friends, once more.' "

Peggy lingered.

"You are sure that you won't come with us, Jerry?" Her sister smilingly shook her head.

"No, I must finish some work. Come back, Goober!" to the dog who had been jumping up to lick the noses of the horses, and who with short joyous barks was preparing to follow them. He threw her a glance replete with injured dignity and flopped down on the porch with head on his outstretched paws. Peggy threw a hasty "I'm sorry!" over her shoulder and urged Bubbles to a gallop. Tommy bore down upon her as she reached the ranch road. He seized the bridle of her horse and pulled him down.

"Where's the fire?" he demanded. "What's the big idea in burning up the road? I want to make this ride last."

"I thought you wanted to get to Lower Field to help Steve," reproachfully.

"Sure thing, but if I break my neck getting there it won't prove much, will it? I wonder why your sister didn't come."

The horses stepped daintily side by side, their glossy coats shining in the sunlight. Peggy's brows met in a suspicion of a frown.

"Tommy—you don't mind if I call you Tommy, do you?" with just the right suggestion of hesitation and a glance from under curling lashes which fanned a spark in the man's eyes to fire.

"I'll say that I don't," fervently. "Formality is silly in a great, God's-own-country like this. What's on your mind?"

"Jerry. I was wondering. There is something queer about Steve and Jerry, Tommy. They don't seem a bit like married lovers; have you noticed it?"

Benson bent far forward to examine the bit in his

horse's mouth. When he settled back in the saddle his face was flushed.

" 'I never knew so young a lady with so old a head,' " he quoted gayly. "What does a child like you, just out of the nursery, know about lovers?" he teased.

She regarded him with lofty condescension.

"I shall be nineteen my next birthday and I'll have you understand that boys have been plentiful in my career, Mr. Benson. Of course if you don't care to talk with me——"

"I do—I do, Peg-o'-my-heart!" Courtlandt's name for her slipped unconsciously from Tommy's lips. He looked at her apologetically but the girl was too engrossed in her troubled thoughts to notice what he called her. Reassured he answered her question. "I think that Steve and Jerry are bully pals."

"Pals! Ye gods, and that's all. Honest now, Tommy, have you ever seen Steve catch Jerry's hand as though he just couldn't help it?" Benson met her triumphant glance with a sternly accusing eye.

"Oh, the precocity and sophistication of twentieth century youth! Look here, young woman, what have you been reading?"

"Reading! Tommy, you're overdoing it. You're too innocent to be true," with a little rush of laughter. "Now I ask you, would you want a wife who was as distantly friendly to you as Jerry is to Steve?"

"I should not," with convincing emphasis. "But why should your sister have married Courtlandt if she didn't love him? I can't conceive of his not being mad about her."

"Dad was the why. I didn't know until I asked him if I might come here. I went to San Francisco with my roommate when school closed, but I intended to come to Jerry as quickly as I politely could. When he gave me permission to come Dad told me that he expected me to marry family as Jerry had—that he had brought her up with the idea and that she had not disappointed him. That's that!"

"In the vernacular of the backwoods, 'She seen her

duty an' she done it,' " interpolated Benson. "Might—
might an humble admirer ask if you are planning to
please your father or—or yourself, when you marry?"
He succeeded in keeping eyes and tone gayly imper-
sonal.

"I don't intend to marry at all, that is, not for years
and years and years."

"You'll be quite a nice old lady by that time, won't
you?"

"You're not nearly as good-looking when you scowl,
Tommy. As I was saying, when so rudely interrupted,
when I do marry it will be to please myself. I told Dad
a thing or two," and Tommy, observing the tiny flames
which memory had set in her hazel eyes, allowed that
she had.

"I'm puzzled about Jerry's money," Peggy went on
thoughtfully. "Dad gives us an allowance fit for prin-
cesses of blood royal; that's an out-of-date simile now,
isn't it? When I asked her this morning for five dollars
with which to tip the man who brought up my trunk,
first she was shocked at the idea of tipping one of the
outfit, and then she grew as red as fire and stammered
that she had no small bills. Ye gods, what do you know
about that?" with slangy amazement.

"Sweet cookie, that's nothing. Many a time I haven't
been able to pry a dollar bill loose."

"That is different. You're—you're working and it
takes time to make a living," with sweet earnestness.
Tommy shot a quick look at her. Was she laughing at
him? No, she was taking his lack of funds seriously.
"About that Alexandrite ring. Once Jerry would have
ordered it by wire before you could say 'Jack Robinson'
—but all she said was, 'I—I'm not buying jewels now,
Peg.' Has she turned miser or has Dad——" her eyes
flew to Benson's in startled questioning. "Dad was
furious because Jerry and Steve left New York. Could
he have stopped her allowance? But—but if he did—
surely Steve would give——" she stopped in troubled
uncertainty.

"Why don't you ask your sister?" suggested Benson gravely.

"I will. I can't believe that Dad would—well he'd better never try to drive me. And that's that," with a defiant tilt of her chin.

"Would you stick to—to a man, a poor man, you loved even if you knew that your father would cut you off with the proverbial shilling?" Her hazel eyes met his turbulent blue ones frankly.

"Indeed I would, Mr. Tommy Benson. I shouldn't be afraid to marry a poor man, that is, a poor man with a future. I should want to be sure that he was that kind. I love to cook and sew and I should adore taking care of a ducky little house and brushing my husband's coat collar when he started off for work in the morning and going to market. There is only one thing I should hate to economize about——" her expression and tone were introspective. Benson was conscious that his heart was in his eyes but he didn't care. She was adorable with that thoughtful pucker of her vivid lips. He had to steady his voice before he asked lightly:

"And what may that one thing be, Peg-o'-my-heart?"

"Children," she answered promptly and with utter absence of self-consciousness. "I want eight and—and I suppose that's rather extravagant for a poor man to start with, don't you, Tommy?"

Benson held his emotions in a grip of steel. At that moment the boy-he-had-been waved good-bye and slipped away forever. The man's eyes were gravely tender as he answered the girl's question with judicial deliberation.

"Perhaps—not. That is, not for a poor man with a future." He tightened on the bridle. "Steve will think we're quitters. Let's go!"

The white road stretched ahead of them. Their horses' feet raised a haze of dust. On either side billowed fields of tall, untrodden grass and beyond the fields lumped the foot-hills. In a pasture a roan mare lay with her head up over her shoulder asleep, while beside her, flat on its side in the sun, dozed a young colt. Insects droned and buzzed unceasingly. The air sparkled with that brand of ozone to be found only among the foot-hills.

Benson and Peggy came upon Courtlandt in Lower Field. He nodded to them absent-mindedly. He was the centre of a group of mounted men, all eager, all armed. Most of them rolled and smoked cigarettes incessantly as they sat their horses. A few of them wore chaps with vests over their colored shirts, some were in khaki riding clothes, all wore bandanas of violent pattern in place of collars, broad-brimmed Stetsons and laced riding boots. They were a clean-cut, self-respecting looking lot, as lean, lithe and brown as a life spent in the saddle could make them. Pete Gerrish on his massive sorrel loomed above them all.

"Understand me, there is to be no shooting," Steve was reiterating as Peg and Benson rode up. "Gerrish, I'll fire the man who shoots unless in self-defense. Do you get me, boys?"

"Sure, we get you," drawled Marcelle O'Neil, so nicknamed because of the irrepressible kink in his straw-colored hair. "No objection, be ther', to ropin' one of Ranlett's gang an' reinin' him up short if he starts to lope?" he wheedled.

"No. Bring every one of them back if you can. Without injury, though. We'll let the law mete out punishment."

"Sure, it's none of my butt-in how you handle the durn polecat, but if I had my way I'd swing Ranlett up to a cottonwood if I got my mazuma fer doin' it. Them were the finest Shorthorns in the world and if Nick-the-time-feeder was back——"

Nicholas Fairfax had been notoriously prompt to discharge a man who slacked on the job, but O'Neil had not intended to let the bunk-house name for the late owner of the Double O slip out. He looked furtively at Courtlandt but he, consciously or unconsciously, ignored the lapse.

"We'll find them, O'Neil. We must. Get a move on, boys. Ride in pairs and ride like——"

Their whoop of enthusiasm drowned his last words. Steve remained motionless until the last one had taken the fence at a jump. His face was white, his eyes strained and tired. He rode toward Peg and Benson who had with difficulty restrained their horses from following the riders.

"That was the nearest approach to the wild-west cowboy of the eighties that you will ever see, Peg-o'-my-heart. Did you notice that Marks and Schoeffleur were missing, Tommy? Why didn't Jerry come with you, Peg?"

"She said that she had work to do, that she would ride after luncheon."

"She understood that she was not to go out of sight of the ranch-house?"

The girl's salaam was as profound as the neck of her horse would permit.

"Your slave heard and obeys, oh Abdul the Great."

A laugh erased the tired lines about Courtlandt's mouth.

"Do I seem such a tyrannous old Turk to you? Well, it is only because I am afraid that Jerry——" He left his sentence unfinished and turned to Benson. "Take a message to Upper Farm for me. Tell—the Devil!"

"Your mistake, Steve; it's only Mrs. Denbigh," Peggy corrected mischievously as she followed Courtlandt's eyes to where Felice Denbigh and Greyson were entering the field. The three rode to meet the newcomers.

"Good morning. I didn't know that you left your downy before noon, Felice."

The woman put her horse through a few paces that were as coquettish as her eyes and voice.

"On with the vamps!" muttered Tommy in a tone intended only for Peg's ear. With difficulty she choked back a delighted giggle as Felice answered in a spoiled-child voice:

"Steve, you're getting to be a barbarian out here. Have you forgotten that last night you invited me to ride with you this morning?"

"Last night—I what?" demanded Courtlandt, a slow color darkening his face.

"I waited for you at the X Y Z and when you didn't come fairly browbeat my host into escorting me to Double O ranch. I thought I should find you there. No such luck. We saw only Mrs. Courtlandt and she thought that you would be too busy——"

"I am too busy," curtly. "Tommy, take Mrs. Denbigh with you and Peg to Upper Farm. You'll find the most up-to-date dairy in the country there, Felice. Its equipment cost——"

"Don't talk like a mail-order catalogue, Steve," the woman interrupted petulantly. "If you can't show me the Upper Farm I will wait until you can. I'm a patient waiter. I always get what I want," with narrowed eyes and an iced smile which sent a queer shiver down Benson's spine. He looked at Greyson to see how he was bearing his equivocal position. The man's fine, thoroughbred face was red and set about the lips. Benson couldn't understand his allowing himself to be placed in such an awkward situation. Why the dickens had he invited the Denbigh woman to the X Y Z? He must have been at the Manor long enough during Old Nick's illness to have found her out. He brought his thoughts back to the present in time to hear Felice say:

"Shall we go on to Slippy Bend, Mr. Greyson? Your sister gave us some commissions to execute there. So long, Stevie! You'll come over for a game of auction to-night, of course. You and I against mine host and Paula." She didn't wait for his answer. Without a glance in the direction of Peg and Benson she wheeled her horse and rode away. Greyson waved his hat to Peg, called something to her companions and cantered after his guest. For one long, silent moment Courtlandt followed the two with his eyes, then he resumed his directions to Benson where he had dropped them.

"Tell Mrs. Simms to have Simms report to me to-morrow noon at the ranch. Show Peg over Upper Farm. She won't insist upon being personally conducted by me, I'll wager. Get your lunch there. Mrs. Simms' jelly cookies will make you purr with repletion, Peggy. I told Ming Soy that we wouldn't be back till late afternoon. Take your time. Don't let Peg ride too hard. Jerry won't be anxious. She knows what distances are here."

"But, Steve, don't you need me? I can take Miss Glamorgan back and join you."

"No, I'm riding alone. I have a few fairly fresh trails to follow up. Be a good child, Peg-o'-my-heart, and do exactly what the best range-rider on the Double O tells you to do." He laughed at her indignant eyes, touched Blue Devil with his heel and loped off. Peggy looked after him and then at Benson.

"I wonder—I don't like that Denbigh woman. Did you see her eyes when Steve turned her down? Careful Cosmetics is the name for her. She must think it's the open season for vamps round here." She looked at Tommy with laughter and a glint of mischief in her hazel eyes. "Now I wonder who Steve could have meant by the best range-rider of the Double O?" she mused in a low voice as though communing with herself.

Benson swept off his Stetson with swash-buckling impressiveness.

"I don't like to talk about myself—but," he murmured with exaggerated humility, "I'll say that I—now who the dickens is that? The Simms kid. Johnny Simms. What does he want? I——" His voice trailed off into silence as he watched a boy who came galloping up on a pony to speak to Courtlandt. Tommy unconsciously caught the bridle of the girl's horse. Bubbles and Soapy, who had been paddock mates, nuzzled noses. The girl and man watching saw the boy hand Steve a paper, then whirl and gallop away as though pursued by a thousand furies.

"That's queer," Benson observed under his breath.

"What's queer?" asked Peggy in the same hushed whisper.

"That the boy should break away like that. He adores Steve. So do the other Simms kids. Now what is

Courtlandt doing? Burning something?" as a wisp of smoke fell to the ground.

"Why don't you go and find out?" in a tone which was own cousin to his.

"Nothing doing. You don't know Steve. I'm here; he knows it. He never misses a trick. If he wants me he'll shout. There, you see? He doesn't," as Courtlandt, after a glance at the ground where the smoke had fallen, galloped across the field toward the ranch road.

"You're fond of Steve, aren't you?" Peggy probed as they headed their horses toward Upper Farm.

"Fond of him! That's a deleted, diluted expression of my sentiments for the Whistling Lieut. We literally went through fire and water overseas; since then I've been on the ranch. You see, the German Inn where Steve and I sojourned for a couple of months didn't have a particularly beneficial effect on my health, so when I got back to the good old U. S. A. I came here to recuperate and I have stayed."

"Haven't you any family?"

"I have. One devoted, in-perfect-condition mother, 1921 model, ditto father. She is coming out next week. Hasn't your sister written you about me?" curiously.

"What conceit! She hasn't written pages about you," with a laugh which sent the color to his face in a flood. "She wrote that you were here, that Steve said that you had a future if you'd stick to ranching and leave celluloid alone—now what did he mean by that?"

"So Steve said that I was a man with a future, did he? Make a mental note of that, Miss Glamorgan," his tone and look brought a startled flash to eyes which had been so boyishly friendly. He steadied his voice before he went on: "I've had a fool idea that I wanted to be a movie-actor—but——"

"But don't you want to any more?"

"No."

"When did you experience a change of heart?"

"This morning at exactly two o'clock, I decided that there was nothing in it, that I wanted to be a solid citizen with a settled abiding place."

"Two o'clock! Why, that was when I reached Slippy
———" With heightened color she tightened her rein
and touched Bubbles with her heels. "I'll race you to
the farmhouse," she called over her shoulder, a curious
breathlessness in her voice. She kept the lead till they
reached the gate of the farm, then Benson caught her
horse by the bridle.

"The back of your head is attractive but I like your
face better. Don't you want to hear the romantic story
of Mrs. Simms before we get there? She's a Heart and
Ringer."

"A—a what?"

It was no longer necessary to hold the bridle of the
girl's horse. She forced him to a walk.

"Heart and Ringer. That is what they call the women
who marry men who advertise in the matrimonial sheet,
Heart and Ring."

"Really, Tommy! Did Mrs. Simms do that?"

"She did, and she got just what she paid for. Simms
is a bounder but he's thrifty as the dickens and an A 1
workman. That's what caught Old Nick in the beginning. He'd have employed the devil himself had he
those characteristics. But the man is ugly and insolent.
How Steve puts up with him beats me. It is because
of Mrs. Simms, I suppose. She is a fine woman and a
corker in the dairy. She lived in Montana. She was the
daughter of a miner who had made his pile and gone to
farming. Montana got on her nerves, so when she saw
Simms' 'ad' in Heart and Ring she corresponded with
him and married him. I'll bet a hat Montana has looked
like heaven to her ever since. That was one of their
children who met Steve. I'd give my Kipling de luxe to
know why."

He drew rein before the white farmhouse which
hugged the ground like a mammoth brooding hen. In
the field beyond was a spatter effect of snowy dairies
and cow-barns. Black and white Holsteins, creamy Jer-
seys, Guernseys and a few Ayreshires grazed epicurean-
ly in the lush pastures that climbed the foot-hills.

A slender, wiry woman, who gave a fresh-from-the-laundry impression, so immaculate, so clear of skin, so smooth of hair was she, greeted Peg and Benson as they dismounted. Her smile was obliterated as Tommy's eyes lingered on her arm. She hastily pulled down her sleeves and buttoned them snugly at the wrists.

"It sure is fine to see you, Mr. Benson. You ain't taken my advice so soon and got a wife, have you?" she asked with a laugh and a twinkle in the eyes which nature had intended for a merry blue, but which Life, aided and abetted by Heart and Ring and—Simms, had threshed to an apprehensive gray.

"No such luck, Mrs. Simms. This is Mrs. Court- landt's sister, Miss Margaret Glamorgan. We came with a message from the Chief for Simms. Where is he? At the dairy?"

"I'm sure pleased to know you, Miss. Simms has gone to—to Slippy Bend, Mr. Tommy."

"She's lying," Benson decided, even as he directed: "When he gets back tell him to report at the office to- morrow noon, sharp, with his accounts. Has he been up to his old tricks again?" His eyes fell as though by accident to her arms.

The woman's eyes, her lips, changed in expression. It was as though her features, red-hot with life and interest, had been run into a mold and hardened.

"He has that, Mr. Tommy."

"Is there any use in repeating what I have said be- fore, that you ought to leave him?"

"An' I say as I said before, you're wrong, Mr. Tommy. I promised in the sight of God and man to stick to him as long as we both lived. I wasn't forced to marry Simms. I did it of my own free will—my own fool will," contemptuously. "I'd be a fine example to my children, wouldn't I, if I tried to get out of mar- riage just because it wasn't the romantic joy-ride I'd expected. It would be different if Simms abused the children; he never lays a hand on 'em. He wouldn't dare," with a glitter in her eyes. "You and Mr. Tom- my'll stay and have a bite of lunch with us, won't you, Miss? Mr. Courtlandt always has his when he comes."

Her change of voice and subject was so sudden that it caught Peggy's hazel eyes, glistening with tears, fixed upon her face. The girl blinked the mist away, slipped her hand under the woman's firm arm and inquired with irresistible charm:

"Will there be jelly cookies, Mrs. Simms?"

The blue came back to the eyes for a moment.

"Surely. Aha, Mr. Tommy, now I know what you came for."

"I didn't tell her about them. It was the Big Chief."

"Mr. Steve!" The blue suffered a total eclipse. "Did he come with you?"

"As far as Lower Field. By the way, what's wrong with Johnny? He galloped up to Courtlandt, stuck out his hand, then beat it."

"But he stuck out his hand?"

"Surest thing you know."

Mrs. Simms exhaled to the limit of her flat chest.

"That's all right, then. Johnny—Johnny found a sparkling stone—and he said as how he thought 'twas gold—and he's—he's pestered me to death till I told him he could ask Mr. Steve if he could stake off a claim. Minin's in his blood. My father was a miner, Miss. I guess I'd better get busy about dinner, not stand talking here," she explained as she hurried away.

Benson's eyes followed her as he perched on a corner of the porch railing and lighted his pipe. Peg had gone into the house to help. He could hear the two voices, the woman's a high strident tone, the girl's like music with a joyous note running through it. The delectable odor of bacon and frying chicken drifted out to him and set his already rampant appetite clamoring for satisfaction. Mrs. Simms had cut that boy and pebble story from whole cloth, if he was a judge of human nature, and he'd bet his last dollar that he was, Benson thought, as he changed his seat to one from which he could look inside the room which served as living-room and dining-room at Upper Farm.

It was for all the world like the pictures one saw in mail-order catalogues, he thought with a smile. There

was an old-time melodion in one corner and an up-to-
date phonograph in another. There was golden oak
furniture in profusion. The walls were covered with a
paper on which impossible roses fought for supremacy
with more impossible alleged birds of paradise. How
could a person think between such walls, Tommy wondered. He had the feeling as he looked that birds and
roses were being stuffed down his throat. In the midst
of his reflections Mrs. Simms called him.

The three children slipped shyly into their chairs after the strangers were seated. They were boys, ranging
in age from four to ten. Johnny had not come home,
apparently. They had almost white hair and eyes
shaped like the eyes of sculpins, which they kept fixed
on Peggy Glamorgan, after the hypnotic effect of the
company blue and white checked table-cloth, the
pressed glass spoon-holder, and the best gold-banded
plates with a big S in a funereal-like wreath on the
border, had worn off.

Benson smiled to himself as he watched them. They
were doing frankly and unreprovedly what he longed to
do. Extreme youth had some compensations. He lost
himself in a radiant dream of possibilities and became
as absorbed with his inward vision as the scions of the
house of Simms were with the material and fascinating
Peg herself. He was quite unconscious that the girl was
observing him in amused wonder.

"What did Johnny mean by staking a claim, Mrs.
Simms?" she inquired as with the air of a dainty
gourmand she set her teeth in a second cookie. "I would
have asked Mr. Benson, but who am I to rouse him
from his dream of—of fair women, perhaps—yes?"
with a ripple of laughter.

Tommy roused with a start and colored generously.
"I beg pardon, I was——"

"That's what miners do when they think they've
found gold," interrupted Mrs. Simms, quite unconscious
of the byplay. "They stake off a lot of land and post it.
Sometimes they don't work it for a year or more."

"Then why take possession? Isn't that dog-in-the-manger stuff?"

"No, because they really want it. They stake their claim so that no other man can get it," broke in Benson. "And if you ask me, I'll say that it's a whale of an idea," he added with a curious light in his eyes. "Young woman, if you have finished your cookie gorge we will depart."

"Cookie gorge! Slanderer! Mrs. Simms, did I eat as many as he?"

"Don't perjure yourself, Mrs. Simms. Come, Peg-o'-my-heart!" He realized that his eyes were acting as towncriers for his emotions and shifted his gaze from the girl to the woman. She sensed their message and exclaimed impulsively:

"My stars, ain't it great to be young and—and free!"

"You've said it, Mrs. Simms," agreed Peg with her woman-of-the-world air as she drew on her riding gloves. "Catch me settling down. Never! And that's that!"

The woman's troubled eyes sought Benson's. He laughed and held out his hand. "Good-bye Mrs. Simms. Don't you worry. Having attained the titanic and imposing age of eighteen the lady would naturally have caustic views on matrimony. It will come out right and—and that's that!" he observed cryptically. "Be sure that Simms reports tomorrow. The Big Chief has about all he can handle now; we don't want him worried."

It was not until Benson and Peg neared the Double O ranch that they came back to the subject of their late hostess. They had spent a lazy, happy afternoon, making Tommy's daily round of inspection which he usually covered in two hours.

"Do you think Simms hurts her?" the girl broke out suddenly, apropos of nothing. "Did you see those marks on her arm? Why, oh why, does she stay with him?" with a shudder.

"You heard why."

"Yes, and do you know what I saw when she said

that about God and man? I didn't see her at all—it was a
closeup of Jerry's eyes at her wedding, and the clergy-
man saying, 'And forsaking all others.' Those words
echoed in my brain for days. Jerry is like Mrs. Simms.
She'd keep a vow like that if it killed her."

"Wouldn't you?"

"You never can tell," flippantly. "At least I don't
intend to get into a position where I'll have to for
years—and—years—and years——" The last words
floated back to him with laughter as she galloped off.
She kept the breakneck pace till she pulled up at the
court entrance. Benson was off his horse before she
could dismount. He lifted her from the saddle and with
his arms about her drew her into the garden.

"I won't take possession till you give me leave,—but
—but I—I'll stake my claim now, and that's that!" he
whispered huskily as he kissed her once upon her
white throat.

"Mr. Tommee! Mr. Tommee Benson!" called a voice
from the path as Ming Soy in her gay silks came running toward them. Her slant eyes were almost wide.
"Misses Stevie went off on horse after lunch. Tlell
Ming Soy just going to flield; Ming Soy bleat glong
when you and little Missis come, but she didn't go to
flield, and she never come back—not all this time."

XIV

JERRY COURTLANDT lingered on the porch to watch
her sister and Benson as they raced down the drive.
Her eyebrows met in a thoughtful frown. What would
her father say if Peg fell in love with Benson, with his
poor-but-honest background? There was no "if" about
Tommy. Cupid had set signal fires to burning in his
eyes already. Benson pere had begun his business career
as an errand boy; now he twinkled a large and somewhat dazzling planet in the select heaven of the multies.

Well, Glamorgan the oil-king couldn't expect both his daughters to marry the man of his choice. She had done it and what had been her reward? Because she had views as to right and wrong and justice he refused to write to her. Evidently Peg didn't know the terms of Nicholas Fairfax's will or she wouldn't have been surprised at her lack of enthusiasm about the Alexandrite. Two thousand dollars! It seemed a more stupendous sum than twenty thousand would have seemed to her a year ago. Values were curious things. What had Steve thought? She was beginning to dread his eyes—they were so searching, so compelling.

If she wanted and needed money, she would earn it; other women had been doing it for years; she wouldn't accept it from Steve any other way. In spite of his prohibition she would work on the books for a while. She paused before she entered the house to draw a long breath and take a look at the glorious world about her. The sky spread like a cerulean canopy flecked with motionless white clouds. It seemed near. She felt more as though she were looking up at a vast, decorated dome than at the heavens. Almost she expected to see Dawn or any one of the symbolic head-liners in the mural world, come trailing her scanty draperies across the blue. The far-off mountains reared a patchwork of purple and blue and gold. The noisy stream was fringed with color. The fields rustled their content in the sunshine. On the road to the X Y Z rose a cloud of dust.

"Somebody coming!" she thought with a thrill of excitement. Then she laughed and looked down at the dog who stood in stately, aloof dignity beside her. "Goober, I'm getting to be like a prairie-dog who parks outside his hole to see the pass," she confided. She still watched the approaching riders. When she recognized in them Felice Denbigh and Bruce Greyson she regretted that she had lingered. It was too late to disappear now. The owner of the X Y Z had seen her and waved his hand. With a feeling of repugnance, which shocked her even as it swept her, Jerry went to the steps to greet the riders. Felice in her smart silvery linen looked as though she had been removed recently from tissue wrappings. Greyson's eyes met Jerry's. Was she mistaken that they were full of a wordless apology, she wondered, even as she greeted the two cordially.

"Doesn't this morning look as though it had just been returned from the dry-cleaner's?" she asked gayly. "Did you ever feel anything more spick and span than the air? Won't you come in?"

"Thanks, no." Felice Denbigh's answer was hurried. "Where is Steve? He invited me to inspect the Double O with him this morning. He was to come for me but I tired of the rôle of patient Griselda and made Mr. Greyson bring me over. Not that I had to work hard to persuade him." Her light tone was tinged with malice as she administered one of those subtle female digs commonly imperceptible to the male intelligence. Jerry caught the obvious reply between her teeth and substituted:

"Steve was called to Lower Field. I—I doubt if he can ride with you this morning, Mrs. Denbigh."

If a glance could have accomplished it, Jerry would have been neatly and expeditiously skinned, then and there. Felice's voice had the edge of a hari-kari sword as she answered:

"Steve is the person to decide that. Which way to Lower Field, Mr. Greyson?" Her host's eyes flamed.

"If Mrs. Courtlandt thinks——"

"Oh, but Mrs. Courtlandt doesn't think," protested Jerry laughingly. "Do show Mrs. Denbigh the way to Lower Field, Bruce. I should be delighted to go myself but for a letter which must be ready for Sandy this morning. You will find——"

Felice Denbigh was off before she had finished her sentence. Greyson followed without a word. Jerry looked after the two with troubled eyes. Her thoughts were in a turmoil.

"What has happened to Bruce Greyson?" she thought anxiously. "His conversational output has shrunk till what he says seems a waste of breath, it amounts to so little. One would think he was under a spell. I wonder —I wonder if Steve did make a date with her?" she mused aloud as she crossed the court on her way to the office. José, busy among his flowers, swept off his hat with his single-tooth smile.

"*Buenos dias, Señora.* My roses bloom brighter as you pass, yes?" Benito, balancing on one claw on the rim of the fountain, shivered, blinked his yellow eyes and croaked hoarsely:

"Piffle!"

With a shocked exclamation José flung a chunk of loam at the parrot. It hit him squarely and knocked him backward into the shallow basin. With frightened squawks and much ruffling of feathers the bird regained his place on the basin's rim. For an instant he indulged in a what-hit-me blink, then with his gaudy plumage looking as though it had been electrified croaked angrily:

"I'll be d——!"

José swooped and muffled the final word beneath his coat. "You weel pardon, Señora? It is Señor Tommee that teaches Benito seence he come to the rancho. I teach heem when he ees so leetle to speak only good. Not till one year ago does he begin to talk like wild devil. Señora weel pardon? He ees all I have, he ees like my child."

Jerry accepted the brown man's apology as seriously as it was offered.

"Children are a great responsibility. You never can tell what they will do, can you, José?"

The office seemed a dull, uninteresting drab in contrast to the light and color of the world outside. Even the silent witnesses to the drama and lawlessness of the country, now guarded jealously by glass doors, failed to spur the girl's imagination. She streamed the curtain up at the window. A light haze of dust lingered above the road Greyson and Felice had taken. The music of the stream stole into the quiet room; down in the corral a horse whinnied intriguingly; the whole gleaming out-of-doors lured, the mountains beckoned.

Jerry resolutely barred heart and mind against temptation and attacked her letters. She worked with single-track intentness until Ming Soy announced luncheon. She looked up in surprise. Her work had burned up the hours. She interned the typewriter and closed her desk with a bang. She flexed her muscles in luxurious enjoyment of the sensation. What a relief to move, but it wasn't even a sliver of the relief she felt when she looked down at the sheaf of letters awaiting Steve's signature. How it would have pleased her father to know that she had resisted the temptation to be up and away on Patches, she thought wistfully. She could see him now, hear his gruff voice saying:

"Jerry, the more you dread the thing you have to do, the more you should hustle to get it behind you. Make that a rule of your life and you'll find you will have all the time you want and some left with which to speculate." He was a resplendent example of the working out of his own precept, his daughter thought. He was the busiest man she knew yet he always had an abundance of time for pleasure.

What should she do with her afternoon, she wondered, as she enjoyed the dainty luncheon Ming Soy served in a shady corner of the court. The air had lost the keenness of the morning. Birds flew to the rim of the basin, observed the girl at the table critically for an instant, then proceeded with the day's ablutions. They chattered, they splashed, they scolded, they preened and dressed their feathers in the sun. Butterflies darted in and out among the blossoms. There were none of the usual ranch sounds to break the stillness. Where were the men? Had Steve taken them all with him, she wondered. What were Peg and Tommy doing? Peg might see some real riding if she caught up with the outfit before they started off in pursuit of the missing cattle, but alas for buckskin fringes and——

Suddenly a plan sprang full panoplied, complete, from her brain. It was born of her what-shall-I-do-now mood. If necessity is the mother of invention, idleness is the father of adventure. She would array herself in one of the cowboy suits behind the glass doors, mount Patches and ride to the field behind the ranch-house, practise with a six-shooter until Peg came, then she'd dash toward her with her gun "spittin' death and damnation" into the air.

Her idea developed with magic-beanstalk rapidity, as all ideas will if they are dropped in fertile and well-cultivated soil. She laughed until she was breathless as she confronted herself in the mirror in her own room an hour later. Over her linen riding breeches she had drawn a pair of flapping black and white Angora chaps. Great Mexican rowels adorned her riding boots. A hectic yellow bandana, with red spots which gave the cheery effect of a geometrical nosebleed, almost covered her delicate blouse. Her sleeves were rolled to the elbows, at her hip swung a six-shooter of sinister portent. A heavy belt filled with cartridges sagged from her waist. She had slipped a silver filigree band above the black and gold cord of Steve's campaign hat.

In a little whirlwind of laughter she blew a kiss to the gleaming eyes of her vis-à-vis and lifted the saddle which she had purloined from the glass case. It was gay with silver. The tapideros were choice examples of Mexican craftsmanship. The head-stall of the bridle was fantastically trimmed with the metal. As Jerry passed through the living-room the huge rowels on her boots caught in the rug. She dropped the saddle with a crash and caught at the table to save herself from falling. Her eyes were bright, her cheeks pink when she had Patches saddled. She had brought him up from the corral herself before she dressed. He rolled his great eyes at her as she came out of the house. He pranced skittishly until she spoke. Then he quieted but he kept an appraising, suspicious eye on her. As the crowning touch of realism Jerry fastened a coil of rawhide rope beside the saddle fork.

It was with difficulty, punctuated by *sotto voce* exclamations, that the girl mounted. The chaps were heavy and perversely unadaptable. As she gathered up the reins Ming Soy appeared at the door. The little

Oriental's eyes were globules of wonder. Jerry antici-
pated her.

"I am off to practise shooting in the field behind the
house, Ming Soy. Don't be frightened if you hear shots.
Watch the road for Miss Glamorgan and Mr. Benson.
They ought to be here within an hour. The moment
they appear in sight sound the gong at the back of the
ranch-house. Do you understand?"

"All light. Ming Soy understan'. Slandy tlell Hopi
Soy he see Clarey range-rider ketch Double O steers,
other day. Said first he thought he doin' it for Hopi
Soy's chief, so he doan't say nodin'. Now he wonder."

"Ming Soy! Are you sure?"

"Slandy tlell Hopi Soy he see um ketch um. Clarey
range-rider drove steers over hill black of Blear Cleek
ranch, Slandy tlell Hopi Soy."

"Ming Soy, don't let anyone know you told me that."

"All light, Ming Soy no tlell."

Jerry didn't know why she put that embargo on the
Chinese woman's tongue. Perhaps a vague fear that a
warning would get to the thief prompted it. The girl's
mind was in a tumult as she raced Patches along the
road. She didn't stop to unfasten the gate, she jumped
it. As she entered the field which led to the stream she
had quite forgotten the exhibition she had staged for
Peg. She had suspected that range-rider of crookedness.
Absorbed in thought she allowed Patches to race across
the rustic bridge. The thud of his hoofs on the wood
brought her back to the present. She pulled the horse
down to a walk. Where was she going? To see what
was on the other side of that ridge beyond which the
range-rider had disappeared!

She followed the pack-trail cautiously. Bear Creek
ranch-house in the glare of sunshine was outlined dis-
tinctly against the dark cliff behind it. Was it only this
morning that she had come out of that door to find
Steve waiting for her? She had the curious feeling of
being in another decade. How were things going with
the little mother, she wondered and—and where was
the Man of Mystery?

She touched Patches lightly with the great spurs and raced along the trail toward the hill. It didn't seem possible that the man who had seemed so concerned when he came for her last night could be a rustler—but Sandy had seen him and the calves were missing. Her thoughts urged her on. She was the one person of authority within reach. She didn't know just what she intended to do, but she must do something. She only knew that a frenzied voice somewhere inside her head kept reiterating:

"He shan't get away with it! He shan't get away with it!"

Once as she climbed the hill she thought she saw a horse's head behind a tree. Her heart choked her with its pounding. The object proved to be nothing more intimidating than a black stump. When she reached the top of the slope she came upon a clump of dead trees standing spectral and white. She rode through them till she emerged in a clearing from which she could look down into the valley.

Below lay a trough of the hills. Heat waves pulsed above it. Over its surface, pockmarked with gopher holes, tumbleweed rolled and billowed and stacked against rocks and fallen timber in uncanny, shifting masses. Purple-gray and green sage-brush dotted it. Alkali whitened it in streaks. Beyond the hollow stretched a belt of upheaved ridges of brick-red sandstone. Between each ridge lay emerald green valleys with little streams cutting through at nearly right angles. Higher and higher rose the hills beyond till they loomed to mountains whose sides were clothed with forests that had never paid toll to the lumber-jack, whose snowy peaks, gold now in the sunshine, bared their jagged fangs to the soft blue of the sky. They lured and beckoned with their mysterious silences.

At the base of the slope on which Jerry stood was a circular hole perhaps three hundred feet in diameter and ten feet deep. At one side of it, near a pool, were the unmistakable traces of a camp. There were the ashes of a fire and beside them the mutilated body of a calf. The place gave an intangible sense of tragedy and terror.

Stepping as though the ground under her feet were a network of mines, any one of which might be jarred into disastrous activity by an inadvertent pressure of her foot, Jerry led Patches among the trees and fastened him. She stole back over the carpet of pine needles, her chaps flapping awkwardly at every step. She threw herself flat on the ground from which she could see the hollow and waited. From somewhere came the howl of a coyote; there seemed a million of them when the hills sent back the echo. High and motionless in the sky a great bird poised to reconnoiter then sailed and wheeled and dove. A gopher in front of his hole beat Jack-in-the-box at his disappearing trick.

Jerry shivered. Now she knew where she was, "Buzzard's Hollow." She hated the wailing coyote and she cared less, even less, for that horrible winged thing by the pool. Had the Bear Creek range-rider joined the campers? If she could only see the brand on that calf. But she couldn't; it would be madness to go down into the hollow. She must hurry back to the Double O and report. Slowman, the corral boss, would be there if no one else was. Someone should see that calf before the buzzards had obliterated all trace of the owner.

The girl sprang to her feet and ran to unloose Patches. Now that she had decided to go her courage was disappearing as rapidly as vapor in the sunshine. How terrifyingly empty of anything human the great spaces seemed. She saw a menace behind every bush, a lurking danger behind every tree. Apparently Patches' imagination was working overtime too. It was a nervous horse she mounted but, as she turned toward the trail which led to the Double O and safety, something drew her round. Perhaps it was a sound, perhaps the lazy blue sweep of the mountains hypnotized her. She guided Patches to the clearing from which she had looked down into the hollow. She couldn't have explained why she did it; it might have been a morbid curiosity to see if the great bird was feasting on the carrion. Her horse showed increased nervousness with every step. He began to shake. Jerry slipped to the ground and laid her face against his soft nose.

"What is it, boy? We're going back——"

A howl, a hair-raising mixture of banshee-wail and wildcat scream, callioped behind them. Patches stood not upon the order of his going but went at once. Snorting with terror he jerked the bridle from the girl's hand and racketed down the hillside toward the hollow. For a moment Jerry was rigid with terror, then she gripped her stampeding senses.

She must think. She was alone with that yelling demon—she couldn't get home without her horse—her next move was to follow Patches—he would get over his fright and answer her call. The dangling six-shooter at her side gave her courage. If her silly masquerading as a cowboy had done nothing else, it had given her that.

She slipped and slid down the slope. She caught at shrubs and stumps to retard her too impetuous progress; they sampled the fringes of her black and white chaps as she went by. She stubbed her toe upon a piece of rock. The next instant it seemed to her excited fancy as though the hillside gave way and took her with it.

"Detour!" she chuckled hysterically as down, down, down she went with a mass of dirt and gravel. She shielded her face with one hand as with the other she made futile grabs at the ground. It seemed as though aeons of time passed as she rolled down the hill. Steve's hat went bounding down ahead of her. "I wonder how many miles I've gone now?" she thought with a frightened laugh. Then, as suddenly as she had started she stopped against something big and weather-stained and unyielding.

She lay passive for a moment looking up in dazed surprise. She was lying beside a wooden shack. Strange that she had not seen it when she looked down into the hollow. It must have been directly under the bank from which she made her reconnaisance. She shut her eyes and stifled a cry as she felt a hot breath on her cheek.

Had the wildcat—she set her teeth and looked up between cautiously parted lids—looked up into the brown
eyes of Patches. The horse was reeking wet, but he had
stopped trembling. His lips twitched against her cheek
with a clumsy, quivering caress. With a sob of thanksgiving Jerry threw her arms about his neck and tried
to rise. She fell back with a frightened laugh. From her
waist down she was buried in earth.

She controlled a frantic desire to attack the gravel
furiously and scooped it away with slow and telling
precision. Patches waited patiently. Possibly he realized
that having landed his mistress in the dilemma it was
only a square deal that he stand by. Jerry's heart
pounded as she scooped. What was on the other side
of that wooden wall? The headquarters of Ranlett and
his gang? Was the calf lying in the hollow one of those
the range-rider had appropriated from the Double O?

The gravel half removed, the girl flung her arms about
the horse's neck and drew herself free. The black and
white chaps remained partially covered in earth and
sand. Jerry took account of the damages. There was a
stinging, smarting scratch along one cheek, the sleeve
of her blouse was torn from the shoulder, her hair was
a mass on her shoulders. Nothing serious, she con-
gratulated herself, as she tidied her hair, removed a
jeweled bar-pin from under the flamboyant bandana,
and fastened her sleeve in place with it. The scratch
was the only real casualty. Now that she was here she
wondered if she couldn't find the brand on that calf
herself.

Cautiously she tied Patches to a stump. The click of
his hoof against a rock sent her heart fluttering to her
throat. She shrank against the house and held her
breath. No sound came from within or from the hollow.
She must have frightened off everything alive when
she came crashing down the hill.

Reassured she picked up her hat which had landed
near her and put it on. It was curious what courage the
touch of it gave her. It was as though Steve had spoken.
She could almost hear his "Steady, little girl, steady!"

She tiptoed round to the front of the shack. The slanting sun shone on two dirty windows in sagging frames from which some of the panes had been broken. In one of the survivors a round hole radiating tiny cracks told a story without words. Desertion had laid its spell on the place. The cabin was roofed with dirt and hay. Its board sides were warped and weather-stained. The door in the middle sagged and swung uncannily in the light breeze. What lay behind it? Evidence that would convict Ranlett?

Her heart pounding out the measure of her racing blood Jerry laid her hand on the rusty iron handle of the door. Its hinges creaked dolorously as she swung it wide. The sound echoed curiously within the empty shack—but—was it an echo? The doubt sent a million little icy shivers pricking through Jerry's veins. Her heart winged to her throat. She swallowed it valiantly and put a hesitating foot across the threshold.

It took an instant for her eyes to adjust themselves to the dimness after the glare outside. Then the furnishings began to take shape. A cracked stove, red with rust, stood against the wall opposite; there was a table with shreds of oilcloth hanging from it; a chair which had been fashioned from a packing-box leaned against the table in three-legged dejection; the door of a cupboard hung on one hinge displaying an array of crockery and tin, in all stages of dilapidation and rust. Across one end of the room was a built-in bunk. A ragged saddle-blanket trailed from the side of it.

What—what—was that! Had her imagination tricked her or had that dirty blanket stirred? Jerry clutched the door. Even as she stood there, too frightened to move, there came the muffled sound which she had thought was an echo. Her vague sense of tragedy merged into something tangible and threatening. Someone was under that blanket! Was it an injured man—or—or—was it a decoy?

XV

JERRY never knew how long she stood with her eyes
fixed in fascinated terror on that heap in the bunk.
Should she mount Patches as soon as her frenzied feet
would take her to him, or should she stay and help the
man if he were wounded? Head urged flight, heart
urged help. She remembered the parable of the Good
Samaritan only to remind herself that the rescuer had
been a man.

Another moan from the bunk decided her. Setting the
door wide she drew the six-shooter from its holster; un-
loaded even, it gave her a feeling of strategic advantage,
and with the gun gripped tight in her hand tiptoed
across the room. Every vestige of color had fled from
her face as with icy, shaking fingers she lifted a corner
of the dingy blanket. Under it a man lay on his face,
his hands and feet securely tied.

"Beechy!"

The four walls flung back the girl's hoarse whisper.
"Beechy!" "Beechy!" "Beechy!" they chorused.

Jerry looked down in dumb incredulity. She recognized the rampant reddish hair, the dent at the corner
of one exposed eye. As though her voice had penetrated
to his consciousness the man rolled toward her. The
six-shooter clattered to the floor. The stunning effect of
her discovery was quickly tempered by the man's condition. Beechy, the man who had saved Steve's life, was
hurt, helpless. Her fingers attacked the knots in the
rope which bound him. She tugged, she pulled without
making the least impression. Was there not something
in the room which would cut? The minutes were flying!
Someone might come. She ran to the cupboard and
seized a tin can. The cover was jagged. She tried to
saw the rope with that but it made no impression on
the twisted hemp. She threw it from her and looked

about the room again—then—she rubbed her eyes; was that a knife sticking in the wall above the bunk—or was she just seeing it?

She stepped up on the edge of the bunk and touched it. It was real! With an inarticulate cry of triumph the girl seized it. With teeth set hard in her under lip she attacked the rope again. She stopped every few moments to listen. Once she caught the far off call of a coyote—then Patches whinnied. She dropped in a little heap on the floor, her hand pressed hard against her heart to still its thumping—but nothing stirred outside. She went on with her work. It seemed ages before she had freed Beechy's arms and another century of time before the cords were cut which bound his feet.

She touched his head gently. There was no trace of blood. He must have been stunned and tied, his captors relying upon the remoteness and abandoned appearance of the shack to cover their work. Why had they done it, Jerry wondered. Beechy had said that he had contracted to work on the railroad. She remembered his answer to Steve's protest, "You know there is honor among thieves." Had he been linked up with Ranlett? But Ranlett had nothing to do with the railroad.

If she could only get him up. When she tried to lift him the clumsy cartridge belt with the dangling holster kept getting in her way. With an impatient exclamation she unfastened it and dropped it to the floor. Then she slid the man's feet from the bunk, put her arms under him and lifted him. His head rolled to her shoulder. How hot it was. If only she had water! Her eyes roved about the cabin. No hope there. Through the doorway, not twenty yards away, she could see the pool with the carcass of the calf lying beyond it. With the possibility of lurking enemies, had she the courage to go out to that?

Beechy stirred and lifted heavy lids. The eyes beneath them were glazed with pain. He looked about the room, then up at the face bending over him. His gaze lingered a moment dreamily, then incredulously, then it seemed as though his brain made a superhuman effort to break the spell which bound it.

"Mrs. Lieut.!" he tried to get to his feet but his head rolled weakly back to the girl's shoulder. "Go! Go!" he whispered hoarsely. He made another effort to sit up. He gripped the edge of the bunk till the flesh under his finger nails showed white. "If I could get water to—to cool this—this devilish fire in my head—go—Ranlett ——" his clearing gaze fastened on the long scratch on her cheek—"For the love of—did they get you too?"

Jerry gently forced him back.

"No—no, I fell. Lie still, Beechy, while I go for water. Every moment that you keep quiet counts. Your head is not cut, there is nothing the matter that I can discover except that you were stunned. Don't move while I am gone. When I come back we will get away from here—we—we must. Remember that my safety depends upon you now and keep perfectly still until I come back."

It was quite the reverse, his safety depended upon her, Jerry thought, but she knew his type. Her need of his help would do more than anything else to clear his mind. She picked up the tin can she had used as a saw and went to the door. She looked back. Beechy was lying with closed eyes, the lines about his mouth relaxed.

The sun had dropped behind a high mountain. The air was sultry. A tinge of rose had replaced the gold of the afternoon coloring. In the southwest an unobtrusive bank of cloud had appeared. The tumbleweed still stirred with every breath of air but everything else was still. Jerry could see now, what she had not noticed from above, parallel grooves in the ground through the middle of the hollow.

"That's strange! Those ruts look like the marks of wagon wheels, but how could a wagon get down here?" she thought. She hesitated an instant on the threshold. Fortunately the pool was on a level with the cabin. Had the shack been on the opposite side of the hollow she would have had a ten-foot drop before she reached the level. The small body of water looked a thousand miles away and the room behind her, which had seemed sinister and forbidding a while before, seemed a haven of refuge now. So quickly do values shift in the crises of life.

"The more you dread the thing you have to do the more you should hustle to get it behind you," Jerry admonished herself and made a dash for the pool. For an instant the air seemed full of flapping, dark wings, then it cleared. She kept her eyes resolutely away from the body of the calf. The water was low. She had to lie flat to reach it. She wasted time in trying to dip deep enough to get clear of the tumbleweed which floated on top. When she had it to her satisfaction she sat back on her heels and inspected the contents of the dripping can.

"This will have to do," she announced to the world at large. "I——"

"That depends on what you're getting it for, don't it?" inquired a voice behind her.

The insolence of it, the portent of it, brought Jerry to her feet. The precious water slopped wastefully. She had the sense of suspended animation as she looked up at the man sardonically observing her, then a sense of sudden, ungovernable panic. It was the late manager of the Double O with the bridle of his horse, The Piker, a big, lanky chestnut, in his left hand.

"Ranlett!"

Her own frightened whisper infuriated her. She had spoken to the man looming over her as seldom as she conveniently could; always she had distrusted him. She looked at him now as though seeing him for the first time. His black hair had a white streak from the middle of his forehead to his neck, which had earned him the soubriquet of "The Skunk," from the outfit; his eyes were steel gray, his thin-lipped mouth was nothing more than a crooked slit in his face, his chin was stubborn. Jerry's gaze returned to that feature and lingered. Apparently he was as amazed to see her as she had been startled at his appearance. She felt as though he had her wriggling under a miscroscope, pinned by the needle points in his eyes as he observed caustically:

"Well, now that you have sized me up it's my turn. What are you doing so far from the Double O alone? Perhaps you're not alone, what?" His attitude, the lines of his shoulders, his voice, bristled with suspicion.

The girl's mind indulged in one frenzied merry-go-round before it settled down to constructive thinking. For the first time in her life she was squarely and uncompromisingly up against danger. Ranlett must not suspect that she had been in the shack, that Beechy was unbound. He might be in no way responsible for the condition in which she had found the ex-sergeant, but she couldn't take a chance with Carl's, "Ranlett—for the love of—did they get you too?" still echoing in her ears. If she could only get him away from the place. The throbbing pulse in her throat, which gave the impression of delicate wings beating futilely against bars, was the only sign of her agitation as she answered the man's question gayly.

"I don't wonder you ask, Mr. Ranlett, I'm a sight." She laid a finger cautiously against her scratched cheek and laughed. That laugh was a masterpiece of its kind. "I started for Bear Creek to inquire for Mrs. Carey, but yielded to the temptation to ride to the top of the hill. Pandora with her box has nothing on me for curiosity. I was born with an irresistible desire to look on the other side of things and places." The sudden narrowing of his eyes set her to wondering what false note she had struck, even as she went on:

"When I dismounted the better to peer down into this hollow, something gave a scream as of a thousand furies rampant." Her shudder was genuine. "The sound did direful things to Patches' nerves. He bolted down the hill. I bolted after him. I stumbled over something which must have been the keystone of the slope, or its twin, for the hillside gave way and landed me in an ignominious heap of dirt and gravel back of that shack. A rolling body gathers some scratches," she paraphrased flippantly as she felt again of her bruised face.

"I'll say you're some little talker, Mrs. Courtlandt, when—when you're frightened. You've never favored me with a word before," observed Ranlett insolently.

Two red spots burned like able-bodied beacons in Jerry's cheeks. She knew that she had been garrulous, that she had been talking against time, but it was maddening to be told so; the sound of her own voice had sustained her courage. Every moment that she held the attention of the late manager of the Double O counted for Beechy. It took all her strength of purpose to keep her eyes from wandering to the door of the shack. It acted like a malevolent magnet.

"Where is your horse?"

"Back of the cabin. I came here to get water for him."

"Have you been in the shack?"

"In the shack!" the shudder with which the girl turned her back upon it would have made Nazimova pale with envy. "That—that gruesome place? Rather not——"

"Then you are not curious when it comes to empty houses? You're not consistent, Pandora. Where did you get that can?"

Jerry felt as though she were under a machine-gun fire of words. The man's insolence infuriated her. She didn't dare resent it for fear he would leave her and investigate the cabin. She looked down at the can she still held between finger and thumb, then at the bed of ashes beside the pool.

"Did I find it there or behind the shack?" she mused as though interrogating herself, then quickly, "Is it yours? Take it if you want it."

"You know d—ed well that you didn't pick it up outside," Ranlett exploded as he caught the girl by the shoulder; she felt his hot flesh through her thin blouse. "You've been in that shack and you've——"

"Take your hand away! Quick!" Jerry commanded, her voice hoarse, her face white, her eyes blazing.

"I'll let you go when I get good and ready." The man sunk his fingers deeper into her shoulder to emphasize his words. "What's that yellow coyote in there been telling you——"

"Nothin' to your advantage, Ranlett. Put up your hands an' put 'em up quick," interrupted a voice. It was Beechy, Beechy leveling Jerry's villainous six-shooter at Ranlett's head. His face was white, one eye was almost closed but he had an air of cocky unconcern.

"Mrs. Lieut., grab his horse. No you don't!" as the late manager of the Double O, arms held high above his head, tried to trip the girl. A bullet whizzed so close to his ear that Ranlett turned a sickly green. "Yer see, I'm a little nervous. I'm not used to this old-time six-shooter; I've been using a Colt 45. I'll get the range better next time and it'll come closer. I didn't get my expert rifleman badge in the army for shootin' crap. Frisk his pockets, Mrs. Lieut." For the fraction of a second Jerry hesitated.

"Quick! Get busy, unless you want more of his pack down on us. That's the stuff! Now you're talkin'," as the girl produced a corpulent revolver from a hip pocket. Ranlett's voice was hoarse with fury as he dared:

"You'll need that gun, Beechy, when Courtlandt finds that you and the missus have been meeting—you sure have a way with the ladies."

Jerry's cry was submerged in Beechy's oath. The man's face was like granite, as gray, as immovable. Only his eyes blazed. His tone was as cold and passionless as his face.

"Meanin'? You'll pay for that, Ranlett, but not now. Just for fear your gang will butt in we'll make our getaway, but remember—I'm comin' back. I want you and I want the feller that cracked my head. Hand me his gun, Mrs. Lieut. Lead his horse and yours to the top of the hill and wait—don't look around—get me?"

"Yes, I get you, sergeant—but you won't——" Jerry hesitated with the bridle of Ranlett's big chestnut in her hand.

"Obey orders and obey 'em quick!"

And Jerry obeyed. With the unflurried agility Tommy had taught her she mounted Ranlett's horse and turned him in the direction of the shack. The animal side-stepped and tried to look in the direction of his master but the girl touched him with her spurs, and urged him on. She unhitched Patches. She looked like a slender boy as she led him by a backward stretched left hand up the slope. The moments that she spent ascending were one long prayer that the hillside would not encore its disappearing trick. She felt an irresistible desire to look back but she remembered the salty fate of Lot's wife and kept doggedly on.

As she gained the shelter of the pines at the top of the hill she heard a shot. Her face went white. Who had fired it? Ranlett or Beechy? Beechy was weak from the blow on his head; he could easily be overcome. She listened. A flock of magpies lighted in the tree above her, observed the strange figure below them for a moment then flew away in noisy haste. As the sound of their raucous voices died in the distance Jerry heard another sound, the sound of gravel slipping. Who was coming? She hastily changed mounts and twisted her hand in the bridle of the big horse. If it were Ranlett she would race at breakneck speed toward Greyson's, the X Y Z was nearer than the Double O, taking The Piker with her. Her breath came so hard it hurt her throat. Eyes dilated with excitement she watched the brow of the hill. The sound of the slipping gravel came nearer and nearer. Then she heard labored breathing. The suspense was unendurable; she felt as though she must scream. A man staggered into sight. It was Beechy. She slipped from her horse and called him softly.

"This way! Quick!" As he stumbled toward her she noted the pallor of his face. She didn't dare leave the horses to go to his assistance. With a bridle in each hand she went forward to meet him.

"I'm about all—in, Mrs. Lieut.," he panted. "The blow and this climb have about finished a job the—war—started."

She slipped her arm under his. Her eyes were tender with concern.

"Lean on me a moment. You mustn't give way now, Beechy. Get on Ranlett's horse. We must get away from here. He may follow." He laughed weakly.

"Follow! Nothing doing. Just to make sure he wouldn't I put a bullet through his leg. I couldn't have him interferin' with the job you an' I have to put across. He'll go as far as the shack while the goin's good."

"But he may starve!"

"You should worry. There are provisions to withstand a siege cached under that cabin. Forget him. If you're the good little sport I think you are you've got a job——"

"Listen!"

Jerry laid her hand over her heart. Beechy raised his heavy head from the side of the horse where he had rested it. His eyes narrowed into mere slits. From the hillside came the sound of slipping gravel.

"Well, I'll be——"

"It's Ranlett! He's creeping up!" the girl whispered tensely. "You must mount. He may have found a gun." Then as he shook his head weakly, "If you don't I shall stay with you and you may never get a chance to tell me what I am to do."

"Help me up!" The white beneath Beechy's skin had changed to crimson. His teeth clenched as he pulled himself into the saddle. He held tight to the horn with his two hands.

"Mount! Quick!" he panted. "Now ride close beside me while I tell you——" for an instant his eyes lost their purpose. He slipped over to one side. Jerry caught him and steadied him.

" 'Tention company!" he drawled foolishly as he tried to straighten in the saddle.

"You must keep on, Beechy! Grip your mind tight till we reach the Lieutenant," pleaded the girl, always with one ear turned to the sinister, slipping sound that drew nearer and nearer up the hillside. It seemed as though the reference to Courtlandt had power to conjure strength. With a stifled groan the man eased himself in the saddle.

"I can ride this way. Don't lose your sand, Mrs. Lieut. I've pulled through worse scrapes than this. We'll beat 'em yet."

They left the pines and began the descent of the hill. The innocent cloud bank in the southwest had spread in great jagged peaks until it darkened the heavens and the fields beneath them. The stream looked like a drab ribbon splashed with white. They rode silently. Beechy conserved his strength. "When we get to the level I'll talk," he vouch-safed once through blue lips. Jerry kept close beside him. Across the valley lights were beginning to appear in the X Y Z. She felt as though she were in a horrid nightmare from which she must waken to find herself safe in her own charming rooms at the Double O. Beechy's voice dispelled her illusion. In obedience to a gesture of his she pulled up her horse as they reached the level.

"We've got to work quick, Mrs. Lieut. This rustling dope of Ranlett's is a bluff. When he cut the fences in Lower Field he figured that the Double O outfit to a man would hunt for the cattle in that direction—away from the railroad."

"The railroad!"

"Yes. Listen. No,—I'm not going to fall.—Not till I've put you wise." The knuckles of his hand showed white as he gripped the saddle-horn. "To-night a car, carrying silver bricks from the mint in Philadelphia goes through on its way to the coast. It's attached to the regular evening train—it's under armed guard—but— Ranlett——" It was characteristic of the girl that instead of demanding how he knew she announced breathlessly:

"We must reach that train before Ranlett's gang——"

"You've said it! Ranlett's staged the party at Devil's Hold-up. It's only fifteen miles from the X Y Z but ten of that fifteen is wilderness. We've got to stop that train before it reaches Greyson's crossing."

"I'll ride for the X Y Z and get Bruce Greyson. I don't know where Steve is," interrupted the girl breathlessly. "You go on to the Double O. The Piker will know his way there in the dark. About ten o'clock, did you say?"

"Yes." Beechy's voice was weaker. "Don't let *anyone* know but Greyson. Ranlett has the place honeycombed with spies. I'll stay here for a while. If he comes— moseying over—the hill———" He slipped suddenly from the saddle to the ground. He stretched flat on his back. "A-ah! That's better," he groaned. He tried to smile up into the concerned face bent over him. *"C'est drôle, ça?* I bragged that I was through with the good old U. S. A. and the minute I find that I'm caught in a plot against her I throw up my hands. I knew that Ranlett would kill me if I backed out but I'd—I'd rather—die."

"But you're not going to die, Beechy, and we'll win out," the girl comforted eagerly. "Oh, how can I leave you like this———"

"Mount that pony again, quick!" He gathered his strength by a superhuman effort. "Don't think of me. I'll rest here and then I'll move on, I promise. I want to—get out—of—this scrape as much as—you want me to. That's right—up you—go." The last word was a whisper. He struggled to one elbow. "Tell Greyson if he gets a chance—to put a bullet through the man— Ranlett took on in—my place—that range-rider at Bear —Creek ranch."

XVI

BENSON regarded Ming Soy in stunned amazement. Her words, "She never come back—not all this time," revolved stupidly round and round in his brain. They had been catapulted into the midst of his passionate declaration to Peggy; what she would have answered he never would know, now. The color which the touch of his lips had brought to the girl's face had faded; she was regarding the Chinese woman with terrified eyes. She laid a trembling hand on Benson's arm. "Thank God, I haven't made you hate me," he thought fervently as he gripped her cold fingers in a comforting clasp. His faith in the wisdom of a surprise attack had been built upon a rock, after all.

"Tell me again, Ming Soy, just when Mrs. Courtlandt started and what she said to you."

In her excitement Ming Soy's English kept tripping her up, but Benson was able to get a fairly clear idea of what had happened.

"I watched her rode—not to the flield she tole me— no—down the road. I listened for shoots. No shoots. No noding. No noding in flield. When Ming Soy see you way down road, Ming Soy bleat glong."

Benson's mind had been working with machine-like speed while he listened. The girl beside him drew a long, ragged breath. He laid his lips upon her hand for a moment.

"Don't worry! I'll find her, Peg-o'-my-heart. She has probably dropped in at Bear Creek ranch to see that new arrival and has forgotten the time. Women are like that when there's a baby." He advanced the theory with a light-hearted laugh which he flattered himself was a marvel of its kind, but it merely drew a long, quivering sob from the girl. "Just for company, I'll ride down to meet her."

"I'll go with you," announced Peggy eagerly.

"Nothing doing! You'll go back to the house with Ming Soy. Don't let Hopi Soy work off any of his thrift ideas on the dinner. If Jerry has been riding all afternoon she'll be famished, and I—I feel as if I could eat a raw mountain lion this minute. I'll take the horses back to the corral and get a fresh mount."

"Please—Tommy—take me?"

Benson closed his ears heroically against the wiles of his own particular Circe. He shook his head; his grave eyes met the girl's squarely.

"Be a good little sport, Peg. I can go faster without you. Besides, Jerry may be back before me and she would be anxious if you were not here."

"All right, Tommy. Come, Ming Soy."

Benson could get no satisfaction from the man in charge of the corral. He questioned him as he watched him shift the saddle from Soapy to a powerful black. Slowman only knew that Mrs. Courtlandt came for Patches at about two o'clock. She was humming and laughing softly to herself as she led him off, quite as though she had heard some good news—or—was up to some mischief; women were like that, when they had something up their sleeves, he'd noticed. None of the boys who had gone after the Shorthorns had returned. Mr. Courtlandt had 'phoned the corral from Slippy Bend that he should not be back to the ranch until morning, and to keep a sharp watch over the horses.

"By cripes, when he said that," Slowman added as he looked at Benson with eyes so curiously crossed that they appeared to regard an object from the north and south extremes of the pole of vision, "it sent the creeps all over me. It was almost as good as though I'd gone back to the days of honest-to-God hold-ups an' rustlin's. I'm sorry about Mrs. Courtlandt, Mr. Tommy, but don't you worry. You'll like as not find her over takin' care of Jim Carey's baby. I hear the kid's a boy," with a sheepish grin.

As Benson rode out from the corral he looked at the bank of clouds in the southwest and put spurs to his horse. Ming Soy, under cross-examination, had held stoutly to her statement that Jerry had not gone to the field back of the ranch-house. He would ride to the B C first. On the rustic bridge that spanned the stream he stopped to reconnoiter then went on and rounded the clump of cottonwoods that screened the Bear Creek buildings from his view. They were beginning to lose their outline in the deepening gloom. The fast spreading clouds were letting down a curtain of darkness.

Benson had ridden but a few hundred yards when he pulled the black up short. What was that! He listened. The air was still with that curious sinister calm which precedes a storm. The sound came again. It was the whinny of a horse but—but—it was not from the direction of the B C ranch; it came from the level at the foot of the hills beyond.

Tommy's imaginings as he raced across the field would have provided material for a five-reel thriller of the most lurid variety. They blew up like a balloon which has been pricked when he was near enough to the whinnying horse to discover that it was not Patches but Ranlett's favorite mount, The Piker. He gave voice to a mild but expressive swear-word.

"Now what's to pay?" he muttered as he flung himself from the saddle and bent over the outstretched figure half buried in the long grass. He knelt. "Beechy!" he exclaimed incredulously. "How the dickens did you ——" The recumbent man lifted heavy lids.

"*Comment ca*——" Returning consciousness cleared the haze from the blue eyes. "Mr. Benson—you—did she find you—instead of——" his eyes closed.

"Beechy! Beechy! Rouse yourself. You must help me," Tommy pleaded. "Have you seen Mrs. Courtlandt? She's—she's lost! Your Lieutenant can't find his wife, Beechy!"

"*Mon Lieutenant,*" the blue eyes looked up at Benson dazedly. "What's that you said, Mr. Benson? Lost his wife? You're wrong, you've got another guess coming." With cautious effort he raised himself on his elbow. "Prop me up, that's better. Don't worry about Mrs. Lieut. She's a good little—sport. She must be getting near the X Y Z by now." His voice was clearer, the color was coming back to his lips.

"She's safe—unhurt?"

"Sure, man—nothin' could happen to a woman like her—don't you know that? She's ridin' like the devil to cut off——" in his excitement he jerked himself erect; in the next moment he was a crumpled heap on the ground.

Tommy emptied the canteen he had tied to his saddlehorn, for the Lord only knew what emergency, over the white face. His tense nerves relaxed. Jerry had been all right when Beechy saw her last and that couldn't have been so long ago. If she was at Greyson's she was safe—but—what the dickens had she been doing all the afternoon, he wondered. Now that he had her accounted for he must get Beechy under cover. With an anxious glance at the threatening sky overhead he spoke to the man on the ground. He was quite conscious again. He listened intelligently as Tommy outlined his plan for getting him to Bear Creek ranch. He wasted no strength on words but with Benson's help finally mounted The Piker. He put his arms around the horse's neck and fell forward on his mane. Benson steadied him with one hand. Side by side the two horses made their way to the buildings now nothing but a blotch of darkness.

Jim Carey dashed out of the corral as the two rode up. He was a tall, good-looking man with black eyes which twitched nervously as he talked.

"Is that you, Small? Where the devil——" he broke off in astonishment as he saw the figure flung forward on The Piker's neck.

"It's not Small, Carey. I'm Benson from the Double O," Tommy called from out the gloom. "I picked up a man at the foot of the hill who was about all in. He was Courtlandt's sergeant overseas. Help me get him down, will you?"

"We'll take him into Small's cabin. This way."

The two men carried Beechy into the shack and laid him on a bed. Carey lighted a lamp. He came back and looked down at the unconscious man as he lay with his red hair roughly tousled and the bruise under his eye a purplish red.

"I'll get Mother Eagan. I—I suppose you know what's come?" Carey asked with awkward pride.

"I heard that the stork was playing a one-night stand in this county. Is Mrs. Carey getting on all right?" Tommy asked as he busied himself unfastening Beechy's clothes. "What is it, Carl?" he soothed as the injured man struggled to one elbow, his eyes blazing with excitement.

"Grab his horse—Mrs. Lieut., I'll get the range better next time—Ranlett——" he dropped back on the pillow; the fever died down in his eyes. He looked up into Benson's anxious face. "Don't mind what I said," he pleaded weakly. "I was dreamin' but—but—I guess you'd better ride after Mrs. Lieut., and be sure she's all right. Ranlett's gang——"

"Ranlett's gang!" both men bent over him. "What do you mean, Beechy?" Benson asked tensely.

"Bolster me up! That's right. That infernal pounding inside me's quieting down." He drew a cautious breath and smiled wanly into the faces above him. "Did you see that? It came as easy as spendin' money. Who's that? Where am I?" he demanded as he caught sight of Jim Carey and looked around the room.

"You are at Bear Creek ranch and this is Carey the owner."

"Send him out, Mr. Benson. I've got something to say to you."

"But Carey is——"

"Send him out," Beechy reiterated weakly and closed his eyes as though he were again slipping into a coma.

"You'd better go, Jim. There's some deviltry afoot and Beechy knows what it is. Send Mother Eagan down in ten minutes if she can be spared."

Carey looked down at the motionless figure on the bed.

"I wonder if he knows anything about Small," he whispered. "He left early this morning and——"

"You mean?"

"The same," answered Carey enigmatically and left the cabin. The wind banged the door after him. Benson could see Beechy wince. Then he was conscious of what was going on about him.

"He's gone, Carl," he whispered.

Beechy's lips twisted in a smile as he opened his eyes, and eased himself on his elbow.

"I reckoned we'd shake him if I played 'possum. I'm feelin' better every minute. Get a paper and pencil, Mr. Benson. I want you to take something down for me. This bogus heart of mine is likely to pound on for years, then again it may shut up shop any minute."

"I'll do it, Beechy, but first, tell me about Mrs. Courtlandt. I must know that she is safe."

"She's safe, all right. She started for the X Y Z and Greyson. I kept my brain steady till she got out of sight. She was ridin' her own horse. I'm not deceiving you. I wouldn't have any harm come to her for her own sake, let alone the Lieutenant's. Now you listen and put down what I tell you, *sabe?*"

Beechy told the story of his acquaintance with Ranlett, with frequent pauses for rest and to get his breath. Someone on the border, he wouldn't tell who, had sent him to the manager of the Double O. Outside the wind rose steadily. It flung itself against the corners of the small building, it shook the window frames as a terrier does a rat; the flame in the lamp flickered and steadied.

"Get me straight, Mr. Benson," Beechy concluded. "I ain't excusing myself. I was dead wrong—but Ranlett caught me when I was bitter and discouraged. He set out as how we were to pull off this hold-up on a carful of gold belonging to some 1917–18 millionaires that had made their money in munitions. Then this morning I got a hint 'twas government money. I up an' had it out with Ranlett. I allowed I'd touch nothin' belonging to the government. His eyes got like red-hot coals. 'You don't think for a minute you'll get away with turning goody-goody after hearin' my plans, do you?' says he, his hand twitching. 'No, I don't, Ranlett,' says I, 'but you want to remember that thievin's one thing an' murder's another.' Then crack! It was like a shell burstin' and I didn't know anythin' more till I looked up into what seemed two shimmery gold stars—the Lieutenant's wife was holdin' me."

"Who hit you? Ranlett?"

"Not on your life! He ain't takin' no chances. He

wasn't even figurin' in the hold-up to-night; he is to direct operations from a dugout in the rear. It was Carey's range-rider."

"What!"

"Somewhere he'd found out I was linked up with the Lieutenant. Now you know why I wouldn't tell before—— Who's coming?"

The knock preceded the entrance of Mother Eagan. She fairly blew into the room. Her round, shining face was red; she was panting from exertion. The man on the bed straightened up, smoothed his hair, adjusted the collar of his shirt and turned reckless, smiling blue eyes upon his visitor. She was a woman, therefore to be impressed, irrespective of age or size or charm. That was Beechy, Benson thought as he watched him. He was a curious combination of characteristics. The woman looked from one to the other.

"Where's the man I was sent down to drag back to life?" she asked with a good-natured chuckle. Her eyes lingered on Beechy. "Sure you don't look sick to me."

Benson slipped the paper he held into his pocket.

"Make him lie down and keep quiet, Mother Eagan, and put something on that bruise. I'll go on to the X Y Z now that you're being taken care of, Beechy."

"Righto. Mr. Greyson may need help in that little matter I was tellin' you about. Mother Eagan, it sure is good to see you. You're the handsomest white woman I've seen since I left the border—you——"

Benson closed the cabin door behind him. Beechy was incorrigible, but Mother Eagan was fool-proof. She'd laugh and volley back at him while she made his poor, racked body comfortable.

When Tommy reached the pack-trail which led toward the X Y Z he pulled up his horse. He looked back at the buildings of the B C ranch, then speculatively at the hill behind them. On the other side of that Beechy had left Ranlett. Suppose, just suppose, that the late manager of the Double O was not incapacitated to the extent his assailant thought? Suppose that he should be able to make his getaway? To put the bandits on

their guard? Mrs. Steve was doubtless with Greyson by
this time planning to checkmate the bad men. Wasn't it
up to him to make sure of The Skunk?

Without giving his bump of caution time to rouse
from its habitual state of coma, Tommy made for the
hill. Lightning crackled the sky, the rain came.

> " 'It ain't no use to grumble and complain,
>   It's every bit as easy to rejoice
>   When the Lord sorts out the weather and sends
>   rain,
>   Rain's my choice,' "

he quoted with cheery philosophy as he pulled the
broad brim of his hat down and the collar of his shirt
up.

The spectral grove was a protection from wind and
rain when he entered it. He dismounted when he
reached the pines on the crest of the hill from which he
could look down into Buzzard's Hollow. Fortunately he
knew every foot of the surrounding country. In the
years he had been at the Double O he had explored
foot-hills and valleys, had fished in the streams that
crossed them.

With flash-light in one hand and his forty-five in the
other Benson waited for the lightning. He must get his
bearings. The storm rattled and crashed among the
mountains. It was deafening—but—what was that? In
the interval between crashes he had caught another
sound. It was the spasmodic roar and hum of a plane.
It was a sinister sound in that place at that hour. In a
flash Tommy's mind reverted to the plane which had
passed over the stream on Sunday. Again he heard
Courtlandt's curt answer to his question, "Nothing, except that your information confirms me in my suspicion
that Marks and Schoeffleur signaled that pilot when he
went over." Was that the reason the two men had been
missing this morning when Gerrish rounded up the outfit to send them in search of the runaway Shorthorns?

Benson's hands were like ice as standing behind the

bole of a giant spruce he watched the progress of the aeroplane. The lightning flashed steadily. Against the glare of the sky the great shape was silhouetted. Almost instantly as though assured of his bearings, the pilot shut off his motor and spiraled down toward the hollow. The machine lighted as softly on the carpet of tumbleweed as might a fluff of thistle-down. It made a smooth three-point landing.

"That pilot's a veteran, none of the amateur's bump in his," Benson muttered, at the same time subconsciously thanking the great god Thor for his coöperation as he took advantage of a reverberating roll of thunder to slide down the hillside. He went so amazingly fast that he would have come up against the wall of the shack with a crash had he not seized a shrub and stopped himself in time. Through the cracks between the imperfectly matched boards that made the wall he could see light. On hands and knees, his heart thumping as only that well-regulated organ can thump in the breast of a brave man who realizes the risk he is running, Tommy put his ear to a crack. He heard the sound of voices, his nostrils were filled with the odor of cigarette smoke. He recognized Ranlett's high-pitched nasal tones. Evidently the pilot had brought a passenger, for Benson could distinguish two other voices. The late manager's was weak, as though with pain, but it held an ugly note.

"That's better, Marks. That'll stop the bleeding. I was a fool to try to follow that fellow Beechy. But—but I was mad to get at him. Bill Small swore that he'd fixed him so that he wouldn't move again—I don't know now whether he believed it or whether he was trying to double-cross me."

"Nice fella, Beechy. We'd better be getting out of this; he may give the alarm." Benson had never heard the voice before. It was thick and guttural and evidently belonged to the pilot. Marks must have been the passenger.

"He can't. He's all in. He could hardly get up that hill. Bad heart. Even if he told the girl——"

"A girl in it! Good day! I'm through!"

"Hold on, young feller! Don't get cold feet so easily. I—I don't know where he met up with her—but—she can't get far. There is no telephone at the B C and the lines connecting X Y Z and the Double O with each other and Slippy Bend are 'Out of order.' " There was a sardonic note in his voice as he mimicked the stereotyped words. "We're safe, I tell you. The boys will pull off that stunt and come winging back here laden with silver bricks before any of that bunch can get anywhere. No one will think of looking here for the loot; it's too near the centre of Sheriffville. We'll take what silver we can in the plane and the boys can cache the rest till the excitement has died down. Simms will be sound asleep in his bed at Upper Farm by the time the authorities get round to him. He can ship us a silver brick in a tub of butter at his discretion. I tell you, it's a cinch," he exulted with a sound midway between a chuckle and a groan.

With a crash, as though the resident giant in a passion of rage had knocked the rocky crowns of the mountains together, the storm spent itself. In an incredibly short time the moon began to peer from between scudding clouds. Benson crept slowly round the shack, his mind seething with anger and resentment. Both ranches cut off! Where was Mrs. Steve?

Moving when the moon was obscured, burrowing in the soaked tumbleweed when it emerged from hiding, Benson made his way slowly and with infinite caution to the aircraft. He crept round it till the plane, which looked like nothing so much as a Brobdingnagian bird of prey, was between him and the shack. He looked up at it. Suppose there were someone in it! For an instant his heart obstructed his breathing. He must know. He scratched one wing with his flash-light. To his taut nerves it seemed as though the sound reverberated among the foot-hills. Surely a person on guard would respond to that.

Reassured by the silence within the machine, Benson groped along the side of the plane until he located the pilot's seat. He climbed in. Silently, expeditiously, he did a few things to the steering gear and wrecked the throttle. "You won't transport many silver bricks in this, young feller," he muttered grimly. Knowledge of any kind was a valuable commodity to have packed in one's kit-bag, he thought, as he cautiously climbed down from the machine. Thanks to the few months spent in the hangar of an aviation field in the spring of '17, he had known where and how to administer body blows.

By a circuitous route he reached the shack. With jaws set hard to keep his lips from twitching with nervousness he peered through one of the dirty windows. The light inside came from a candle stuck in a bottle which stood on the range opposite the door. Its weird, wavering light threw ghostly shadows on the walls. Someone was stretched out on the bunk. A man with an aviator's helmet pushed back on his head sat on the range, another sprawled on the floor. It was Ranlett on the bunk; Benson recognized his voice as he replied to a question.

"Ten o'clock. Better begin to watch out for the rockets soon. Remember, two green lights if they have pulled it off and want us to wait; two red lights if we are to beat it. Help me up. I'll get into the plane and then we won't waste time making our getaway when they come."

Benson stood rigid. Should he let them get out of the shack or should he cover them where they were? If they reached the aeroplane they would immediately discover the damage and be on their guard. He must keep them in the shack. Before the two airmen could help Ranlett to his feet he fired a bullet through the window. It lodged in the wood over the bunk.

"Stay where you are! Hands up!" he shouted in a gruff voice which excitement hoarsened. "We have you covered from each window. The man who moves gets his good and plenty. Gerrish, you cover the chap with the helmet; O'Neil, make a target of Marks and I'll devote my entire attention to the Skunk."

Would his bluff work; would it? Tommy wondered frantically. It did. With muttered imprecations the two men ranged themselves against the wall, their hands above their heads. Ranlett sank back on the bunk. They weren't taking chances. What should he do next, Benson wondered, with a nervous desire to shout with laughter. He had placed himself so that without moving he could see any signal which might come from the direction of Devil's Hold-up. At imminent danger of becoming cross-eyed for life, he kept one eye on the men and one on the sky above the region where he knew the railroad to lie. At signs of restlessness in his prisoners he stole to the other window. He fired a shot which had a miraculous effect upon their sagging muscles. They stiffened. Benson with difficulty repressed a chuckle. He had them dancing to the tune he piped, all right. But what the dickens should he do if the bandits successfully pulled off their raid on the treasure car? If he stayed where he was he would be one against a dozen or more desperate men. If he made a break for safety Ranlett and his choice aggregation of bad men would escape with their plunder. If—what was that? A green light! Then Mrs. Steve had not reached Greyson. Another emerald star shot into the sky.

"Two green lights if they have pulled if off and want us to wait!" That was what Ranlett had said. Some fugitive lines flicked tantalizingly on the screen of Tommy's memory, then steadied:

> "But to every man there openeth
> A high way and a low,
> And every man decideth
> The way his soul shall go."

That settled it. He'd hold his prisoners and take his chance.

XVII

SHE had been right in her suspicions of the Man of Mystery, Jerry thought, as she put spurs to her horse. The words Beechy had called after her echoed in her mind. "Tell Greyson if he gets a chance—to put a bullet through the man—Ranlett took on in—my place —that range-rider at Bear—Creek ranch." It was growing dark. Heavy clouds had rolled up. She had some difficulty in forcing Patches from the old pack-trail which eventually led to home and supper. She cut across fields, splashed through the stream, then headed for the X Y Z ranch-house whose lights seemed like will-o'-the-wisps. The longer she rode the more they receded.

She determined not to worry about Beechy. He had promised that he would try to get to the Double O and she knew that he would win out. The unexpected would happen to help him, as nine out of ten times it did when one was in dire straits. With the thought came a vision of her father; she could see his massive head, his shrewd eyes, hear his deep voice saying:

"I have a firm conviction that a person can put through any worthy thing on which he is determined; how else do you account for the seeming miracles of heroism men got away with in the World War? The test is, how much do you want it? I've gone on that principle all my life and it's worked, I tell you, it's worked."

It was curious how that memory of her father vitalized her. Jerry straightened in the saddle. She felt as though she had been warmed, fed, had had the elixir of courage poured through her veins. Beechy would come through. All she need think of was her part.

It was quite dark when she reached the X Y Z. The air stirred in hot gusts; from far off came the rumble of thunder. Patches was matted with sweat and dust.

Ito, the Jap, opened the door in response to her knock. From behind him came the sound of voices, the tinkle of silver, the ripple of a woman's laugh. Felice Denbigh! Jerry had forgotten her. For an instant she visualized the gold hair, the gold eyes with their tigerish spots, the alluring chiffoned daintiness of the woman. With a shrug she looked down at her own torn, dusty riding clothes. She would hate to meet the ultra fashionable Mrs. Denbigh now. Felice must not know that she had come; she might ruin everything. Jerry had an intuition that she would stop at nothing to humiliate the girl Steve had married. She caught the astonished Ito by the lapels of his coat and drew him into the shadow.

"It is Mrs. Courtlandt, Ito. I must see Mr. Greyson. Don't tell him who it is, though. Say—say that—that the ranch boss wants to see him."

The Jap's yellow mask of a face did not for a moment lose its imperturbability.

"All lie will I tell him, honorable lady. Keep in dark when I door make open."

Jerry sank to a bench among the vines; weary Patches sagged in the shadows. For an instant it seemed as though life drained out of her, as though she were being swept along the tide of indifference to unconsciousness. For the first time she realized that she had had but two hours' sleep in almost forty-eight hours. She forced herself erect. She pulled off her hat which she had crushed down over her forehead when she started on her wild ride to the X Y Z. It was a relief to get it off. She could think better. She dropped it to the bench beside her. A ray of light from somewhere set the gold in the cord glinting. Where was the owner of that hat, she wondered. Had Steve gone into the mountains? Would Tommy and Peg be anxious when she did not appear for dinner? She did not dare 'phone them for fear that in some way Ranlett might get a clue to her errand. She started forward as the door opened and closed and Greyson's voice demanded sharply:

"What's to pay, McGregor?"

"It isn't McGregor, it's Jerry Courtlandt," the girl

whispered. "Shs-s! Take me somewhere we can talk and not be overheard."

He led her to a clump of trees near the entrance to the drive; her horse followed with his head close to the girl's shoulder. The branches swayed in the wind. Even in the dusk she could see the eddies of dust in the road. The atmosphere seemed electrically alive. Jerry shivered and seized a fold of Greyson's sleeve.

"I—I just want to make sure you're really here—it's so—so dark I can hardly see you," she apologized shakily. His hand closed over hers. His voice was tense as he demanded:

"What has happened, Jerry? What has brought you to me like this?" For the first time she was conscious of the absurdity of her costume, of her delicate, torn blouse with its bandana addition, her linen breeches and riding boots. She flung the thought of her appearance from her mind and plunged into explanation. Greyson questioned when she had finished:

"Are you sure? How did Beechy know?"

Jerry's eyes widened.

"I never thought to ask," she confessed. "I just believed what he told me and I know, I know that he was telling the truth. What shall we do? We must hurry—hurry——" For what seemed an eternity of time to her Bruce Greyson was silent. The wind rose and whistled and whined. Jerry was quivering with impatience when he spoke.

"The train must be flagged before it reaches the X Y Z. I'll run the flivver to the crossing and try to get down the track. It's a mad scheme but it's the only chance. We couldn't get to the station at Slippy Bend in time if we tried. I'll take one of the men to wave a lantern——"

"You'll take me," interrupted Jerry breathlessly. The amazing audacity of the plan thrilled her with its possibilities. "We mustn't take a chance with a third party. Beechy warned me that Ranlett had sympathizers everywhere. We can't trust one of the men."

"But there is a tremendous storm rising. What if Steve——"

"Steve may not be at home to-night; what he doesn't know won't trouble him. Tommy and Peg will have to worry. Individuals must be sacrificed to the good of the government, or words to that effect." Her spirits were mounting now that she had secured an ally. "Felice must not know that I am here."

"I'll have Ito make my apologies to Mrs. Denbigh. He can tell her that I have been called away suddenly. He can also tel—slip down to the front gate and wait for me. I'll take your horse to the corral. If the men notice him at all, they will think merely that you have taken refuge from the storm."

Crouched against the shrubs near the gate the girl waited. A lurid flash in the heavens gave an instant's glimpse of the ranch-house, the white fences of the corral. Then came the crash of thunder and utter darkness. There was a sound as of a fusillade of bullets on the hard road. "Here comes the rain!" Jerry murmured. The words were drowned in a sudden hissing downpour. She peered at the illuminated dial of her watch. Nine o'clock! In just one hour the train was due at Devil's Hold-up. Could they stop it? She listened. Was that the sound of wheels? Yes. Greyson was coasting the machine down the slight incline toward her; there was no sound of the engine. While it was still in motion she sprang to the running-board, took her seat and closed the door softly. Not a moment had been lost. For the first time she felt the rain beating on her bare head; it stung her shoulders through her thin blouse. The top of the car had been thrown back. She put her hand up. Her hat! Where was it? Then she remembered that she had flung it on the bench beside Greyson's front door. "Being hatless is the least of my troubles," she thought buoyantly as she peered forward into the darkness. At the foot of the incline Greyson bent to the lever.

"Now we're off," he whispered. "There is a lantern at your feet. Light that."

On her knees in the bottom of the car Jerry struggled with the lantern. The flivver bounced and swerved as the driver tried to force the engine belonging to the hundreds class to speed achieved only by the thousands. After using a profusion of matches, and—anathemas when she burned her fingers, Jerry lighted the lantern. She gave a long sigh of relief as she slipped back into her seat.

"It's done! The bottom of the car looks as though there had been a massacre of matches, just as the floor round Steve's chair looks when he is smoking his pipe, but what are a few matches at a time like this? What can I do next?"

"Jerry, you amazing girl! Nothing—nothing seems hard or impossible when you have a share in it," Greyson burst out impetuously. He steadied his voice and directed, "When we come to the gate get out and open it. I'll run through to the crossing. Be sure that you fasten the gate securely behind you. No sane person will think of our getting down the track this way. No sane person would think of attempting it," he added under his breath.

Once through the gate Greyson cautiously steered the car off the crossing on to the track which paralleled that on which the west-bound train would come. He manipulated the motor until the left-hand wheels of the car hugged the inside of one rail and the right-hand wheels were in the road-bed. He waited for flashes of lightning to show him the way. They came almost incessantly. The thunder crashed and rumbled as though the gods of the mountains were playfully pitching TNT shells for exercise.

"This is going to be one little stunt," the man confided to the girl as she took her seat beside him. "Keep the lantern in your hand. When I say 'Ready' stand up on the seat and wave like mad. Now we're off, and may the gods be good to us!"

It wasn't a heathen god whom Jerry Courtlandt importuned. She never looked back upon that wild ride without a renewed thanksgiving that the prayer in her heart had been answered, without a reminiscent ache in every bone of her body, without seeing a close-up of Greyson, tense-jawed and wrinkle-browed bent over the wheel. He drove with his eyes intent on the tracks which seemed glistening streaks of fire when the lightning flashed. The swift transitions from dazzling light to inky darkness blinded her. It would always remain one of the inexplicable miracles to the girl that the flivver did not capsize. She felt no fear at the time. Only when from behind them came the sound as of a hundred furies let loose did she shudder.

"Is—is that a pack of wolves?" she whispered hoarsely.

"Coyotes. Two can make as much noise as a dozen of anything else. Hear that? Begin to wave! Ready!"

Jerry scrambled to the seat. She lost her balance as the car careened tipsily. She clutched Greyson's hair with a violence which wrung a stifled "Ouch!" from the victim.

"I'm sorry. My mistake! I wasn't trained as a bareback rider," the girl apologized with an hysterical ripple of laughter.

"Wave! Wave!" Greyson shouted above the din of the storm.

The girl waved her lantern in curving sweeps. At first she could hear nothing, see nothing, then above the noise of their own wheels she heard a rumble which quickly increased to a roar. Then came a light and behind it a creature which might have belonged to the ancient order of Compsognatha, so long was it, so sinuous, so sinister. It was the train. Jerry waved frantically. Surely, surely the engineer must see her light. She caught her breath and held it as the roar grew deafening and the monster came leaping, writhing, pounding on.

"They see us! They see us!" she shouted, and laughed exultantly all the while waving the lantern madly. The whistle of the oncoming engine blew a frenzied warning. Greyson turned his wheel way over. The flivver literally jumped the rails and ran along a siding which joined the main track. The girl slid into her seat limp with exhaustion. With groaning and grinding of brakes and clanking of wheels the long train trembled to a stop. Which one of the cars carried the treasure, Jerry wondered, just as a rough Irish voice thundered in her ear:

"For the love of Mike! What we got here? Escaped lunatics, or I miss my guess." The light of a lantern was flashed in the faces of the occupants of the car. The man who held it swore with an ease and facility which took Jerry's breath. "It's a man and a woman, crazy as coots," he called to someone behind him. Then in a magisterial tone, "It's a hunch we got the new division superintendent aboard this trip. He can see for himself what held us up; he'd never believe it if I told him. Now what'd you flag this train for?" demanded the violator of the second Commandment, truculently. A group of men had gathered round him.

Greyson stepped from the flivver and drew Jerry after him. What would he say, she wondered anxiously. Their errand must not be suspected. They must get aboard the train and interview the division superintendent. A sudden mad thought suggested itself. Without an instant's hesitation Jerry slipped her arm under Greyson's, rested her head against his sleeve and smiled audaciously into the broad, weather-beaten face glowering at her.

"Don't scold, Mr. Brakeman. It was reckless, but—but—you see, we just had to flag this train. We—we want to get to the coast. We're—we're—eloping."

"Good God!"

Greyson's inarticulate protest was submerged in the hoarse ejaculation. Jerry wheeled. Behind her stood Stephen Courtlandt.

XVIII

IT seemed to Steve as he looked at the girl, with her hair, which wind and rain had lashed into clinging tendrils of glinting bronze, pressed close against Greyson's arm, that his universe tore itself from its orbit and hurtled into fathomless space. For thirty throbbing seconds the blue eyes challenged the brown, then he turned away.

"Courtlandt!" called Greyson dominantly, but Steve was speaking to the division superintendent who, white with anxiety, had hurried up.

"Sure they'll have to go along with us, Steve," reassured the autocrat of the train. He turned to Greyson. "We'll take you to the coast, all right, but you won't get off the train till you've paid a good fat fine for stopping it. You and the lady get aboard, pronto. Steve, lock her up in one of the compartments. I'll look after the man. Mac, if anything else tries to hold us up you shoot and shoot quick, no matter if there are skirts mixed up in it." He rushed off in company with the burly brakeman. Greyson caught Courtlandt's arm.

"Look here, Steve, you must listen. Jerry——"

"You needn't apologize for my—my wife, Greyson. She's coming with me." He put his hands none too gently on the girl's shoulder.

"But, Steve, you don't understand," Jerry protested. "I——"

"All aboard there!" yelled the brakeman angrily. Steve fairly lifted the girl to the platform of the Pullman. He hurried her along the corridor to a compartment.

"Come in here, Jerry, and no matter what you hear don't come out. I'll send the maid to help you get your clothing dry." He turned to go, but she laid her hand on his arm.

"Steve, you must listen to me. I want to tell you——"

"What can you tell me except that you love Greyson and ran away with him? I can't hear that now—I won't. You're mine and I keep what is my own. And remember this, if you try to communicate with him while you are on this train—I'll shoot him." His eyes were black; there was a white line about his nostrils.

"Steve, you're all wrong,—but if you won't trust me——" she shrugged the remainder of the sentence. Then her voice was pleading. "Did Bruce—Mr. Greyson,—get a chance to speak to the division superintendent?"

"Did he? I'll say he did. What Nelson isn't saying to your—your gallant friend at this minute, isn't worth saying." He looked at her suspiciously as she laughed. He took a step nearer.

"No, I shan't have hysterics, Stevie. Now that I know that my gallant friend, as you call him, is explaining our late plan to the division superintendent, I haven't a care in the world,—in fact," with a dainty, politely repressed yawn, "if I could have this place and the maid to myself, I might take a nap. I shall have plenty of time. It is a long way to the coast," with another irrepressible ripple of laughter. Then as he lingered, "You needn't stand guard. I shan't run away again. An encore lacks the snap of a first performance," audaciously.

Courtlandt opened his lips to reply, thought better of it, closed the door smartly behind him and went in search of the maid. Back in the compartment which the division superintendent used as an office he lighted his pipe, and paced the floor back and forth, back and forth as he tried to marshall order from the chaos of his thoughts. Why didn't the fool train start, he wondered, as he listened to what seemed an endless amount of backing and starting and grinding of brakes.

His mind went back to the moment in Lower Field when Johnny Simms had handed him a letter and bolted. He could see every word on the tear-blotted page now:

"Ranlett doesn't want the cattle. He cut the fences so that the Double O outfit would follow the Shorthorns into the mountains. He and his bunch are figurin' to rob the west-bound to-night at Devil's Holdup. Government silver. Watch out! Ranlett has spies everywhere."

There had been no signature, no mention of Simms, but Courtlandt felt sure that he was in on the deal and that the wife was trying to keep her husband from being caught in what might easily prove to be more than robbery. His first reaction from the message had been amused incredulity. It was absurd to believe that in these enlightened days a man of Ranlett's intelligence, and he was infernally intelligent, would try to get away with such a mid-eighties stunt. The sense of amusement was succeeded by startled conviction. The fact was that Ranlett did think he could put it across and was to make the attempt that night. He must hustle through his work and make Slippy Bend in time to board the train. He could neither wire nor 'phone if it were true that Ranlett had spies everywhere. He must keep his own counsel until he could talk with the official in charge of the west-bound.

After that he had followed trails and conferred with ranch section heads. As clouds began to spread out from the southwest he galloped into Slippy Bend. He had supper in a leisurely fashion at the one hotel, dropped into the post-office for a chat with Sandy, who was sorting his mail for the morrow's trip, and discussed crops and stock and tractors with the group of men gathered there. He had reached the railroad station about ten minutes before the treasure train was due. He hailed the railroad man-of-all-work whose slouch relegated him unquestionably to the preëfficiency era.

"West-bound on time? I'm going up the line to follow some steers that have mysteriously wandered off. I'm not looking for trouble, but——" He tapped the holster which hung from his belt. Baldy Jennings, whose head resembled a shiny white island entirely surrounded by a fringe of red hair, chewed and spat with intriguing accuracy as he listened. Steve's explanation had precipitated a flow of observation.

"Shucks! The world's sick. Most of it don't want to work and them that does won't be let by them that don't. The majority seem to figur' that it's a darned sight easier to pick the other man's pocket than to fill their own by honest sweatin' labor. Sure, it never wa'n't none of my butt-in, but I used to tell old man Fairfax that Ranlett was narrer between the horns. Oh, you don't hev to mention no names, I know who took them steers,—but cripes, it didn't do no good, he wouldn't listen to Baldy Jennings. And now the coyote's knifed you! An' your old man given' him every chanct. Human natur'! Human natur'! Well, I gotta get busy. The railroad don't pay me sixty bucks per fer swappin' talk even with the owner of the Double O. Here comes the west-bound." A shrill whistle echoed back and forth among the hills like a shuttlecock. The vibration of the rails announced the coming train.

Courtlandt's pipe went out, he stopped his restless pacing of the narrow compartment as he visualized the first person who had stepped from the train. It had been Nelson who had been a captain in the battalion in which Steve had served overseas. His face, which had been white and tense when he reached the platform, had suffused with color as he recognized Courtlandt.

"Well, you can knock me for a gool, if it isn't the Whistling Lieut.!" he cried eagerly. "What are you doing in this teeming mart of trade?" he added, as he glanced at Baldy Jennings staring open-mouthed at the meeting and beyond him to the few coatless, vested, bearded favorite sons who leaned against the sagging building.

Courtlandt had laughed. When the fog of surprise had lifted he had seen that the years had not changed Nelson. His black eyes were as keen as ever, his little mustache had the same moth-eaten effect, the network of veins on his slightly bulbous nose were redder perhaps, and he was in civilian clothes. That realization wrinkled Steve's brow in perplexity.

"What are you doing here? Last I heard you had joined the regular army and were stationed somewhere around Phila——" Perception of the situation came in a blinding flash. Nelson's eyes met his steadily.

"There are some occasions when a soldier appears in mufti. Especially when he is passing as the newly appointed division superintendent of a railroad." Steve drew a breath. So that was it. His eyes traveled over the train. Which was the treasure car? Obviously the one in the middle which looked like an ordinary baggage-car. The rest were brilliantly lighted coaches, from the windows of which eyes peered out curiously, indifferently or interestedly as the temperaments and minds behind them dictated. His glance came back to Nelson.

"You're the man I'm looking for. I've lost some cattle, and I'm going up the line a way to look for them. I must give you all particulars. I'm counting on you to help me, if there should happen to be any rough stuff pulled off, see?"

The two men had stood apart from the confusion of the station. The rain beat down. Over among the mountains thunder and lightning held high carnival. Courtlandt drew Nelson into the lee of the building. He struck a match and held it above his pipe till the wood burned down to his fingers. In the flickering light he and the superintendent, pro tem., had regarded one another steadily. Nelson moistened his lips:

"Sure, I see, Steve. Glad to have you along." He raised his voice as one of the train hands approached. "Make yourself comfortable in my quarters. Perhaps I can find a couple to make up a little game."

Courtlandt was quite unconscious of the rumble of the train as in imagination he relived the time he had spent waiting for Nelson to join him in the double compartment which had been fitted up as an office for the superintendent. Minutes seemed hours. When he did come the smile had left his lips. His eyes were stern. He closed the door with a bang.

"Deal out what's coming, quick!" he had commanded

and Steve had told him almost word for word what Mrs. Simms had written. "You're sure of this?"

"I've given the message as it came to me. The person who sent the warning had every reason to keep mum."

"I get you." Nelson pulled down a map which was rolled against the side of the car. He studied the maze of lines and dots and dashes. "Going along with us?" he had asked casually.

"The surest thing you know." Steve remembered how absurdly light-hearted he had felt. Nelson looked so thoroughly equal to his job.

"Then you'd better—now what the devil is *that?*" he growled as the engine blew a furious warning and the brakes ground on with a suddenness which threw both men against the desk. "We can't have reached Devil's Hold-up yet."

And then—Courtlandt's crowding thoughts had reached the moment when he had heard a girl's voice say:

"Don't scold, Mr. Brakeman. It was reckless—but—but, you see, we had to flag this train—we—we want to go to the coast. We're—we're eloping!"

Jerry and Greyson! And he would have staked his life that she was true blue, that even if she felt that she could never love the man she had married she would have trampled temptation. The intolerable ache in Steve's heart maddened him. She should not carry out this mad plan. He wouldn't let her go if she hated him eternally. He'd make her love him, love him as he had loved her from the moment he had looked up to see her enter the living-room of Glamorgan's apartment. He had been so infernally proud that he had tortured himself by pretending indifference and now he had been brutal. He should have let her explain—he'd go now and listen to what she had to say. God help him to act the man no matter what it was. He would be tender, he would be sympathetic—but—he'd never give her up.

Nelson entered and closed the door softly behind him. His face was white, there were tiny flecks of foam on his lips, his eyes blazed.

"In five minutes we'll slow down to a crawl before entering Devil's Hold-up. The bandits counted on that. I'll go forward to the cab. Trail along after me. Leave your holster here. The passengers mustn't get the idea that we're packing guns; get me?"

"I get you. Where is Gr—where is the man who flagged the train?"

Nelson turned with his hand on the door-knob.

"In the car back locked into a compartment with an armed guard before it. He wanted to talk but I wasn't taking chances with any middle-aged Lochinvar until after we'd passed the Hold-up. Got the woman in the case locked up, haven't you?"

"Yes, she——" Courtlandt cut off the explanation he was about to offer. Why enlighten Nelson? If he could keep Jerry's name out of the mix-up, so much the better. Greyson wouldn't be likely to talk.

"All right, see that she doesn't break loose. A girl who would flivver along a railroad track would have to be roped and tied to keep her out of a wild party like this or I miss my guess."

Steve looked unseeingly at the door as it closed behind Nelson. He was right; it would be like Jerry to get into the mix-up. He would stop at her compartment as he went forward and make sure that she was there. He unfastened the holster from his belt and flung it to the desk. With a slight bulge in the region of the hip pocket of his riding breeches he left the office. At the door of the compartment in which he had left Jerry he knocked.

There was no answer. He tapped again and listened. There was no sound inside save the creaking of woodwork and springs as the car swayed with the grinding of wheels. Courtlandt whitened. Could she have left her room? With quick impatience he opened the door and stepped inside. In his surprise he slammed it behind him. Jerry, rolled in a blanket, lay in the bunk asleep.

Even the noise he had made did not arouse her. Evidently the maid had taken her clothing to dry it, for she was blanketed like a mummy from her feet to her dimpled chin. Courtlandt crossed the narrow space between them and looked down upon her. Her hair was spread over the pillow to dry, her dark lashes lay like fringes, the one cheek visible had a long red scratch, a bare foot hung over the edge of the bunk. Her sleep was so profound that she barely breathed.

Why was she so exhausted, Steve wondered anxiously. In a flash he remembered. She had been up all the night before with Mrs. Carey. Was it only last night that he had taken her to the B C ranch? It seemed weeks ago. No wonder that she was tired; she couldn't have had much sleep in the last forty-eight hours. What did the bruise mean? He leaned over her and touched it lightly. It was not a recent scratch. Very gently he raised the pink foot which swayed with every motion of the car and covered it with the blanket. He looked down upon the girl for a moment. With jaw set and the veins in his temples standing out like cords he went out and closed the door behind him.

The train barely crawled as Courtlandt swung from the step of the coach to the ground. His eyes were strained; there was a white line about his lips as he pulled himself up into the gangway between tender and engine. The storm had rolled eastward. Above the distant mountains a broad and yellow moon played at hide-and-seek with fleecy remnants of cloud. Stars appeared dimly, reconnoitered for a moment, then shone with steady brilliancy. Nelson, seated on a tool-box in the cab, rolled a cigarette with slightly unsteady fingers. The engineer had his head out of the window; his assistant was tinkering a bit of balky machinery. Nelson looked up as Courtlandt appeared.

"Did you come out to see the wheels go round, Steve? I'd rather ride here than anywhere else myself. What the devil! What's to pay now, Hawks?" as the engineer ground on the brakes.

"Boulder on the track," rumbled the sooty man. He turned white under the soot as his eyes crossed in a futile endeavor to look along the shiny blue nose of an automatic in the hand of his grimy assistant.

"Hands up, all of you! Come over here, Hawks. You gentlemen can talk to me while my friends give the train the once-over."

"Well, I'll be——"

"You sure will if you talk," growled the grimy one, looking like a popular conception of his satanic majesty sans horns. Courtlandt and Nelson who had been caught completely off guard by this attack from within, stood with upraised arms. "Now, what t'ell!" The gun swayed for the fraction of a second as a figure slid down over the coal in the tender and landed in a crumpled heap in the gangway. Courtlandt seized the opportunity. By the aboriginal expedient of kicking his victim smartly in the shin he surprised the grimy one into a howl of pain. Instinctively one hand reached for the aching member. Steve seized the revolver.

"You're some gunman," he jeered. "Go back into that corner and sit down!" And Satan's understudy, shorn of all of his gun and two-thirds of his bravado— went. "Hawks, tie his feet and hands. Here's his gun. Nelson, I can manage if you want to give orders elsewhere. What have we here?"

The man who had fallen from the tender had struggled to his feet. He braced himself against the side of the cab. His hair was matted down over his eyes, his khaki shirt was in strips, his breeches and riding boots were caked with mud; evidently he had been a rider before he turned bandit, Courtlandt thought as he covered him with his forty-five. Hawks was standing guard with his prisoner's own automatic. Fate has a keen sense of comedy.

"What's your business?" Steve demanded. The man made an evident effort to rally his senses. His voice was low and broken as he answered:

"There are twenty men in the gap—waiting for this train—the silver—bricks. Here—here are the names——" He fumbled in his shirt. Steve watched him with wary eyes his finger on the trigger of his gun. The trussed man in the corner swore volubly. The engineer silenced him with the toe of his boot. Courtlandt took a step nearer the gasping, groping man. The light was dim, if he were tricking him—but he wasn't. With painful effort he produced a paper. His right arm hung helpless. A red spot the size of a nickel appeared on the breast of his shirt. "Here it is. I—I played into Ranlett's hands with the steers—Steve." He collapsed in a heap on the floor.

"Steve!"

Courtlandt was on his knees beside him echoing his name. He slipped his arm under the bent head. The man looked up with a laugh that died in a painful rattle in his throat.

"You didn't know me, Steve?"

"Denbigh!"

"Don't take it so hard, this—this scratch isn't anything. I—I swore I'd square myself with the world and —and my conscience. I've been playing my cards for this grand slam for weeks. Somehow Ranlett got wind that the silver—was to—be shipped sometime this month. When I found that Beechy was your man I dropped him a hint as to the ownership of the treasure he was after—then—then—I took care of him for Ranlett—see? You'll find him stunned but unhurt in the shack in Buzzard's Hollow. No—don't interrupt—let me talk while I can—they'll be here in a minute. Tonight they must have been watching me. When I tried to slip away Simms fired. I—I rolled over the cliff— they must have thought that finished me—it did—almost—but I was determined to get here. Keep those names—I—hope—I've saved the government's money."

His head fell back on Courtlandt's shoulder, his eyes closed for a moment. Then with almost superhuman effort he rallied:

"I can't drift off yet. Two green rockets—in my shirt. As—soon as you've caught the gang—send those up. They'll keep Ranlett and—and the others in the Hollow till—you get there. They mean that—that——"

Courtlandt had to put his ear close to Denbigh's lips to

hear the last words. He laid him down and reached into his shirt for the rockets. Nelson appeared.

"Leave him, Steve, I need you. I've sent a gang out to move the boulder. We'll let the bad men think they've fooled us. Half the passengers on this train are regulars in mufti. Little ol' Uncle Sam isn't taking chances when he ships silver bricks to the coast. Here they come! Look!" in a hoarse, excited whisper.

Out from between crevices and behind cottonwoods stole sinister shadows. The men trying to remove the boulder from the track worked steadily. The night was so still after the storm that Steve could hear their hard breathing, their gruff commands and the clink of metal against rock as they attacked the granite. The man in the corner opened his lips to shout a warning but Hawks stuffed his mouth full of oily waste before he could utter a sound. Nelson oozed delighted anticipation.

"Good Lord, man!" Steve exploded, "you haven't crossed the bridge yet. Those men are after the government's money and they're going to put up a stiff fight for it."

"So they are, so they are, little ol' Steve, but they won't get it. We dropped the treasure car, the last lighted Pullman with the silver bricks in it, off on the siding where those crazy elopers flagged us. Your Uncle Dudley wasn't taking any chances."

XIX

"AFTER all, it has been absurdly like the fake attack and repulse of bandits in a musical comedy, except— except for Phil," Courtlandt thought two hours later. "And here's where the female portion of the audience would adjust hats and grope under the seats for missing articles," he added, as from the platform of the train he watched a splotch of darkness move slowly up the main street of Slippy Bend, en route for the jail. The act had lacked none of the usual colorful stage setting. There had been a starry heaven overhead, the dim outlines of the rocky gap for a back-drop, clumps of cottonwoods and aspens for side wings and for the crowning touch, two green rockets had sped skyward.

The attacking party had boarded the train with just the right amount of theatrical bravado, but something went wrong. Someone must have hopelessly mixed the cues, for instead of towering over their shrinking victims the bandits had found themselves staring dumbly along the snubnoses of Colts in the trigger-quick hands of veterans. Denbigh's list had been checked off and, save for Ranlett and Marks, every man named on it was now being personally conducted up the silent street.

Phil had made good, gloriously good, Courtlandt exulted as he made his way to the baggage-car where Denbigh lay on the floor, his eyes closed, his face flushed with fever. Steve knelt beside him, and laid a cool hand on his forehead, but the wounded man did not move. Nelson climbed into the car.

"They've brought the stretcher, Steve. I'll attend to moving him while you get the girl off the train. I've sent for a doctor."

With his pulses hammering Courtlandt knocked at the door of the compartment in which he had left Jerry asleep. There was no answer. Had she gone? He knocked again, this time with a peremptoriness augmented by the fear in his heart.

"Come in!" a cool voice answered.

Steve entered the compartment. From across the small room Jerry, dressed as she had been when she flagged the train, contemplated him with unfriendly eyes. Her blouse and linen breeches showed stains of mud and weather but they had been mended and pressed. Her boots, with the big rowels still attached, had been cleaned. Her hair, brushed till it shone like satin, had been coiled in place; even the scratch on her cheek had been reduced in color if not in length. Her lips were disdainful, her face curiously colorless as she challenged:

"Well!"

"We are back at Slippy Bend. We must leave the train at once. There has been——"

"I know. The maid told me of the hold-up and that—that someone was hurt. I feared—I feared"— even her lips whitened—"I—I've been so anxious——" She caught her breath in a strangled sob. "She said that it wasn't one of the train-hands or—or—a soldier, and I—I thought——"

"Don't worry, it wasn't Greyson," Courtlandt cut in brusquely; his eyes flamed a warning. "It—it was Phil Denbigh."

"Phil Denbigh! You don't mean the man Felice married?"

"Yes—alias Bill Small, the range-rider at the B C."

"And he—a man like that—was one of the gang?"

"No, no! Phil was in it to get information, to give warning. He is entitled to an honorable discharge from his conscience now. His testimony will rid this part of the country of about twenty undesirables, the missing Marks and Schoeffleur, among them."

She looked up in dumb incredulity for a moment, then she laughed.

"So-o, the treasure would have been saved anyway without—without——" There was another irrepressible ripple of mirth before she asked, "Has Bruce—has— Mr. Greyson been told?"

Her laughter, her reference to Greyson snapped Courtlandt's self-control, which already strained to the limit of endurance. Even his lips were white as he caught her by the shoulders.

"I don't know what Greyson has been told, but he'll get it straight from me that you are mine—mine——" With sudden savage ruthlessness he caught her in his arms and kissed her shining hair, her throat, her eyes. He let her go. "Now perhaps *you* understand it too," he announced huskily.

Jerry shrank as far away from him as the narrow space would allow. The color burned in her cheeks, her eyes blazed.

"You—you have no right to—to do that!" she reminded breathlessly.

"Haven't I?"

"Don't stand there looking like a lion ready to spring. I—I won't have it! You promised——"

"That is humorous. When you ran away with Greyson were you keeping your promise? At least, you'll acquit me of making love to—another woman. I——" the door was thrown open violently and Nelson shouted:

"Get that girl off quick, Steve! We leave in five minutes." The last words died in the distance as he hurried along the corridor.

"Come!" Courtlandt commanded, and with a curious look up into his eyes Jerry preceded him from the compartment. As she stepped from the train she fell almost into her sister's arms.

"Peggy!" she gasped in astonishment.

"Where the dickens did you drop from, Peg-o'-my-heart? Why are you at Slippy Bend at this unholy hour?" Steve demanded peremptorily.

"Ye gods! Don't ask me why! For information apply to Ito. I only know that while I was walking the floor at the Double O, wild with anxiety, that Jap tragedian appeared and announced that he must see the excellent Mr. Benson. When I succeeded in convincing him that I couldn't produce the excellent Mr. Benson, he explained that he must take me to Slippy Bend to meet Mrs. Courtlandt, by order of his honorable master."

"His master!" Jerry and Courtlandt echoed in unison.

"That was what he said. He did deign to explain that he had been told to telephone, but that as all lines were out of order he came himself to give the message to Mr. Benson. When he found that Tommy wasn't there he insisted upon bringing me to Slippy Bend himself."

"Where is Tommy?"

"Don't snap, Steve. I don't know. I'm one little walking encyclopedia of ignorance to-night," with a sob which she valiantly tried to strangle at its birth. "Jerry, where have you been? That Chinese woman of yours met Tommy and me when we returned from our ride with some incoherent stuff about your having gone off with a gun. That sent Tommy in a mad rush after you. All I could get out of the Oriental while I was waiting was, 'Missee tlell Ming Soy when she see little Missee and Mr. Tommee Blenson she bleat glong.' If I hadn't locked her into the pantry she'd be beating it yet." She snuggled her arm under her sister's as she asked again, "Where have you been, Jerry?"

"I'll tell you all about it, honey, while we are riding home; that is, if we are going home." With tantalizing daring she looked up at Steve and asked with exaggerated humility, "Am I to be permitted to return to the Double O in the care of Bruce—of Mr. Greyson's man, Mr. Courtlandt?"

He flushed darkly, but without answering led the way to the big touring car. The Jap sat behind the wheel in bronze immobility. When Courtlandt had laid the rug over the knees of the two girls in the back seat he closed the door and gave Ito his order.

"Drive Mrs. Courtlandt and Miss Glamorgan to the Double O as quickly as you can with safety. Jerry, in some way get word to Gerrish that I need him at Slippy Bend as soon as he can get here. I'll try 'phoning from the hotel as well; the lines may be in order now."

"Aren't you coming with us, Steve?" Peggy's tone was aggrieved.

"No. I have Blue Devil here; I'll ride out. Goodnight!"

He watched the red light on the departing automobile until it became a mere spark in the distance. Then he returned to the train. He was still puzzling over the message Greyson had tried to get to Benson when Nelson hailed him. He was near the step of the last car.

"Oh, Steve, get a hustle on! I've been waiting for you." Then as Courtlandt stood beside him he added in a grave voice, "It's about Denbigh. When we lifted him he—he went out like a candle. Never saw anything like it. They've taken the—him to the hotel. You'll have to notify the authorities, Steve. Simms shot him, and I hope they make that surly brute pay the piper. I'll give my testimony when they want it. Now I must get on with this train." He sprang to the step of the car and seized the rail. Brakeman and conductors stood rigidly awaiting his signal. Courtlandt stepped back.

"Just a minute, Steve! Lord, I almost forgot to tell you. There is just one glint of humor in this infernally tragic night. It seems that Lochinvar is Greyson of the X Y Z ranch. Don't know where that is; perhaps you do. His lady friend got the dope about this hold-up, too. She rode to his place for help and the two flivvered down the track to stop the train, she standing on the seat grabbing his hair with one hand while with the other she waved that fool lantern. Can't you see the picture? I'll say she's some little sport."

"But—but the elopement?"

"Lord-ee, Steve, don't take this whole rotten business so to heart. You're livid. That elopement stuff is the glint. The girl had been told that there were traitors on the train. She knew Greyson's reason for flagging it mustn't be suspected; just there the elopement excuse flashed into her mind. Said she reckoned that elopers were the only people who would do such a fool stunt. She told the maid about it after things had quieted down. I'll say she's a peacherino. If I hadn't a perfectly good wife at home she could have me. Happen to know who she is?"

"Yes. I happen to know. She is—she is Mrs. Stephen Courtlandt." Nelson almost fell off the step.

"For the love of Mike! I don't wonder you're white. She—she was so darned convincing." With a chuckle he swung forward and gave the signal to the waiting crew. In a fairly successful imitation of Jerry's voice he called softly:

"Go on, Mr. Brakeman. We—we want to get to the coast."

As he made his way along the street in the starlight Courtlandt felt as though he were traveling with his double. It was as if his shadow had suddenly developed a mind which occupied itself exclusively with thoughts of Jerry, leaving his own brain free to concentrate on the business ahead. In a spirit of detachment he turned over and over her reason for the elopement announcement, pictured her ride, her furious indignation when the flesh and blood Steve had held her in his arms. There was nothing shadowy in Courtlandt's reaction to that memory.

The foyer of the small, ramshackle hotel was filled with men, tobacco smoke, and the hum and buzz of excited voices, all but the space near one closed door. When they looked in that direction men spoke in whispers, many of them dragged off their hats. It was as if the insensate wood had an aura of mystery and tragedy into which no person in the room cared or dared penetrate. Greyson was the first person to whom Courtlandt spoke.

"Bruce—I know now——" With a smile the elder laid his hand on the younger man's shoulder.

"Forget it, Steve. Had I been in your place I couldn't have carried off the situation as well. I am glad that I stand exonerated of that unspeakable treachery. I—I only hope that later when you learn——" he cleared his throat and went on irrelevantly, "Who's to tell Mrs. Denbigh about her husband? After all, he was her husband. You were his friend. She'll take it better from you, Steve."

A furious protest rose to Courtlandt's lips but he looked at the closed door and answered instead:

"Somebody's got to do it. I'll ride over to the X Y Z in the morning. There is no use in consulting her about any of the arrangements here. Has anyone wired Denbigh's mother for instructions?"

"No, we waited for you. You'd better get her on long distance. A train goes East at two A.M."

"I understand. While I'm doing that try to get the Double O on the 'phone, will you? Tell them to get Gerrish here as soon as possible."

"I will. The sheriff wants to see you at the jail when you can manage it. He's sent a posse after Ranlett. He's in or near that shack in Buzzard's Hollow, that is, he was."

"He's there, all right. I signaled with the rockets as Phil directed. He may be getting a little uneasy at the non-arrival of his bad men by this time though. How the dickens did you know about it?"

"Beechy put a bullet into his leg. Jerry will tell you——"

"Beechy and Jerry!"

"Don't look like that, Steve. Jerry is safe and Beechy has made good, gloriously good. Get the little girl to tell you about it. She—she's a wonder! Meantime the sheriff waits. He wants to talk to you about Simms. There can be no doubt that he shot Denbigh. He wants your deposition. Perhaps it is a cold-blooded way to look at it, but I can't help thinking that with Simms out of the way his wife and kids will have a chance at real living. That's an awful indictment of a man, isn't it?"

It was morning when Courtlandt dismounted in the corral of the Double O. Slowman hurried up to take Blue Devil. The two men talked in low tones while dawn streaked the sky in rosy peaks and the stars paled. The grass glittered with diamond-like dew, the fairies had spread their squares of gossamer everywhere. The boys had come in with the Shorthorns, the corral boss reported, not one missing. The outfit had got news of the affair at Devil's Hold-up and were fit to be tied that they hadn't had a chance to clean up Ranlett and his gang.

After the turmoil of the last few hours the ranch-house seemed weirdly quiet as Courtlandt entered the living-room. The night air had been keen and a few coals, like observant red eyes, glowed at him from the hearth. Scherherazade, the white Persian cat, occupied the wing-chair. She opened her topaz eyes wide as Steve approached the mantel; she watched unblinkingly as he laid his arms upon it and looked up at the portrait above him. He spoke softly as though he and the smiling woman were comrades and confidants.

"They said that Phil went out like a candle, Mother.

Where did he go? Where are you? It can't be the end.
If it were I shouldn't feel as though you were with me
wherever I am. Was I a brute to Jerry? Will she ever
forgive me? Would you if you were in her place?" The
tender eyes must have reassured him for with a husky,
"Good-night, Betty Fairfax!" he straightened his shoulders and turned away. For an instant he stood looking
across the room. As he went toward his own door he
whistled softly his favorite "Papillions." Scherherazade
craned her ruffed white neck to follow the sound, her
eyes narrowed to ruby slits. The coals on the hearth
crumbled and fell. She sprang to the back of the chair
and listened. Across the room a door had latched softly.

Out in Buzzard's Hollow a white-faced, haggard-eyed
man was turning over his three prisoners to the deputy
sheriff. Overhead a great bird hung motionless for an
instant as it glared down at the curious creature with
mammoth outspread wings that lay below.

XX

BREAKFAST in the court was a late affair the morning
after the hold-up. Steve did not appear. Tommy had
given Jerry a sketchy account of his adventure of the
night before, minimizing his part in it. Ming Soy hovered about the table with what, in an Occidental, would
be tearful devotion. The world was as clean and fresh
and sweet as wind and rain and sunshine could make
it. Faintly from the corral came the voices of riders
coming and going; the skip and cough and stutter of
tractors drifted in on the breeze. Benito, with much
fluttering and shivering and croaking, was taking his
matutinal plunge in the basin of the fountain. Goober
lay beside Jerry's chair, his tawny eyes fixed unblink-
ly on the parrot, his tongue hanging, his white teeth
gleaming.

The girl, in a pink and white frock that suggested the

daintiness of morning-glories, had been absorbed in the thoughts induced by Tommy's story. It was some time before she became conscious of the obstinate silence maintained by the usually talkative Peg, who was a bit more bewilderingly lovely than ever in a frock just a trifle less blue than the sky above her. Benson was tenderly solicitous of her comfort. Would she have more honey? Hopi Soy had broken his own record with the waffles; sure she wouldn't have one? Peg answered his questions with an indifferent shake of her head. Jerry observed the two in silence for a few moments before she protested:

"Don't grovel, Tommy. I don't know what you've done to displease her royal highness, but knowing you as I do I am sure that it was nothing to warrant such rudeness. 'Fess up, children, what has happened? 'Who first bred strife between the chiefs that they should thus contend?' " she quoted gayly. "That is worthy even of you, Tommy."

"You may think it's funny, Jerry," flared Peg indignantly. "But if you had been—been——"

"Say it! Tell the gentlemen of the jury just what happened, Miss Glamorgan," prompted Benson in a judicial tone and with a glint of his blue eyes. "You won't?" as the girl responded only with a glance of superb scorn. "Then I will." He disregarded her startled, "Don't dare!" and announced, "I—I kissed her yesterday, Mrs. Steve."

"I won't stay to hear!"

"Yes, you will!" He caught Peggy gently but firmly by the shoulders. He stood behind her as he explained. "You see—I want—I intend to marry your sister, Mrs. Steve. Yesterday I staked my claim. I kissed her once."

"Hump! Squatter's rights!" interpolated Peggy angrily.

"Only once! Are you—sure, Tommy?" Jerry's voice was grave but there was a traitorous quiver of her vivid lips as she asked the question.

"Only once, on honor. I told her that I should never

do it again until she gave me permission. I meant it. I know that she is young. I expect to wait until——"

Peggy twisted herself free from the restraining hands on her shoulders. Half-way across the court she turned. Her hazel eyes were brilliant with laughter, her lips curved tormentingly as she flouted the two at the table.

"I—I hate—quitters!" she flung at Benson before she disappeared in the path which led to the office. Tommy followed her with his eyes, then turned to Jerry.

"I always watch where my ball falls so that I can find it quickly," he explained. The assurance had drained from his voice when he asked, "What—what do you think of my pronunciamento? Will your father stand for it, Mrs. Steve?"

"If you and Peg decide that you really care for one another he will have to," encouraged Jerry gravely.

"Peg has told me how he feels about family. Mine is the finest ever—but we don't date back to Colonial days on this continent. I suppose that we must have existed somewhere before we came to this country, we couldn't have been prestidigitated out of the everywhere into the here, could we? There is plenty of money behind us but—but that angel girl thinks I'm poor."

"Don't enlighten her. Let her think so—it may—make her kinder. When the time comes I'll talk with Dad. I'm with you heart and soul, Tommy, but I am afraid you have a long road to travel before Peg says 'Yes.'"

"You are wasting your sympathy. 'I scorn to change my state with kings!'" he declaimed dramatically before he disappeared into the path which had swallowed up Peggy.

Jerry rested her elbows on the table, her chin on her clasped hands, and gazed thoughtfully after him. Subconsciously she noted the sound of horses' hoofs on the hard road in front of the house. Who was arriving at ten o'clock in the morning, she wondered idly before she returned to thoughts of Peg and Tommy. She sat motionless for so long that Goober rose, stretched and poked his cold nose under her hands. She stroked his head gently.

"Where is your master?" she whispered into one of his big ears. The dog shook his head, sneezed violently and looked up, his eyes eloquent with reproach. "Did it tickle? I'm sorry." She reached for a lump of sugar in the squatty Dutch silver bowl. "If you could say please——" Goober rose on his hind feet, dangled his crossed forepaws and with head on one side avidly regarded the enticing white morsel in the girl's fingers. He gave a short, sharp bark. She tossed him the sugar which he crunched between his strong teeth. She patted his head. "Do you know, Goober, I think that any dog is more interesting than the average human. Wait for me. I'll get my hat and we'll take Patches a lump of sugar."

Obediently the dog took up his position beside her chair. Humming lightly Jerry went toward the house. What a glorious morning. The nightmare of yesterday already seemed like an impossible dream. Some day she would explain that elopement business to Steve and they would laugh about it together. She caught her breath as a vision of his face as he had held her in his arms crowded itself into her mind. She raced up the court steps to elude her clamorous thoughts. At the door of the living-room she stopped as though galvanized. She brushed her hand impatiently across her eyes. Coming into the shadowy room from the gleaming world outside certainly did queer things to one's vision. That——that couldn't be Steve with a woman's arm about his neck! There was an inarticulate sound in her throat as she took a step forward. Courtlandt heard it. With a muttered imprecation he loosened the clinging arm. His face was white, his eyes inscrutable as they met Jerry's.

"Felice, here is Mrs. Courtlandt. I have been telling Mrs. Denbigh of her husband's——" the woman beside him interrupted.

"Steve forgets that I haven't had a husband for several years. I confess the news was a shock. I had no idea that he was in this part of the country. I suppose

that detestable Fairfax man knew it when he suggested
to Bruce Greyson that he invite me here for the summer. Does that surprise you, Steve?" as Courtlandt
stifled an exclamation.

"If—if I can do anything to help you——" Jerry
had produced an apology for a voice at last.

"Thank you, no. Steve is all I need. He is such a comfort. Would anyone but he have had the sympathetic
understanding to wait until he thought I would be
awake before coming with such news to the X Y Z? But
I came here to help him. I have had his happiness on
my mind since I found this on the bench outside the
door just after Mr. Greyson had received a mysterious
summons." She held out Steve's campaign hat with its
black and gold cord and the band of silver filigree
which Jerry had added the day before. There was malice thinly disguised with solicitude in the tone in which
she added, "Then—then I understood that—that you
and he had gone——"

"Felice, cut that out! When I want your intervention
in my affairs I'll ask for it," Courtlandt's tone lashed.
"Now that you have returned the hat you may go.
Greyson has made arrangements for you to leave on
the east-bound train in the early afternoon. Your maid
is packing for you."

"But why should I go East, Steve? Phil Denbigh is
nothing to me, while you——" her tone was drenched
with significance. She looked defiantly at Jerry who was
conscious that she was giving an excellent imitation of
an automaton. Only her eyes felt alive, they burned,
and the pulses in her throat throbbed. She knew that if
she opened her lips it would be to hurl words at Felice
of which she would be utterly ashamed later, that if
she unclenched her hands it would be to strike the
mocking woman. She was terrified at the tumult which
shook her. Without a glance toward the two near the
window she crossed the room, entered her boudoir and
closed the door behind her. She leaned against it and
listened. She heard the front door close, footsteps on

the porch, voices, then the sound of horse's hoofs. They had gone!

With the realization, something inside her seemed to crash. The barrier of ice which she had erected between her heart and Steve was swept away in a surge of passionate emotion. She knew now why she had been so terrified last night when she had heard that a man had been wounded, she had feared it might be Steve; why she had been so furiously angry at Felice; why it had hurt so intolerably to see her in Steve's arms. It wasn't because she thought him false and untrue—it was because she loved him.

With confused consciousness that she must escape from her own thoughts she ran into the living-room. She and Goober would take that sugar to Patches and then—— The smiling, tender eyes of the portrait over the fireplace drew her like a magnet. She crossed her arms on the mantel and smiled back at them, valiantly.

"Mother dear——" she implored breathlessly. "Mother!"

Comforted in some inexplicable way she dropped her head on her arms. In retrospect she went back to that evening in her father's apartment when she and Steve had entered into their matrimonial engagement. He had staked his future for money, she for social advancement. Old Nick had been right. How could a man love or respect a girl who would marry for position? Now that Felice was really free, not merely legally free, would Steve—— Absorbed in her thoughts she was conscious of nothing in the room till Courtlandt's voice behind her announced authoritatively:

"I have something to say to you, Jerry."

To the girl's taut nerves it was the voice of the conqueror laying down terms of surrender and clemency. In a flash she was back in the library of the Manor, hearing Steve's cool, determined voice announce, "I shall consider myself in a position to dictate terms to one member of the family." If he had meant separation then, what would he mean now with her silly elopement

declaration of the night before to infuriate him? Was
he about to reproach her again for that? Felice had
supplied the last shred of evidence he needed when she
produced the hat, if he needed more than her own
statement to the brakeman to convict her. Her anger
flamed. He shouldn't get a chance to indict her. To put
one's opponent on the defense meant strategic advantage. Before he could speak she fended:

"You can't reproach me for last night, Steve, after—
after what I saw when I came into this room. Honors
are even," flippantly.

He caught her by the shoulders and looked steadily
into her angry eyes. They met his defiantly. His voice
was grave as he probed:

"After last night and—and this morning, Jerry, do
you still—still want to go on with it?"

"Go on with it? Do you—you mean our comedy of
marriage? Why not? 'Rather bear those ills we have
than fly to others that we know not of.' You see I
have contracted Tommy's pernicious habit of borrow-
ing from the classics when I wish to express myself
with force and distinction. Let me go!"

Courtlandt's grip on her shoulders tightened. His
face was white. There was a rigidity about his jaws
which should have warned her.

"Flippancy won't save you. You are to listen to me
now, girl."

"While you boast to me again as you did last night
that you had not made love to another woman? Not a
chance!" she twisted away from him and gained the
threshold of her own room. "Don't—don't let me keep
you from your alluring—friend," she flung back at him
before she closed and locked her door on the inside
with grating emphasis.

Then she listened with hands clasped tight over her
heart. The anger which was so foreign to her character had been a mere flash in the pan. Already she was
sorry and humiliated and ashamed. She had maintained
always that a girl who could not keep her temper, who
wrangled, belonged in the quarter where shrewish wom-

en, with shawls over their heads and forlorn little babies
forever under their feet, fought and brawled. Hadn't
she seen them in her childhood? And she—she who
thought herself superior hadn't been much better under
the skin. She could have scratched Felice's eyes out
and as for Steve——

Where was he now? The living-room was portentous-
ly still. Had he gone? Why couldn't she have listened
to his explanation, have assumed a friendliness which
this new, disturbing riot in her veins made impossible
as a reality? Her eyes which still smarted with unshed
tears traveled round the dainty, chintz-hung boudoir. In
a detached way she noted that the one picture on the
wall, which served as the key-note to the color scheme
of the room, needed straightening. She must speak to
Ming Soy—— Her heart hopped to her throat, then
did a tail-spin to her toes as a low, stern voice outside
her room commanded:

"Open the door, Jerry."

She stood rigid, motionless.

"Open the door!" there was an undercurrent in
Courtlandt's words which seemed to paralyze her
muscles. In a voice the more compelling because of its
repression he threatened, "If you don't open it at once
—I'll break it in!" The shake he gave the barrier between them broke the spell which held the girl. She
turned the key and flung open the door.

With a sudden fierce movement he caught her hands.
She had a confused sense of flinging herself against an
inflexible, determined will as she struggled to free them.
She met his steady, dominant eyes.

"Steve! What—what rank melodrama! Are you quali-
fying for the movies?" she essayed a nonchalant tone
which to her hypercritical senses seemed horribly frightened. "What—what do you want?"

"That door open. Nothing else—now," Courtlandt
answered as he dropped her hands and turned away.

XXI

"WHAT shall we do this afternoon, Jerry?" Peggy Glamorgan asked as she, her sister and Benson sat at luncheon three hours later. The table was spread on the broad, shadowy veranda on the north side of the ranchhouse. The sun beat down upon fields and white roads; insects droned lazily to the accompaniment of the faint roar of the stream swollen by the heavy rain of the night before. "Ye gods! If here isn't Abdul the Great," she mocked saucily as Courtlandt appeared at the door. "Are his humble slaves to be honored with his presence at the noonday meal? Allah, oh Allah! Jerry, aren't you overwhelmed at this tribute to our charms?"

"Can't a man lunch beneath his own vine and fig tree without creating a panic? From now on I shall make it a daily rite that you may get used to it," Steve laughed. He laid his hand on Benson's shoulder. "Tommy, you're a hero. Slippy Bend is agog with admiration. What the populace can't think of to say in praise of you the deputy sheriff supplies in the most colorful vernacular the locality produces. Don't run; I won't say any more," as Benson, fiery red, half rose from his chair. Steve seated himself opposite Jerry.

She observed him resentfully from behind a screen of lashes. He looked more care-free and debonair than she had ever seen him while her heart still contracted suffocatingly at any thought of the morning. It was just like a man, nothing went deep, she thought. Ming Soy fluttered about in devoted anticipation of his needs; Peggy poured cream into his tea with a lavish hand. Benson laughed.

"You're a master tactician, old dear. You let your light shine upon us but seldom and behold the devotion when you do appear. Alas, 'Maidens, like moths, are ever caught by glare.' I'll say your beatific expression would put the twinkle-twinkle-little-star effect out of business. Got a load off your mind, haven't you? Slow-man tells me that the Shorthorns are back to a hoof, that our temperamental late manager is being securely, if not luxuriously accommodated with quarters in the jail and that—that Mrs. Denbigh is en route to the effete East via Slippy Bend. Is my information correct?" He stole a surreptitious glance at Jerry who, with the aid of a pink-tipped finger, was nonchalantly sailing rose petal boats on the sea of her crystal finger-bowl.

"It is. The tangle of the last few months is straightening out. From now on I'll subscribe to that bit of philosophy of Doc Rand's, 'Things have a marvelous, unbelievable way of coming right.' The late unpleasantness has resulted in one thing: we have an All-American outfit on the Double O ranch on whose honor I'd stake my last dollar. They may come of varied and contending races but when it comes to ideals of service and loyalty to the nation, they're united. Next week I'm going to Uncle Nick's camp in the mountains to inspect the silver mine, and incidentally to fish. There is a lake there where the trout are so thick they form bread-lines to get a chance at the bait."

"You tell 'em!" jeered Benson.

"It's a fact. I want to shake the memory of the last two months, to get away so that I can come back and make a fresh start. I'll leave you in charge of the ranch, Tommy."

" 'When Caesar says, "Do this," it is performed.' "

"What's on for this afternoon? Let's do something. I want to get yesterday out of my mind."

"Miss Glamorgan and I thought—I thought—that if you didn't need me, we'd ride over to Buzzard's Hollow; that spot seems to be occupying stage center now. I'll personally conduct you and Mrs. Steve over the abandoned aeroplane if you'll mosey along with us."

Jerry tried to control a shudder. She wondered if she could ever again hear the name of the hollow without seeing a close-up of Beechy and Ranlett and that muti-

lated calf. She sensed Courtlandt's quick look at her
and answered hurriedly:

"Don't count me in. I shan't ride again until—until
I have forgotten the hours I spent in the saddle yesterday. Buzzard's Hollow as an objective leaves me cold.
If no one else wants the roadster I shall drive over to
the B C to inquire for Mrs. Carey. Mother Eagan may
allow me to see the baby."

Jerry could have cheerfully bitten out her too con-
fiding tongue when an hour later she found Steve waiting beside the roadster at the front door. He had
changed from his usual riding togs to sport clothes. He
reddened under her surprised eyes.

"Have you gone saddle shy too?" she asked flippantly to conceal her frightened suspicion that he was going
with her.

"No, but I must see Beechy and as you were going
to Bear Creek I thought we'd go along together."

"But—I—would rather——"

"Get in, please. It will take time to get to the B C
by the road in this car, which is far from being the
last word in speed-limit violators."

With teeth set in her lips to steady them Jerry stepped
into the roadster. What motive was back of Steve's decision to accompany her, she wondered, as the car
shot smoothly ahead under his skilful driving. She regarded him covertly from under the brim of her rose-
colored hat. He was gazing straight ahead, his brows
knit in a slight frown. The silence between them seemed
heavy with portent. She must say something. From far
off came a faint whistle.

"Is that the east-bound train?" she asked and then
wished fervently that she hadn't.

"Yes. Just pulling out of Slippy Bend. Felice is on it.
Jerry, I want you to understand that the situation you
stumbled on this morning was merely some of her
theatrical clap-trap. When I told her about Phil she
flung herself into my arms and pretended to be overcome."

"Don't apologize," the girl mocked, then as she

caught a dangerous gleam in his eyes she abandoned thin ice. "Has Mr. Denbigh——"

"I got Phil's mother on long distance soon after midnight. Gerrish took him—went East in the early morning."

"Was he a dear friend of yours?"

"No. He was in my class at college but he was always aloof, unfriendly. While the rest of us were in athletics he was devoting himself to his violin. We thought him indifferent but I understand now that his position had corroded his sensitive heart."

"Position? Wasn't he of the elect?"

"Sarcasm doesn't suit you, Jerry. Phil's father and mother were among the great army of incompatibles. His heritage of misery as the child of divorced parents, tossed back and forth between their habitations, ruined his life but—but he made royally good at the last, poor chap."

Jerry blinked furiously to rid her eyes of the tears which had flooded them at his tone. They rode on in silence. The road ran through the fragrant, chill quiet of dense pines, which creaked and swayed a mournful note in the slight breeze. When they emerged into the willow-fringed, sun-dappled road again Courtlandt spoke.

"I want you to tell me everything that happened yesterday, Jerry. I—I know now that that elopement stuff was all a bluff but—but it was an infernally dangerous one. It was lucky for Greyson that an interest bigger than any individual was concerned in last night's work or—forgive me for my lack of faith and tell me what happened, won't you, girl?"

Jerry snatched at her stampeding composure and dragged it back. Her answer was tantalizingly slow.

"That 'won't you' was a master stroke of diplomacy. Machiavellian, I call it. Had you demanded an explanation I wouldn't have given it. Where shall I commence?" She saw him stiffen at her levity but he had his voice well in hand as he answered:

"At the beginning."

"Only on condition that there are no interruptions."

"Then be merciful and tell your story quickly."

Jerry began the recital of her adventures with her determination to amuse Peggy. She forgot herself, she was quite unconscious of the unevenness of Courtlandt's driving as the story unrolled of its own momentum. He did not interrupt with words but at times the car shot forward as though propelled by a furious impulse. They passed Jim Carey herding some lank-bodied, big-kneed calves before him. He waved and shouted a greeting. As they entered the cottonwoods by the Bear Creek corral Jerry described the culmination of the wild ride on the track, her stunned amazement when she had heard Steve's furious exclamation behind her. Her voice was traitorously unsteady as she added:

" 'O ye of little faith!' Even when I saw you there, knew that you had heard my explanation, I—I thought that—that somehow you would understand."

"Why would I? You had told me that you had been engaged to Greyson. You never can tell what a man will do when he is mad about a woman, when he loves her crown of shining hair, her eyes, her smile, the—the tip of her bare pink foot." Memory sent a surge of red to his face. He brought the car to a stop in front of the shack. Beechy, his face white, his hair redder and more rampant than ever, called eagerly from the open window at which he sat bolstered up in a chair.

"Wait for me at the house. I shan't be long."

Jerry nodded dumbly, and drove on. Courtlandt's words had set her heart beating a furious call to arms. What had he meant? Who was mad about a woman? He or Greyson? Whose bare pink foot? Involuntarily she tucked one suede shoe under her, her cheeks flushed warmly. He—he couldn't have meant her.

In the living-room of the cabin Jerry held the cocoon of soft flannel, which in turn held the Carey baby, in her arms. She laid her soft cheek against his.

"Isn't—isn't he the dearest!" she crooned as she felt the sweet warm thrill of his satin-soft skin against her face. Doc Rand, before the fireplace, flapping his long

black coat-tails in time to his heel-and-toe teeter,
blinked at her through lenses which had become unaccountably misty. His russet-apple face showed a new
set of lines.

"I—I am so glad that he arrived safely," Jerry observed innocently, punctuating the words with cooing
sounds directed at the crease in the baby's neck. Indignation at the possible slur on his professional skill
served as a safety valve for Rand's emotion which had
been so unaccountably stirred by the sight of the lovely
girl with the child in her arms. He had seen the same
thing unmoved hundreds of times before, a woman
with her face snuggled against a baby's.

"Arrived safely! Why shouldn't he arrive safely in a
home like this? Take it from me, the Almighty's going
to pick his mothers carefully from now on. He's just
had a demonstration of what ought not to happen in
poor Denbigh's case. He'll find a way to make women
realize what a great and glorious privilege it is to be the
mother of an American citizen."

"Of either sex?" probed the girl mischievously.

"You've said it. The female of the species has got to
take her share in the responsibility of the government.
If we have another war, God grant we don't, the young
women will be drafted to work, just as the men will to
fight. There'll be no feminine slackers infesting the
neighborhoods of the camps next time."

"Hear! Hear!" applauded a low voice from the door.
Doc Rand beamed at the newcomer paternally.

"Steve, you scoffer, come in! Take a look at what
your wife has in that bundle."

Jerry wished passionately that she were a thousand
miles away when Steve loomed over her but she didn't
intend to let him suspect it. She pulled away the soft
blanket that he could see better and challenged breathlessly:

"Isn't he a sweetie peach?"

"Isn't he—it—very red?" Courtlandt stammered in
honest embarrassment that he could not conscientious-

ly voice a paean of praise of the beauty of the Carey
heir. Doc Rand indulged in a denatured guffaw.

"Lord-ee, Steve, your mental propeller showered
sparks of originality that time, didn't it? The baby isn't
appreciated here; you'd better take him back to his
mother, Mrs. Eagan," as the nurse beaming with full-
moon effulgence, entered the room. Jerry smiled up at
the portly woman as she laid the little bundle in her
arms.

"Give my love to Mrs. Carey and tell her that he is
the loveliest baby I ever saw," she whispered eagerly.

"What do you think about Beechy, Doc?" Courtlandt asked as Mrs. Eagan left the room.

"He'll pull through now that he has eased his conscience by confession. I had to let him talk and un-
burden his mind before I could heal his body."

"I've just come from the shack. Carl told me that if—
if it hadn't been for Denbigh he would have been in on
that deal last night."

"Yes, Steve, but Beechy was out of the hold-up for
good when he found that it was government money
they were after. He was prepared to take what was
coming to him for quitting; he knew mighty well that a
man couldn't double-cross Ranlett and—and live, that
is, not if the Skunk knew it. He knows now that Denbigh saved him. Beechy isn't bad at heart. He and a
lot of others like him are suffering from an acute attack
of disillusionment, that's all. They'd been fed up on
'Hail-to-the-conquering-hero' stuff and when the shout-
ing was over and they spent weary months in hospital
forgotten by the world at large, and in particular by
that female portion of it that had fed them, written to
them, married them during the war, do you wonder
that they were ready for any deviltry that was afoot?
I don't. But you see, in spite of his loud talk, when
Beechy came slam up against the proposition of de-
frauding his government, ungrateful government that
he thought it, there was nothing doing. He couldn't
get away with it. He'll never be able to do much hard
work, but there must be a place for him."

"A place for him! If he ever escapes my clutches again he's more slippery than I think him."

"Go to it, Steve! Even you and I salaam when he speaks in that tone, don't we, Mrs. Jerry?"

The sun had dropped behind the mountains; fields and foot-hills lay luminous and still as Courtlandt drove the roadster past the corral at the Double O. A bunch of horses was being turned into the pastures for the night feed. They nipped, they kicked, they rolled. The riders who were driving them out tolerated their antics patiently, with an occasional admonitory "Hi-yew!" Jerry turned to look after them.

"I wish Peg could have seen that. In this light, in their broad-brimmed hats, their colored neckerchiefs, their gloves, their costumes are picturesque. They would have satisfied even her craving for local color."

Courtlandt drove on to the ranch-house without answering. It had been a silent ride home. Jerry had been tensely apprehensive of what might be coming when they started, but as the man beside her drove steadily with only an occasional inquiry as to her comfort, she had relaxed and allowed her thoughts to drift.

Steve followed her into the living-room. As she opened the door of her boudoir he spoke from where he stood under his mother's portrait.

"Come here, Jerry! Please——" he added with a smile as she hesitated.

"I must dress for dinner. I——"

"There is plenty of time. I want to talk to you. Come here!" As a safe and sane compromise she took refuge behind the back of the wing-chair.

"Well?" she queried defensively.

With startling suddenness he caught her hands and drew her to the hearth beside him.

"That's better! I can't talk to you when you are so far away." His grip on her hands tightened. "Jerry, do you remember that day at the Manor when Uncle Nick's will was read? You——"

"The—the day we decided to make the detour? It—it has proved an adventure, hasn't it?" she interrupted in a breathless attempt to gain time. Courtlandt ignored the question.

"You asked me if I wanted his fortune. Do you also remember my answer?" Then as with downcast eyes she nodded assent, he repeated, " 'more than I ever wanted anything, except one, in my life.' You thought that that one thing was Felice and I—I let you think so. I meant you, Jerry. No, you can't go, you've got to listen now. We've been playing at cross purposes long enough. I wanted Uncle Nick's money because I wanted to be rid of the humiliating load of obligation we Courtlandts had shouldered. I wanted to meet you on equal terms. I loved you the first day I saw you in your shimmering orchid gown with the great fan which you wielded with the air of an empress. Who was I to tell you so? You wouldn't have believed me, you would have despised me as a hypocrite. I had no money, nothing but debts to offer you. But if I hadn't loved you nothing could have forced me, nothing could have tempted me to ask you to marry me. On the way in to meet you that first night, I promised Sir Peter that if in any way you were repellent to me, I would let your father take possession of our property. I—I— well, I had to bluff some to my father going home to cover my bowled-over condition. I don't ask for anything now, I only want a promise that you won't close your heart against me—that you will—oh, what's the use—you must love me!"

The girl looked down upon the head pressed against her hands then up at the tender eyes of the woman above the mantel. Were they misted or were there tears in her own eyes? She choked back a sound that was half laugh, half sob as she observed with tantalizing charm:

"Of course when you say 'must,' O Abdul the Great ——" Before she could finish the sentence Steve had her crushed in his arms.

"It's your own fault, Mr. Tommy Benson. I told you that I shouldn't——"

It was Peggy's voice at the door. In breathless haste

Jerry freed herself from Courtlandt's arms. He caught her hands and drew her back. His voice was tenderly exultant, his eyes disconcertingly possessive as he reminded huskily:

"About that honeymoon I promised to show you, Mrs. Courtlandt—— Can I interest you in a silver mine?"

XXII

THE two men were in striking contrast. Glamorgan, massive, shrewd-eyed, of big affairs and world interests and Peter Courtlandt patrician, dreamy-eyed, who dwelt largely in the realm of books and art, were smoking on the terrace of the Manor. They could look down the box-bordered paths of the garden to where stone steps led to a small landing on the shore of the river. A tender swung at its moorings. Motor-boats and steam-boats plied busily back and forth on the water which rippled into scales of gold. From a man-o'-war anchored down-stream came the sound of a ship's band. The sun was setting with lavish prodigality of color, spreading great swaths of crimson and gold and violet above the hills. One steady brilliant star shone in the west. From the garden drifted the scent of heliotrope. The light breeze stirred the awning over the terrace, gently lifted the soft rings of white hair on Peter Courtlandt's head, impertinently flicked the sheets of the letter Glamorgan held.

Courtlandt withdrew his eyes from the river and looked at his guest. The large man was smiling broadly, at his thoughts, doubtless, as his eyes were fixed unseeingly on the star. His host suddenly remembered that he had not seen the oil-king smile like that since Jerry and Steve had left the Manor; he had appeared like a man spiritually burdened. Could his furious indignation because his daughter had gone West with her husband

have accounted for his gravity? Courtlandt tossed the
remains of his cigar over the terrace wall and addressed
his companion.

"You said that you had a letter to read to me," he
suggested. Glamorgan's eyes flashed to his—was there
a hint of tears in them?—the smile on his lips spread
and spread until his host was reminded of the moon in
all the glory of its fullness. He laughed in sympathy. "It
must be amusing, if one judges by your expression."
The oil-king indulged in a throaty chuckle; it sounded
like the delight of a boy in some satisfactorily accomplished bit of mischief.

"It isn't the letter which is so amusing, though I'll
hand it to Peg when it comes to expression that has
punch, it is what I can read between the lines. Listen to
what she writes and you'll understand." He settled
huge horn-rimmed eye-glasses in place and began to
read from the letter in his hand.

"DEAR DAD:
    "By this time you must have received my letter
about the near hold-up, *poor* Mr. Denbigh, Beechy,
Tommy (Benson the Bluffer the outfit call him now)
and your she's-a-hero daughter. I penned that throbbing epistle on the morning after our return from
Slippy Bend when my mind was a red hot molten
mass of *thrills*. Well, to quote Scripture (don't give
me the credit of this, Tommy Benson reeled it off
when I expressed amazement at what was happening
and I copied it from the Bible), 'There be three
things which are too wonderful for me, yea, four
which I know not: The way of an eagle in the air;
the way of a serpent upon a rock; the way of a ship
in the midst of the sea; and the way of a man with a
maid.' It is that last phrase which has to do with the
situation here. When I first came Steve had *about* as
much expression in his face when he looked at Jerry
as has that granite civil war veteran in the park at Oil
City. Jerry was as bad. They were the nearest to
cold-storage newly-weds that I had ever seen. Now—
ye gods!—when I· look up and see Steve's eyes
on Jerry my heart *stampedes*. I feel as though I had

made the unpardonable break of opening a closed door without knocking. Jerry behaves a little better. She keeps her eyes to heel but her *voice*——

" 'The devil hath not in all his quiver's choice an arrow for the heart like a sweet voice.' Tommy Benson again. He is a more liberal education than English 27 at College. I asked him if the lines were Shakespeare or the Bible and he said that a gentleman named Byron wrote them but that I was *not* to cultivate his acquaintance indiscriminately. I have sent east for *all* of Mr. Byron's poems. But I digress.

"To return to Steve and Jerry. They start on a camping trip to-morrow, up into the wilderness to inspect some silly old silver mine. Steve has sent Marcelle O'Neil ahead with packhorses, guns, provisions, and rods. Thank heaven they didn't ask *me* to go. I'm to stay at the Double O with Tommy Benson's mother, who arrived yesterday. She's a stylish-stout of about fifty with wonderful skin and teeth, eyes that make you feel you'd like to *drown* in them they are so like clear-blue pools; hair like dull gold and a smile—well, I walked *straight* into her arms when she turned it on me.

"I wrote you that Jerry seemed terribly short of money. You *must* do something about it. Her Tiffany flame has found an Alexandrite that she wants. When I told her the price, a *miserable* little two thousand dollars, you would have thought I'd mentioned the amount of the Allied war debt. Why don't you send her the ring?

"From my limited observation (there's been something doing every minute since I set foot on the Double O), I should say that ranching was a great life when the coyotes didn't steal your chickens, when the Shorthorns didn't break away, or when a disgruntled fragment of your outfit didn't shoot up the neighborhood. Jerry says that she and Steve will spend their winters at the Manor after they have been here a year, something to do with Uncle Nick's will, *you* probably know about it. Steve will take Tommy Benson into partnership and he will be manager-in-chief. It's a *great* chance for Tommy. He is the poor-man-with-a-future type. He's *super*-sensitive about his lack of money, though. Bruce Greyson brought a perfectly

stunning man to call the other day, heir to a fortune.
Of course I had to be nice to him. Ye gods! You
should have seen Tommy while he was here. After
the plutocrat had departed I asked him why he had
looked as though he could have crunched mountain
lion in the raw. He just *glowered* and quoted:

> " 'O what a world of vile, ill favoured faults
>   Looks handsome in three thousand pounds a
>   year.'

"From my window I can see Sandy's flivver in the
distance; that means that I must wind up this letter
—pronto. That carrier is the *funniest* sight. He wears
a tall white hat and a linen duster and looks for all
the world like the Mad Hatter in 'Alice.' I almost expect to hear him snap when he sees me coming,
'Your hair needs cutting,' the way the Hatter does in
the story. *Heaps* of love,

"PEG.

"P.S. Praise be! Careful Cosmetics has departed.
That's what I call the Denbigh woman."

Glamorgan removed his glasses and threw back his
head with a chuckling laugh. Courtlandt laughed with
him.

"Peggy certainly wields a facile pen. I—I am glad
of what she writes about Steve and Jerry. I confess that
I feared——"

"I want to talk to you about that, Courtlandt," interrupted Glamorgan eagerly. "It has taken all my
strength of will and then some, not to take you into
my confidence but——but I promised your brother-in-
law that——"

"Nicholas Fairfax!"

"I don't wonder you are astonished. You see, from
the moment I saw him I fell for him. I'd known a lot
of men like him. Chestnut burrs outside but sound and
sweet in their hearts. He must have felt that I understood him for he hadn't been at the Manor long before
he confided his doubts and hopes to me. Old Nick was
keener than you or I. He hadn't been here twenty-four
hours before he had sized up the situation between

Jerry and Steve. He realized that they were heading straight for the matrimonial reefs where so many of their friends had come to grief. I guess he realized also that I was a little more anxious for that marriage to turn out a success than even he was. The Lord only knows the burden of guilt I would have carried the rest of my life if it hadn't."

"You wouldn't have been the only one."

"I know that, Courtlandt. Nick realized that he hadn't long to live. He felt sure of Jerry's loyalty, that all that was needed to right matters between the two was to give Steve money and make the girl dependent on him. He knew the boy well enough to know that his pride would stand between them as long as Jerry was spending my money. That was where I came in. He had me cast for the stern parent act. I was to oppose Jerry's going to the ranch. Opposition, he figured, would steel her determination to go with her husband, if she was tempted to waver. I knew my girl better. I knew that she would keep the covenant but I consented to please Old Nick. I almost caved in the day she went away, when I saw her watch the gate wistfully until the train started, but I kept out of sight."

"Who would have believed to have seen Nick in those last days that he was planning so shrewdly."

"That wasn't all he planned. He had the dickens of a time with Greyson. He wanted him to invite Mrs. Denbigh to the X Y Z for the summer as a sort of acid test for Steve."

"What a diabolical idea."

"I'm not so sure of that. His argument was that if the woman had the slightest lure for Steve——"

"But she hadn't," Courtlandt denied sharply.

"I couldn't see how she could have, but then vamps aren't in my line. Nick was possessed by the idea. Greyson kicked like a steer against it, but finally gave in. You can't tell. Fairfax may have had other reasons up his sleeve. Denbigh was at the Bear Creek ranch. He might have thought, have hoped, that he and Felice would come together again. In spite of his ill-health and absorption in his ranch, your brother-in-law was a profound thinker on social and economic questions. I spent hours arguing with him. He contended that the great weakness of the American people lay in their lack of stability, that they could be swept along on a wave of enthusiasm but that when it came to the steady tide of determination they wouldn't even tread water; that lack of stability was at the root of the divorce habit, which if it wasn't checked would insidiously undermine the character of the nation."

"He was right, but," with a profound sigh of relief, "it looks as though Jerry and Steve had escaped the reefs, doesn't it?"

"I'll say it does," with a reminiscent chuckle. "Now you know why I gloated over that letter of Peg's. The child didn't realize how she was easing my mind. Do you know, I like what she writes about that Benson boy. Next to a man with family background I have a deep and abiding respect for a man who has the best in literature at his tongue's end. He's a rare bird these days."

"Then you wouldn't object if Peg and Tommy—he hasn't the kind of family you want behind him."

"I don't care who Peggy marries if he is clean and upstanding, with self-respect and love for my girl. I'm through meddling, though I'm not sorry for what I did with Jerry. She stood nine chances out of ten of marrying a fortune-hunter; Steve wasn't that; he had to be forcibly fed with money. In spite of that fact I haven't drawn an easy breath since Nick told me his suspicions, until now." He glanced at the letter. "I think I'll send that Alexandrite as a sort of peace offering."

"You're too late. Steve wired to me to have it sent."

"He did! Then you knew all I have been telling you?"

"No. I only put two and two together when I got Steve's message."

Glamorgan rose, shook himself like a bear and extended one hand to his host. His voice was curiously rough as he laid the other on his shoulder and confided awkwardly:

"Good-night! I—I hope they'll name the first son Peter, Courtlandt."

Courtlandt put his free hand on the big man's shoulder. His laugh was unsteady but his voice was vibrant with feeling as he countered:

"And I—I hope they'll name the second one—Dan. Good-night." They stood shaking hands furiously, laughing boyishly, and patting one another's shoulders as the lights flashed up on the river and night rang down the curtain of dusk.

BRING ROMANCE INTO YOUR LIFE

With these bestsellers from your favorite Bantam authors.

Barbara Cartland

☐ 13942	LUCIFER AND THE ANGEL	$1.75
☐ 14084	OLA AND THE SEA WOLF	$1.75
☐ 14133	THE PRUDE AND THE PRODIGAL	$1.75
☐ 13579	FREE FROM FEAR	$1.75

Catherine Cookson

☐ 13279	THE DWELLING PLACE	$1.95
☐ 14187	THE GIRL	$2.25
☐ 13170	KATIE MULHOLLAND	$1.95

Georgette Heyer

☐ 13239	THE BLACK MOTH	$1.95
☐ 11249	PISTOLS FOR TWO	$1.95

Emilie Loring

☐ 12947	WHERE BEAUTY DWELLS	$1.75
☐ 12948	RAINBOW AT DUSK	$1.75
☐ 13668	WITH BANNERS	$1.75
☐ 13757	HILLTOPS CLEAR	$1.75

Eugenia Price

☐ 13682	BELOVED INVADER	$2.25
☐ 14195	LIGHTHOUSE	$2.50
☐ 14406	NEW MOON RISING	$2.50

Buy them at your local bookstore or use this handy coupon: